"Come away with me. Let me teach you what love means," exclaimed Sir Guy.

Karina did not speak, but her face was troubled.

Sir Guy's words were deep with passion. "I want you! Dear God how I want you!"

Karina finally answered, her voice low with shock, "But if I went away with . . . you, we would . . . be living . . . in sin! You know full well that I am . . . married, that I promised to be a complacent wife."

"What the hell does it matter?" Sir Guy asked violently. "That man is not worthy of having a wife like you simply because he does not look after you. If you had a husband who loved you, Karina, you would not make mistakes. You would never make them with me!"

Books by Barbara Cartland

THE ADVENTURER
AGAIN THIS RAPTURE
ARMOUR AGAINST LOVE
THE AUDACIOUS
    ADVENTURESS
BARBARA CARTLAND'S BOOK
    OF BEAUTY AND HEALTH
THE BITTER WINDS OF LOVE
BLUE HEATHER
BROKEN BARRIERS
THE CAPTIVE HEART
THE COIN OF LOVE
THE COMPLACENT WIFE
CUPID RIDES PILLION
DANCE ON MY HEART
DESIRE OF THE HEART
THE DREAM WITHIN
DESPERATE DEFIANCE
A DUEL OF HEARTS
ELIZABETH EMPRESS OF
    AUSTRIA
ELIZABETH IN LOVE
THE ENCHANTING EVIL
THE ENCHANTED MOMENT
THE ENCHANTED WALTZ
ESCAPE FROM PASSION
A GHOST IN MONTE CARLO
THE GOLDEN GONDOLA
A HALO FOR THE DEVIL
A HAZARD OF HEARTS
A HEART IS BROKEN
THE HIDDEN EVIL
THE HIDDEN HEART
THE HORIZONS OF LOVE
THE IRRESISTIBLE BUCK
JOSEPHINE EMPRESS OF
    FRANCE
THE KISS OF THE DEVIL
THE KISS OF PARIS
A KISS OF SILK
THE KNAVE OF HEARTS
THE LEAPING FLAME
A LIGHT TO THE HEART
LIGHTS OF LOVE
THE LITTLE PRETENDER
LOST ENCHANTMENT
LOST LOVE
LOVE AND LINDA
LOVE FORBIDDEN
LOVE AT FORTY
LOVE IN HIDING

LOVE IN PITY
LOVE HOLDS THE CARDS
LOVE IS AN EAGLE
LOVE IS CONTRABAND
LOVE IS DANGEROUS
LOVE IS THE ENEMY
LOVE IS MINE
LOVE ME FOREVER
LOVE TO THE RESCUE
LOVE ON THE RUN
LOVE UNDER FIRE
THE MAGIC OF HONEY
MESSENGER OF LOVE
METTERNICH THE
    PASSIONATE DIPLOMAT
MONEY, MAGIC AND
    MARRIAGE
NO HEART IS FREE
THE ODIOUS DUKE
OPEN WINGS
OUT OF REACH
PASSIONATE PILGRIM
THE PRETTY HORSE-
    BREAKERS
THE PRICE IS LOVE
A RAINBOW TO HEAVEN
THE RELUCTANT BRIDE
THE RUNAWAY HEART
THE SECRET FEAR
THE SCANDALOUS LIFE
    OF KING CAROL
THE SMUGGLED HEART
A SONG OF LOVE
STARS IN MY HEART
STOLEN HALO
SWEET ADVENTURE
SWEET ENCHANTRESS
SWEET PUNISHMENT
THIEF OF A HEART
THE THIEF OF LOVE
THIS TIME IT'S LOVE
TOWARDS THE STARS
THE UNKNOWN HEART
THE UNPREDICTABLE BRIDE
A VIRGIN IN MAYFAIR
A VIRGIN IN PARIS
WE DANCED ALL NIGHT
WHERE IS LOVE
THE WINGS OF LOVE
WINGS ON MY HEART
WOMAN THE ENIGMA

BARBARA CARTLAND

9
THE COMPLACENT WIFE

A JOVE BOOK

Six previous printings
First Jove edition published January 1981

10 9 8 7 6 5 4 3 2 1

Printed in the United States of America

Jove books are published by Jove Publications, Inc.,
200 Madison Avenue, New York, NY 10016

ABOUT THE AUTHOR

Barbara Cartland, the world's most famous romantic novelist, who is also an historian, playwright, lecturer, political speaker and television personality, has now written nearly 300 books and sold nearly 200 million books over the world.

She has also had many historical works published and has written four autobiographies as well as the biographies of her mother and that of her brother, Ronald Cartland, who was the first Member of Parliament to be killed in the last war. This book has a preface by Sir Winston Churchill and has just been republished with an introduction by Sir Arthur Bryant.

Love at the Helm, a novel written with the help and inspiration of the late Admiral of the Fleet, the Earl Mountbatten of Burma, is being sold for the Mountbatten Memorial Trust.

Miss Cartland in 1978 sang an Album of Love Songs with the Royal Philharmonic Orchestra.

In 1976 by writing twenty-one books, she broke the world record and has continued for the following three years with 24, 20 and 23. She is in the Guinness Book of Records as the most prolific author alive.

In private life Barbara Cartland. who is a Dame of the Order of St. John of Jerusalem, Chairman of the St. John Council in Hertfordshire and Deputy President of the St. John Ambulance Brigade, has fought for better conditions and salaries for Midwives and Nurses.

She has championed the cause for old people, had the law altered regarding gypsies and founded the first Romany Gypsy camp in the world.

Barbara Cartland is deeply interested in Vitamin Therapy and is President of the British National Association for Health.

AUTHOR'S NOTE

Readers interested in history may like to know that at Ascot Races on July 5th, 1831, the horse of King William IV did actually break down during a race.

Also the description of the Royal Procession down the Course at the Meeting and later the Dinner Party at Windsor Castle—the guests and the treasures shown by the King—are all authentic.

The excitement over the Reform Bill and the statesmen concerned with it are a part of history.

I am told that "complacent" is now an obsolete word and that "complaisant" is the acceptable spelling. This, however, does not have exactly the same meaning and "complacent" was used in 1832!

1

Two people walking with studied slowness and an acquired elegance across the green lawn, passed through a hedge of rhododendron bushes into a small enclosed space where there was an arbour covered with rambler roses and honeysuckle.

Here they were out of sight of the gaily dressed crowd moving around the Duke of Severn's garden at what was the most important social event of the summer. In this hidden retreat the band was only a far-off musical accompaniment to the buzz of the bees.

It seemed as if the two people who had sought sanctuary there instantly cast aside their formal reserve.

Lady Sibley turned swiftly, her head flung backwards in an almost abandoned posture as she said with a quiver of excitement:

"At last! I thought we were never to be alone together!"

"Let me compliment you, Georgette," the Earl of Droxford replied in his deep voice. "I have never seen you in better looks."

He spoke the truth, for Lady Sibley, an acknowledged beauty for the past five years, was in love, and this emotion naturally brought a softness to her classical loveliness and a gleam to her somewhat hard eyes.

For the moment she felt and looked romantic, and it was in keeping with the exotic fragrance of tuberoses which seemed to impregnate the air around her. It

7

was a perfume which she had made essentially personal.

"Oh, Alton, it is over a week since I have seen you!" she sighed. 'George insisted on repairing to the country, and you know how I loathe being here when there is so much gaiety and amusement in London!"

"I have missed you too," the Earl said.

"Can we meet tonight in our usual place?" Lady Sibley enquired. "George is certain to fall sleep when dinner is finished and he will expect me to be fatigued after the party this afternoon. I will retire early and slip out to meet you as I have done before."

Her words were impetuous, but suddenly she stopped and looked up into the Earl's face. He was a very handsome man—perhaps the most handsome man in the whole of the *Beau Ton*—but now he was frowning so that his eyebrows nearly met across the bridge of his nose.

It gave him an almost sardonic look, which even to those who knew him well could be quite awe-inspiring.

"What is the matter?" Lady Sibley asked anxiously. "For I can see that something is amiss."

"I am extremely disturbed, as it happens," the Earl replied.

"But why? What has occurred?" Laby Sibley enquired.

"I hardly like to tell you this, Georgette," the Earl answered, "but the fact is that I have to be married."

"You have to marry!" Lady Sibley hardly breathed the words.

They were obviously such a shock to her that she took a step back from the Earl's side to stare at him in astonishment, her eyes no longer warm and inviting, her mouth tightening into a hard line.

"Yes, married!" the Earl repeated bitterly. "Wed to some simpering miss! And what is more, I have to find the girl, offer for her, and go through the ceremony of marriage, all within a month!"

"But why? What has happened? Who is the girl? I cannot understand what you are trying to tell me!" Lady Sibley ejaculated.

"It is not surprising," the Earl answered, " for I can hardly comprehend it myself."

"Then tell me, tell me quickly," Lady Sibley cried, "for I can promise you, Alton, that the idea of your marriage is something I can hardly contemplate without screaming."

"Let us sit down," the Earl suggested.

For a moment it seemed as if Lady Sibley would refuse him. Then she moved towards the seat in the arbour and sat down clasping her hands together, her eyes raised to the Earl's face.

As he did not speak, but having sat himself beside her remained silent and scowling, his eyes not on her but staring ferociously at a lilac bush, Lady Sibley prompted:

"Relate what has happened, for I cannot believe what you have just said is the truth."

"You know that the Lord Lieutenancy of this County has always been held in my family," the Earl began. "My father was Lord Lieutenant before he died, and my grandfather and great-grandfather before him.

"It was only because I was considered too young on my father's death to represent His Majesty that Lord Handley was appointed, although it was made quite clear at the time that as he was an old man he was only filling the position until such time as I should be old enough to succeed him."

"I think I have heard you speak of this before," Lady Sibley interrupted, "But I cannot conceive what this has to do with your marriage."

"Lord Handley, as you know, died a fortnight ago," the Earl continued as if she had not spoken. "Yesterday I went to see the Prime Minister and asked how soon it would be before the announcement was made that His Majesty had appointed me as Lord Lieutenant."

The Earl paused. He was seeing so clearly in his mind's eye the Prime Minister—tall, slender and the most finished orator of the day—facing him across the writing-desk in No. 10 Downing Street.

The Earl had known Lord Grey since he was a boy, for he had been a friend of his father's and had frequently stayed at Droxford Park.

Now he was surprised to see that the Prime Minister seemed almost embarrassed at what he had to say.

"It is with deep regret, Droxford, that I cannot promise you the Lord Lieutenancy."

The Earl had sat up sharply in his chair.

"You mean that His Majesty intends to appoint someone else?" he asked incredulously. "But who? Who is there in the County who has my standing? Damn it all, My Lord, I own over fifty thousand acres of land, apart from the fact that it has always been a traditional appointment."

"I know the circumstances as well as you do yourself," Lord Grey replied. "But the King has given me new instructions as regards the appointment of Lord Lieutenants."

"What are they?" the Earl enquired.

"His Majesty requires that the noblemen who represent him be married."

It seemed to the Earl at the time as if the Prime Minister drove a naked sword into the table which lay between them.

"Married!" he ejaculated harshly.

"I was afraid this would be a shock to you," the Prime Minister said.

He spoke in the quiet, beguiling voice which had been known to soothe the most violent agitator in the House of Commons.

"But His Majesty, he continued, "is determined to bring in a new era of respectability with anything which concerns the Monarchy."

He smiled apologetically.

"The excesses of his brother's reign must be forgotten and being happily married himself, His Majesty has decided that marriage has a stabilising effect on all men and therefore those who represent him best are those who are in this stage of conjugal bliss!"

"Really, if that is not the height of hypocrisy!" the Earl exclaimed angrily. "With the King's ten bastards by Mrs. Jordan being handed out titles by the dozen one can hardly believe that His Majesty would have the presumption to deny his subjects the joys of bachelorhood—in which he wallowed so blatantly!!"

"I know, I know," Lord Grey agreed. "But that is past history. The King now wishes to do what is best for the country, and he and the Queen are determined to set an example which they hope their subjects will follow."

"Are you therefore saying categorically," the Earl asked, "that unless I find myself a wife the Lord Lieutenancy will pass to someone else?"

"I have no alternative," the Prime Minister replied.

"I know what has upset his Majesty," the Earl said. "It is the behaviour of Lord Beaton who is living openly with a "bit o' muslin" he found in the *Corps de Ballet*. He takes her to every public function he attends. I am told that all the respectable ladies of Wessex are in an uproar because he insists that they should meet her!"

"Lord Beaton has certainly caused His Majesty a number of headaches since his Accession," the Prime Minister agreed. "In fact, His Majesty has decided to ask for His Lordship's resignation."

The Earl raised his eyebrows.

"A new precedent? I thought it was very seldom, if ever, that a Lord Lieutenant was sacked?"

11

"I believe one of my predecessors—George Grenville—dismissed his brother from the Lord Lieutenancy of Buckinghamshire," Lord Grey said with a smile.

"But I agree with you, Droxford, it seldom happens, and that is why His Majesty is determined to be very careful in the choice of his new Lord Lieutenants."

"Can I speak with His Majesty about this?" the Earl asked, knowing that William IV, the genial, good-humoured Sailor-King, could seldom refuse a favour when it was asked of him personally.

Lord Grey shook his head.

"I am afraid it would be useless. This is not the first time I have discussed it with the King, and he has the support of the Queen in this matter. You know well what that means!"

"I do indeed," the Earl agreed. "I received a letter yesterday from Mr. Greville who is in Brighton. He writes: *The Queen is a prude and will not let the ladies come* décolleté *to her parties.*"

The eyes of the two men met across the table.

"Times have changed," the Prime Minister said. "George IV, who liked expanses of that sort, would not let them be covered."

The Earl laughed—he could not help it—but his smile quickly faded as he asked:

"How long can you give me to find myself a wife?"

"Does it mean so much to you?" Lord Grey asked.

"I have a great pride in my ancestry," the Earl replied. "My father was both respected and loved. He carried out his duties in the County to the best of his ability and with a wisdom and kindliness which was appreciated by people in every walk of life. You knew him, My Lord. Am I exaggerating?"

"No indeed," Lord Grey answered. "Your father was a great friend of mine and I am not in the least biased when I say he was a truly remarkable man."

"And I have every intention of following in his

footsteps," the Earl said. "I find my bachelor state extremely pleasant but you will admit that I have given rise to no scandals, I have not behaved in such a way as to give offence to those in authority. I therefore could not tolerate seeing anyone else represent the King in the Country."

His eyes were hard as he continued:

"Indeed, thanks to my father and my forebears, there is no organisation, association, charity or school in the County in which my family has not played an important part. My father always spoke of the County as "his." I have thought of it in the same terms."

The Earl paused then added hastily:

"Let me ask you again, My Lord, how long have I in which to find myself a wife who will ensure for me the Lord Lieutenancy?"

"I am sure His Majesty, if I ask it of him, will wait at least a month," the Prime Minister replied. "But I will be frank with you, Droxford, and say it would not be wise to procastinate longer than that. In fact, His Majesty already has someone else in mind!"

"The Duke of Severn —I presume?" the Earl snapped.

"Precisely," the Prime Minister concurred.

"He owns but ten thousand acres which are badly cultivated, meanly administrated, and his parsimonious treatment of his tenants is a by-word in the County."

"He is married and highly respectable," the Prime Minister said and there was a twinkle in his eye.

"Damnit!" the Earl exclaimed. "The Duke is appointed over my dead body! Your Lordship will be hearing from me!"

He had left No. 10 Downing Street with a scowl on his face which had made his coachman and footmen look at him anxiously.

When His Lordship was in one of his rages the whole of his establishment trembled. And there had been an apprehension that evening at Droxford House

13

in Park Lane from the lowest pantry-boy to the upper hierarchy of the household servants.

Now, as he finished speaking, the Earl brought his clenched hand down sharply on his tight lavender-coloured trousers and exclaimed:

"I will see the Duke in Hell before I allow him to take the place that is rightfully mine!"

"No, indeed, it is something which could not be tolerated," Lady Sibley agreed. "I know that George dislikes the Duke as much as you do."

"Then find me a wife," the Earl commanded.

"It should not be difficult," Lady Sibley answered, "And perhaps, Alton, it might make things easier."

"What things?" the Earl asked sharply.

"I was thinking of us," Lady Sibley told him in dulcet tones. "You see, dear man, you are so handsome that as soon as you appear every husband becomes insanely jealous. George has already arrived at the growling state.

"But if you were married, then it is far more difficult for a man to protest that you should not be invited to the house when the invitation also includes you wife!"

The Earl did not answer. She put out her hands, from which she had drawn her long white kid gloves, and laid them in his.

"Dear, dear Alton, do not let it perturb you," she pleaded. "I will find you a complacent, conformable wife who will look well at the head of your table wearing the Droxford diamonds, and then you can forget about her."

"I have no desire to be wed to some vacant-faced nitwit," the Earl said sharply.

"As long as she behaves herself and does not encroach on your other—interests," Lady Sibley answered with an accent on the last two words, "then it may indeed be all for the best."

14

The Earl lifted her hands to his lips and kissed them.

"You are trying to cheer me up, Georgette. But I assure you the whole idea disgusts me. I have no desire to be married. I have no wish to be tied to a wife for whom I have no affection and little interest!"

"Think how disagreeable it would be for me if you had," Lady Sibley said. "We have been so very happy these past months. Nothing must disturb our relationship; for if indeed you had fallen in love with someone else it would have broken my heart!"

Her voice was vibrant with feeling and almost for the first time since they had met he looked deep into her eyes.

"You are very beautiful, Georgette."

"I want you always to think so," she whispered.

Her lips were very near to his and he drew her closely to him. He bent his head and found her mouth and for a long, long moment they were locked together.

Then Lady Sibley moved away from him and began to draw on her discarded gloves.

"You must meet me tonight, Alton, for I swear I cannot live any longer without your love."

"I will be there," he promised, "and do not keep me waiting too long."

There was a depth in his voice which told her that she had aroused him. She glanced at him sideways with the sly, self-satisfied look of a woman who knows her own attractions and is well aware that she is irresistible.

"I will now go and choose you a wife," she said. "There is a wide selection on the lawn at this very moment. Country girls are best, they are less spoilt, and as your wife has to be satisfied with an infinitesimal amount of your attention, we must look for someone both ignorant and innocent."

"My God, Georgette, you make it sound like a milk pudding—something I could never abide as a child!"

Lady Sibley laughed.

"I have every intention of supplying the champagne in your life, Alton, for a long time to come!"

She rose to her feet, then gave a little gasp as the Earl, rising too, put his arms round her.

"You excite me," he said, "you always do. And perhaps no other woman would have taken the news of my marriage so calmly and sensibly as you have done."

"As I have already told you," Lady Sibley replied, "you will find it will work out splendidly and make things far easier for us."

She turned her lips to his and he kissed her with a controlled passion. Then, as she disengaged herself from his embrace, she said:

"Give me time to mingle with the guests. We must not be seen emerging from here together, it is too obvious."

"Very well," he answered. "Until tonight, Georgette."

"I promise I will not keep you waiting," she said and her voice was very seductive.

She disappeared through the rhododendrons. The Earl drew his watch from his waistcoat-pocket, looked at the time, and picking up his top-hat from where he had set it beside him on the bench in the arbour, he put it on his head at a rakish angle.

He was just about to leave when a voice, low but clear, called:

"Lord Droxford!"

He started and looked around him, but there was no one to be seen.

"I am here," the voice said.

Looking up almost incredulously, he saw through the thick leafy branches of the oak tree which overshadowed the place where he was standing, a small heart-shaped face staring down at him.

16

"What are you doing up there?" he asked sharply.

"If you wait a moment I will come down and explain, the voice replied.

The Earl squared his chin and his expression was grim. It was obvious that he and Lady Sibley had been overheard and he wondered if it would be advisable to obtain the child's silence by bribery.

If so, should he give her a guinea or half a one?

"It might be rather difficult," he told himself, "For a child to explain away the possession of a guinea!"

He was already seeking in his waistcoat-pocket for the smaller coin when there was a sound of somebody scrambling down the bark of a tree and into the clearing came not the child he was expecting, but quite obviously an older girl.

She was dressed in a faded cotton frock which was stained with green bark but she had grown out of it and there was no mistaking the soft swelling of her breasts above a faded sash of pale blue satin.

But after he had realised that this was no child who could be bribed to silence, the Earl was concerned only with the eavesdropper's face.

The girl, whoever she might be, was lovely, there was no doubt about that. Small and delicately made, her face seemed hardly big enough to hold her large eyes.

Dark-lashed, they were the most amazing eyes the Earl had ever seen and he noted the fact that they were green flecked with hazel rather than the obvious blue which should have gone with her hair, which was the colour of ripened corn.

There was a hint of red in it which perhaps accounted for the whiteness of her skin- transparent white in which the flush on her cheeks was as lovely as the dawn.

"So you were listening," he said accusingly.

The girl nodded.

"Elizabeth and I have always used this tree as a

17

lookout," she replied, "but this year Elizabeth is among the guests."

"Who is Elizabeth?" he enquired.

He was not really interested in the answer, he was thinking that the girl's hair, which had just caught the rays of the sunshine as she moved, was a colour that he had never before seen in its natural state.

It was indeed the hue painstakingly emulated by the ladies of the chorus from the dye-pot!

"Elizabeth is your host's daughter," was the reply. "This year she is a débutante, so she is being introduced to the important personages of the County, like yourself."

"So you know who I am?"

"Yes, of course. You are the Earl of Droxford. I saw you last year and everyone gossips about you!"

The Earl raised his eyebrows as if such a remark was an impertinence.

And what is your name?"

"I am Karina Rendell. You used to know my father some years ago."

"You mean Sir John Rendell, who was the Member of Parliament for this constituency?"

"Yes, that is Papa."

"Of course I know him, and you live not far from here, if I am not mistaken."

"Our Estate, such as it is, marches with that of the Duke," Karina answered.

"Then why are you not at the party?" Lord Droxford enquired.

She smiled at him and it seemed to light her whole face.

"Would you like the truth?"

"Of course!"

"Then firstly I am too pretty, and secondly I have nothing to wear," Karina replied.

"Too pretty?"

"The Duchess does not like competition where her

daughters are concerned. I am invited to Ducal meals only when there are no outsiders present."

The Earl felt his mouth twitch at the corners; this girl was certainly original. He glanced at his watch again.

"I think I should be returning to the party."

"One moment," Karina said. "I should not have revealed myself or let you know I was listening if I had not wished to ask something of Your Lordship."

"What is it?"

The Earl seemed suddenly on his guard.

The green eyes looked up at him steadily but the flush on her cheeks deepened.

"I was wondering," she said slowly, "as you are looking for a wife, whether you would consider me?"

For a moment the Earl was too astonished to reply. Then he said sharply:

"You overheard what was not intended for your ears. You had no right to listen, and I can only ask you to forget it."

"But why should I?" Karina enquired. "Lady Sibley said she would find you a complacent, conformable wife. I could be both those things, and as you are prepared to marry someone you have never seen before and about whom you know nothing, I am only asking you that I should at least have your consideration!"

"Do you usually go about asking strange men to marry you?" he asked.

He meant to be crushing but he only brought a smile to Karina's lips.

"No indeed," she said, "for I do not meet many men, only Papa's old hunting cronies who try to kiss me in the passage when he is not looking and who are usually married with half a dozen children older than I am myself!"

"You have an urgent desire to be married?" Lord Droxford said somewhat unpleasantly.

"You would want the same if you were in my position," Karina replied quite seriously. "You see, since Mama died, Papa has given up everything that used to interest him.

"He is no longer a Member of Parliament; if he is well enough he goes hunting in the winter but we can only afford to keep two horses; and in the summer he just sits in the house and . . ."

Karina stopped suddenly but the Earl could fill in the word she had been about to say. He could vaguely remember someone telling him that Sir John Rendell was drinking deep.

"So I would like very much to marry you," Karina went on before he could speak. "And if you are just looking for a wife who will ensure your becoming Lord Lieutenant, I cannot collect why I should not suit you better than what you call those vacant-faced nitwits which Lady Sibley will undoubtedly be producing for you."

"I think it would be best if Lady Sibley's name were not mentioned in this connection," the Earl said firmly.

"She is very beautiful, is she not?" Karina asked. "And you are much the handsomest and most attractive Beau she has ever had. She brought Sir Hubert Bracket here last year but Elizabeth and I did not like him at all!"

"Brought him where?" the Earl asked angrily.

"Here to the arbour," Karina replied. "She always brings her current lover here for a flirtation during the garden party. The one the year before made us laugh . . ."

"Will you be quiet!" the Earl interrupted. "You should not be saying such things to me!"

"I apologise," Karina replied in surprise. "But surely you do not think you are the first Gentleman to be beguiled by Lady Sibley's beauty?"

The Earl did not answer and she continued:

"Elizabeth and I have always called her "The Serpent" because she seems to fascinate men as if they

20

were rabbits. Not that I have ever seen a snake fascinate a rabbit, I have only been told it happens!"

"If you do not cease speaking in such a manner," the Earl thundered, "I will give you a good shaking, which is what you deserve! You have no right to creep up trees and listen to other people's conversation!"

"Please do not be angry," Karina pleaded. "I am sorry if I have said things you do not like, but I thought you were the sort of man who would perfer the truth to "Yes, My Lord," and "No, My Lord" and "casting-down-of-the-eyes" which is the manner in which the Duchess likes her daughters to behave."

"Perhaps they will make better wives because of it," the Earl retorted.

"I thought you did not want a nitwit!"

"I certainly do not want a wife with a tongue like an asp!"

There was a sudden silence.

"I think that was needlessly unkind, My Lord," Karina said quietly with a dignity which despite himself brought a twinkle to his eyes.

Because she looked so lovely with her face turned away from him, her chin held high in protest at his words, he said more gently:

"I think you were explaining to me why you think that you would make me a conformable wife."

She looked up at him, her eyes alight.

"You mean you will consider making me an offer?"

"Shall I say that I will consider your application for the position?" he replied. "Of course the other young ladies may not be as keen as you."

"But their fathers and mothers will," Karina said wisely. "You must not suppose that the girls will have any choice in the matter."

"Surely you are exaggerating!" he said. "Girls are not coerced into marriage in 1831. If they do not wish to marry someone, they say so!"

"Not to someone of your consequence," Karina answered. "You are what the Duke calls a "matrimonial catch"! It always seems to me rather a vulgar expression but His Grace uses it, so I suppose it must be a phrase approved by the *Ton*."

"And you think that is what I am?" the Earl asked in an amused voice.

"But of course you are, and if you even so much as look in Elizabeth's direction she will be forced to accept you, just as her sister Mary was forced to accept Lord Hawk."

The Earl recalled a pretty, unhappy face which he identified in his memory as that of Lady Hawk.

"You mean that Lady Mary had no wish to marry His Lordship?" he asked.

"Of course not," Karina said scornfully. "He is a horrible man, gross and unpleasant. He once tried to put his arms round me but I punched him in the stomach and while he was coughing I ran away!"

"I see you can take care of yourself!" Lord Droxford said mockingly.

"I was only fourteen at the time and it is not always easy to escape," Karina replied confidingly, then continued.

"But we were talking about Mary. She fell very much in love with a young soldier, but he had no money. The Duke threatened to beat her and lock her up in her room with nothing but bread and water to eat and drink if she ever tried to see him again.

"Then to be quite sure, His Grace complained to the Colonel of the young man's regiment and he was posted abroad!"

"Good heavens!" the Earl exclaimed, "And you think that sort of treatment would be meted out to any young woman who refused to marry me?"

"I am quite certain of it," Karina answered. "After all, you have more money, more presence and you are certainly a better matrimonial catch than Lord Hawk!"

"So you think it unlikely that anyone will marry me just for myself," the Earl enquired.

"No, I think that you might easily find someone who would like to marry Your Lordship," Karina replied, "And who would even fall in love with you. But you would have to love them a little first and as it is you have other . . . attachments and very little time!"

The Earl's face darkened as he recalled with anger the expedition with which he had to act.

"That is why I am suggesting . . . only suggesting," Karina went on, "that I might be quite a suitable wife for you. You see, I would like to marry you. I think you are very handsome, very elegant, and you certainly make love better than anyone else I have seen with Lady . . ."

She stopped suddenly and added hastily:

"I mean, some men look so stupid when they are enamoured."

"I am glad you approve of my deportment," the Earl said sarcastically.

"I expect you think I am being impertinent," Karina said, "And of course how you made love would not be of consequence where I was concerned because I have only to be a complacent wife.

"But I would certainly not interfere with your affairs and I expect you have a lot. I am not quite certain what is meant by comformable but I imagine it means doing the right thing, being nice to the tenants and visiting the poor on the Estate. Is that correct?"

"Something like that," the Earl agreed.

There was a little pause until Karina said hesitantingly:

"You may have noticed, My Lord, that I am not very tall so you might think the tiaras would perhaps be too overpowering for me! But I am a little like Mama, who was considered very beautiful, so perhaps I would look quite presentable at the end of your table."

"I am sure you would grace it very adequately," the Earl said politely.

It was impossible to be angry for long with this amusing child.

"And about being well-bred," Karina continued, "the Rendells have lived in this County since before Henry VIII and Mama's father was the Earl of O'Malley.

"Her relations live in Ireland so I have never met them. We have never had the money to go there and I expect they are impoverished too. But Mama said that the O'Malleys were at one time Irish Kings so you would not consider it a misalliance for my family tree to be mixed up with yours, would you?"

There was an anxiety in the green eyes which made the Earl reply gently:

"I consider you very well-bred, Miss Rendell."

"Thank you," she answered. "I would not like you to think that I would do anything loud or vulgar, but that is, of course, covered by my being conformable, is it not?"

"I imagine so," he answered.

"And, lastly, you said you did not want a nitwit," she said. "Well, Mama was insistent that I should speak French and Italian well.

"I know a little German but I think it is a horrid language, and I am fairly proficient at Greek, which used to be one of Papa's favourite subjects, which was why I was christened Karina. But I am afraid my Latin is . . . lamentable."

She looked at the Earl with a worried expression on her face.

"I do not think Latin is entirely necessary in a wife," he assured her.

She gave him a grateful look before she continued:

"I am somewhat shaky in mathematics, but I used to help Papa with all his political speeches until he retired from the House of Commons, and I have read a great deal."

Again the green eyes were anxious.

"I am afraid I am not very up-to-date as we have not been able to afford to buy new books or the newspapers lately.

"But I have borrowed some occasionally from the Duke's library so it would not take me very long to catch up on what I have missed."

"I see that you have had an adequate education," the Earl remarked.

"I must tell Your Lordship the truth: when I play the piano, even the dogs howl," Karina said, obviously determined to be frank with him. "And you may have observed that I have a number of freckles on my nose.

"That is only because since Mama died I often forget to wear my hat when I am out riding. If you were kind enough to consider me as your wife, I would promise always to wear a hat."

"That is undoubtedly very reassuring," the Earl said, and again he was unable to repress the twitch at the corners of his lips.

"I think perhaps you are laughing at me," Karina said accusingly. "But I am trying to be absolutely honest with you. I think that if we were to be married it is essential between a man and his wife. Do you not agree?"

"Absolutely," the Earl replied gravely. "In fact, I shall insist that my wife, whoever she might be, would always tell me the truth. I shall also expect her to obey me."

The green eyes looked at him enquiringly.

"In everything?"

"In everything," he replied grimly.

The idea flashed through Karina's mind that His Lordship would be a difficult man to cross for beneath the somewhat lazy exterior and the almost bored expression in his grey eyes, there was something steely, something that made her feel that if he set his mind on something, nothing would turn him from his objective until he obtained it.

Once again the Earl drew his watch from his waist-coatpocket.

"I am convinced I should return to the party."

"If you do consider what we have talked about," Karina said, "would you be calling on Papa tomorrow? I am not pressing you . . . please do not think that . . . but I would just like to know what time you were coming so that I could keep him . . ." she paused ". . . in the house."

It was not what she had started to say, the Earl realised.

"Whether I consider you as my future wife or not," he replied, "it would give me great pleasure to meet your father again. I will call at Blake Hall, which I recall is where you live, just before noon, if that will be convenient?"

"That would be most convenient," Karina told him. "And when Your Lordship meets the other prospective brides whom Lady Sibley will be collecting for you, you will remember me?"

"I have a feeling I will find it hard to forget you," the Earl answered. "I cannot help thinking, Miss Rendell, that we have had a most unusual conversation."

"You mean," Karina said with a look of mischief in her eyes, "that you are not in the habit of receiving proposals of marriage from young women!"

"That is certainly one of the reasons," he agreed.

"But you see, if I had not asked you, you would not have been introduced to me at the garden party, and unless I stood waving to you on the roadside, which would be even more reprehensible, how could we ever have become acquainted?"

"It does indeed seem that you have taken the only

26

possible course open to you," the Earl told her. "May I say I am delighted to have met you, Miss Rendell, and that I shall look forward to renewing my acquaintance with your father when I call on him tomorrow."

He bowed as he spoke and Karina dropped him a curtsey.

"How do you get home from here?" he asked curiously.

"Were you thinking of offering me a seat in your Phaeton?" she enquired. "That would cause a sensation! No, I shall leave as I came—over the dividing wall between the two Estates. My horse is waiting for me on the other side."

"Do you always ride as you are dressed now?" he enquired.

"I am afraid so," she replied. "I have no other method of coming to the Castle except on one of Papa's horses, and it is too far to walk two miles in this heat."

"I see you have an answer to every question," the Earl said. "Good-bye, Miss Rendell, you have certainly given me a great deal to think about."

He turned away as she smiled and he noticed that she had a dimple, just beside her mouth, on the left-hand side of her face. She was extremely attractive and he thought that, well-dressed, she would undoubtedly be a success. But she was not the type of wife he had in mind—far too perceptive, undoubtedly inquisitive.

No, Karina Rendell was not the sort of female, lovely though she might be, whom he wished to install as the Countess of Droxford. All the same, she would undoubtedly grace the diamonds, or better still, the sapphires.

He had always thought that fair women looked their best in sapphires and turquoises.

He had a sudden vision of his mother coming into

27

his bedroom when he was a little boy wearing a turquoise tiara and necklace which had made her skin seem dazzlingly white and her hair like living gold.

It was peculiar that he had never cared for fair women where his love affairs were concerned. Georgette Sibley, with her raven-black hair and magnolia skin, had a beauty which aroused his desire whenever he looked at her. She was at her best adorned in rubies.

Diamonds would glitter like stars in that ripe gold hair with the faintest touch of red in it, untidily arranged on Karina's small head. He had an idea that it must, when it was down, be very long.

"It is a strange thing," he thought, "that brunettes hardly ever have such long hair as fair ones."

His mother's hair had trailed over the pillows to fall over the side of the bed. He remembered as a small boy asking her to sit on it.

"Show me how you can sit on your hair, Mama!" he had cried. "Papa says that all beautiful women should be able to sit on their hair."

His mother had laughed and obliged him.

As he walked back across the lawn, the band getting louder and louder, the chatter of voices becoming almost deafening, he realised that he had never made love to a woman who could sit on her hair.

"Perhaps one day I shall find one," he told himself.

It was with a cynical but amused twist of his lips that the Earl moved through the crowds to where he saw in the distance the crimson feathers which trimmed Lady Sibley's bonnet.

2

The Earl of Droxford turned his Phaeton into the drive and stared ahead of him at the great mansion where his forebears had lived for generations.

Partially rebuilt by Vanburgh, who had built Blenheim Palace, he had made Droxford Park one of the largest private houses in England.

Magnificent, awe-inspiring, it dominated the landscape and at the same time had an almost ethereal beauty as if its builder had a vision of a fairytale Palace when he designed it.

"There is nothing finer in the whole Kingdom!" George III had exclaimed on his first visit.

To the Earl the colossal house with its lakes, gardens and parks laid out by Capability Brown was a part of himself. He was exceedingly proud of his home and thought of it as a heritage which he must cherish and improve before he handed it on to his children and grandchildren.

Every generation of Droxford's since the first Earl—who had received his title after the battle of Agincourt—had contributed to the wealth and treasurers owned by the family.

The pictures themselves were remarkable. The collection of Vandykes and Gainsboroughs were rivalled only by that possessed by the Crown.

The carvings and stone enrichments by Gibbons were his best work; the Thronhill ceilings and Laguerre murals left those who saw them bereft of adequate terms of praise.

But apart from the pictures and furniture the state in which the Earl lived was in itself almost regal. There were three hundred horses in the stables, there were over a thousand people employed on the Estate, and these included farmhands and gardeners, saddlers, glaziers, brewers and carpenters, woodman and foresters, blacksmiths and iron-mongers.

In fact, as Lord Grey had once said when staying at Droxford Park, "this is a State within a State".

But as the Earl drove down the drive there was the same scowl on his face that there had been when he had left No. 10 Downing Street the day before.

"How can I contemplate," he asked himself, looking at the pinnacles and towers which gave the house a romantic skyline, "bringing her as a chatelaine to take my Mother's place, any of the females who have just been presented to me at the Castle."

Never, he thought, had he seen a plainer and more umprepossessing collection. Granted, he was not very conversant with young girls, spending his time as he did amongst the gay, married set and taking very good care he was not inveigled by the hostesses at Almack's into dancing with some wench who had only just fallen out of the nest.

But if he was forced to marry one of these unfledged little birds, then he despaired for the future line of descendants who would inherit Droxford Park.

"Yes, My Lord"—"No, My Lord," they had simpered at him.

And he remembered with increasing irritation that as each one spoke she cast down her eyes in a maidenly manner which was exactly what Karina had told him they would do.

The things she had said to him in her artless, frank manner seemed as he thought about them, to infuriate him more and more as the afternoon passed on.

He could not help recalling that she had told him Lady Sibley was in the habit of taking her latest lover to the arbour, and the Earl found himself wondering whether her eyes had looked at other men with the same smouldering passion with which she looked at him.

He asked himself if she had lifted her lips to them with the same eagerness and if indeed she had invited them to meet her, as she invited him, in the small Grecian Temple which stood in the wild garden of Lord Sibley's Estate.

For the first time he asked himself why the Temple was so comfortably furnished, with the couch piled with soft cushions, with easy chairs, and with shutters which covered the windows and prevented a lighted candle being seen from the outside.

He had never contemplated that there might have been other men who had had assignations with the entrancing Georgette in this very place! But now, when Lady Sibley had whispered "Tonight" as he kissed her hand good-bye on the Castle lawn, he found himself beset by a number of questions which had never troubled him before.

He glanced back for a moment at the Duke's guests conversing politely around the band and under the trees. They had an elegance which made them, in such an attractive setting, look like a masterpiece from his own Picture Gallery.

And then he thought of the girls whom Lady Sibley had just introduced to him and felt inclined to swear loudly and forcibly.

It would be almost a pleasure, he thought, to see the shock on the faces of those who heard him and to drive away the ingratiating smiles on the face of every ambitious Mama.

He had known that they were looking at him speculatively as Lady Sibley introduced each pale, insignificant chit standing obedient and apparently tongueless beside her mother.

"The Marchioness of Melchester—Lady Mary

Fortesque—Lord Droxford," and "Lady Longforde—Miss Amelia Longforde—Lord Droxford."

The introductions had come one after another. Lord Droxford had made an effort to speak to the girls, one of whom he knew must eventually be his pass-key to the position of Lord Lieutenant.

"It is a lovely day, Miss Longforde."

"Yes, My Lord."

"Do you enjoy these sort of functions?"

"Yes. My Lord."

"And you do miss the gaieties of London when you are in the country?"

"No, My Lord."

"God!" he thought, "is there nothing else they can say?"

Driving away from the Castle he had felt his repressed anger boiling over.

"The Devil take it! There must be women in the world who are not so obviously to-let-in-the-attic that they can only mouth monosyllables!"

He spoke aloud and the groom behind him said:

"Did you speak, M'Lord?"

"Only to myself," the Earl snapped.

"They were impossible, quite impossible!" he told himself now, looking at his house and wondering if Lady Sibley had deliberately chosen the plainest and most unattractive girls for his inspection, or was it perhaps that every other woman paled into insignificance when she was present.

Georgette was beautiful, there was no mistake about that, and as that impudent child Karina Rendell has pointed out, he was obviously not the first to think so.

"The Serpent" was what she and the Duke's daughter, who looked like a small, frightened rabbit, ca'led her. And the Earl was sure that it was not Elizabeth who had thought of the nickname!

"Damn the girl! She had no right to eavesdrop!"

He felt his anger against Karina increasing as he remembered she had warned him candidly that no girl was likely to marry him for himself unless he first made the effort to make her fall in love with him.

The Earl admitted now that his first conception of marriage was that his wife would love him dutifully; he would give her a little attention from time to time, while making sure that she did not interfere with his other interests and attachments.

He supposed that in truth he thought that she would stay at Droxford Park having babies while he enjoyed himself in London.

Perhaps that indeed was what any of those sheep-like creatures he had just met would be prepared to do. But could he tolerate the thought of coming home to find them in charge?

Could he bear to see them sitting in Mother's place? To find them in the Drawing Room, which had been so essentially her own room and where she would entertain so delightfully the distinguished guests who had filled the house in his father's time, and who often still honoured his present bachelor establishment?

He could remember his Mother charming the Regent when he had stayed at Droxford Park.

He himself had been very young, home from Eton for the holidays; but he could still see the beautiful women who had graced that particular house party; hear the brilliant politicians like Lord Melbourne, Sir Robert Peel and Lord Palmerston; and recall the elegance of the Bucks and Corinthians with whom the Regent surrounded himself.

Their wit and laughter had made every hour glow like some brilliant jewel.

How could any of those awkward tongue-tied creatures he had just met ever become a great hostess?

"Curse it, but I will find myself a widow! Someone who is up to snuff," the Earl vowed.

33

But try as he would he could not think among his vast acquaintance of a single widow young, beautiful and important enough to play the part he desired of her.

He drew up his horses outside the great porticoed front door with its flight of wide stone steps. The afternoon sun threw a purple shadow over the courtyard but the upper windows of the house still gleamed iridescently and the flag flying in the warm wind was silhouetted against a cloudless sky.

The Earl stood for a moment on the steps looking to where the lake was bridged by the drive, and beneath which swam the black swans for which the Park was famous. Against the silver of the water they had a dark elegance and he thought for a moment that they reminded him of Georgette Sibley's hair.

The lilacs, purple, white and mauve, were in bloom and he could smell the fragrance of them on the wind. He could see the pink blossom of the almond trees his mother had planted down at the lake's edge, so that the landscape had an ethereal quality and the blossoms that had fallen into the water floated like tiny boats on the ripples which splashed against the yellow iris.

The whole place had a beauty that was almost indescribable, and the Earl turned away as if it hurt him to look at anything so lovely.

He entered the Great Hall with its marble statutes set in alcoves and the ceiling painted by an Italian artist who had been brought from Florence for this very purpose, and walked through the line of liveried footmen towards the Library which was situated on the other side of the house overlooking the formal gardens.

The Butler opened the door for him and said as he entered:

"Is there anything you require, My Lord?"

"Yes, brandy," the Earl replied.

Masters, who had been with His Lordship's father and had served the family for over forty years, made a gesture with his hand and a footman hurried to obey the order.

The Earl walked across the room, which was lined with valuable books and in whose great stone chimney-piece was set a painting by Stubbs of his grandfather on his favourite hunter.

"Tell me, Masters," he said, "what do you know of Sir John Rendell, who used to be the Member of Parliament for this constituency?"

"I am afraid the news of Sir John is not good, My Lord," Masters replied.

The Earl raised his eyebrows and waited.

"After Her Ladyship died Sir John went to pieces," Masters continued. "They say, My Lord, he gambled away every penny he possessed and indulged until he was brought home in such a deplorable state that they almost despaired of his life!"

"A pity," the Earl remarked. "I seem to remember him as a fine-looking man and a good goer to hounds."

"He was indeed, My Lord. His late Lordship always said that one could be certain that Sir John, if no one else, was in at the kill."

"And he gave up the constituency?" the Earl questioned.

"I understand Sir John was not in a fit state of health to attend the House of Commons, My Lord."

"Thank you, that is what I suspected."

The Earl's tone indicated that the conversation was finished, but Masters lingered.

"Lady Rendell used to come here in the past, My Lord," he went on. "There was never a sweeter-spoken lady, but Sir John was always a difficult man. There are some hard stories going around about him now."

"What sort of stories?" the Earl asked sharply.

"They say, My Lord, that because he is so dis-

35

traught at Her Ladyship's death—and she was the one person who always brought out the best in him—he vents his sorrow on his daughter. He only had one child, My Lord, and for all I hear she is as pretty as her mother."

"What do you mean, 'vents his sorrow'?" the Earl enquired.

"I am only repeating gossip, My Lord, but of course one hears things living year after year in close proximity to one's neighbours. But they allege that Sir John, when he is in his cups, knocks the young lady about!"

Masters coughed respectfully,

"She cannot be very old, My Lord, and if she is like her mother, she will be a small delicate creature. It is not right that such things should happen, but what can anyone do? A gentleman can behave as he wishes within his own household!"

"He can indeed," the Earl agreed and wondered whether all his neighbours were peculiar in their habits or whether he had never before been particularly interested in other people's behaviour.

There was the Duke, according to Karina, threatening to beat his eldest daughter and lock her up with nothing but bread and water to eat and drink until she bowed to his will.

And now Sir John Rendell, whom he had always thought of as a decent, intelligent man, knocking about—so Masters believed—that small, fairy-like creature with large green eyes who was quite unlike anyone he had ever seen before.

It was monstrous that the child, for she was little more, should be ill-treated by a drunken man, whatever their relationship, and yet as Masters said so truly, there was nothing that could be done about it!

Anyway, whether it was true or not, he would see Sir John Rendell tomorrow as he had promised to do.

In the meantime he had his own problems to think

about. He certainly could not waste time on Karina's and yet annoyingly he kept thinking of her while he ate a lonely dinner in the huge Banqueting Hall where at least a hundred persons could sit down in comfort.

It had been devised in Vanburgh's most grandiose style, with murals on the wall, with a heavily painted and gilded ceiling and embellished with furniture and ornaments of such inportance that they could not be valued in terms of money.

The table at which the Earl ate was decorated with orchids from his garden and gold plate which had been in the Droxford family since the time of Charles II.

Dish after dish had been prepared by the chef whose culinary efforts were known to be superb. But the Earl ate little and waved most of the dishes away.

He found himself looking at the chair opposite him at the far end of the long, polished table. He imagined the girls he had met this afternoon seated there, conversing with him, glittering with either the diamond, sapphire, ruby or emerald set which consisted of a tiara, ear-rings, necklace, bracelet and corsage, which lay awaiting in the safe for the future Countess of Droxford.

He knew he could not stand looking at Miss Longforde with her vacant eyes and loose mouth, or Lady Mary Fortesque, who had, he was certain, a suspicion of a squint.

There was another chit who had a chin covered in pimples, and yet another who had giggled nervously when they were introduced and who was too shy even to lift her eyes to his.

Was Georgette Sibley insane that she could think for a moment that he could consider one of them? Yet he was well aware that they were all socially eligible and that the *Beau Ton* would accept without question such creatures as his wife.

Moreover, the Earl thought savagely that any of

them would undoubtedly win the King's approval as being the right type of wife for the Lord Lieutenant of the County.

"I will not do it!" he almost shouted aloud.

Then pushing his chair back from the table the Earl left the Dining-Room before Masters had poured him out a glass of port.

The old Butler stared after him in consternation, while the footmen winked at each other, quite certain in their own minds that the only explanation for His Lordship's strange behaviour was a disagreement in love.

The Earl would have been infuriated if he had known how accurately most of his household knew his plans for the evening.

He imagined, when he asked for his horse and rode away alone into the dusk, that they really believed he was just going for a ride; but the groom who brought round the spirited stallion, the footman who saw him off from the door, and old Masters bowing as he rode away, were all well aware of his destination.

The Earl galloped his horse for some way to get the freshness out of him, then he turned the animal's head north and rode through the woods which lay between the Droxford Estate and that of Lord Sibley.

About five miles as the crow flies, it took the Earl a very short time to reach the wood through which he must pass before he came to Lord Sibley's garden.

The Sibley Estate was a small one and His Lordship, who found that his wife's extravagances in London left him little money for the upkeep of a large staff in the country, was content not to farm the land himself but to rent it out to tenants.

It was therefore unlikely, the Earl knew, that he would be seen by anyone in Lord Sibley's employment as he passed through the wood, crossed several fields of grass and came at last to the shrubberies and plantations which sheltered the house itself.

He dismounted and tied his horse to a wooden fence. Then walking quietly through the trees and bushes he came to a small white Temple which had been erected in the garden by Lord Sibley's father, who had a passion for Grecian remains.

The Temple appeared deserted, but when Lord Droxford opened the door there was a golden glow from two candles and he saw that Lady Sibley had kept her promise and he would not have to wait for her.

She was laying on the couch against the silk cushions and she was looking particularly alluring as she held out her bare arms towards him. The diaphanous négligé of pink gauze which she wore revealed the soft nakedness of her body beneath it.

The Earl closed the door behind him and automatically locked it. He put his tall hat, his gloves and his riding-whip down on a chair and moved across the room, the frown lifting from his forehead and a sudden fire glowing in his eyes.

"You look very beautiful, Georgette," he said hoarsely.

"I have been waiting for you," she answered.

And now her face was lifted to his, her red lips parted, a passionate hunger that was unmistakeable in her expression.

He bent towards her. Her arms were drawing him down to an embrace—urgent, persuasive, compelling—and he found that the warmth and desire of her lips blotted out thought.

Karina went to the front door and looked down the drive for perhaps the sixth time. There was no sign of a carriage or a horseman and she gave a little sigh.

"I never really expected him to come," she told herself.

At the same time she felt suspiciously like tears.

It had been hard to get her father dressed this

39

morning, to insist on his shaving and to seat him looking comparatively respectable in the Study with his gouty foot dressed in fresh bandages raised on a footstool.

He had sworn at her, cursed her for interfering, and then with one of his quick changes of mood which she knew only too well, had become full of remorse and apologised for his disagreeableness.

"I am a bad father to you, Karina," he said, "and, as you say, few decent people come to the house these days. If Droxford wants to visit me—I should be grateful. I will behave myself, I promise you. But give me a drink, I cannot face him without one."

"You have had one already," Karina said, "And you know full well, Papa, that you are much more amusing and entertaining without that horrible brandy muddling your speech and making you forget what you were going to say!"

"Goddammit! Can I not have a drink in my own house . . ." Sir John began, only to add hastily: "No. No, I will do as you say!"

"I will get you some coffee, Papa."

"Filthy stuff—but it will be better than nothing," Sir John growled.

Karina ran hastily to the kitchen to ask Mrs. James to make a pot of coffee quickly. She did not dare leave her father to see to it herself, though she knew that Mrs. James, very old and half blind, would take an unconscionable time in preparing the coffee.

There were only two servants left in the house and as they were seldom paid they would not have stayed if they had had anywhere else to go.

James had been with her father and mother since they first married. He was over seventy now, very deaf, and shuffled around the house in carpet slippers as his feet were too swollen to wear any other footgear. And Mrs. James was so forgetful that if Karina

40

had not done most of the cooking they would not have had anything to eat!

This morning, Karina had begged and bullied James into putting on his livery coat and polishing the buttons. His trousers were threadbare and patched in several places, but at least he looked better than he did habitually—wandering round the house with a shawl over his shoulders because he felt the draughts with his rheumatics.

Her father had been difficult from the moment she had informed him that Lord Droxford was calling to see him.

It had been foolish of her to tell him last night, she thought now. He was already drunk when she got back from the Castle and as his gout had been bad, anything unusual was likely to put him a bad temper.

"Droxford! Who is Droxford?" he asked, slurring the words.

"You cannot have forgotten the Earl of Droxford, Papa," Karina replied. "His father was Master of the Fox Hounds, and you used to tell me how much you enjoyed the Meets at Droxford Park."

"Droxford! Why did you not say so?" Sir John asked querulously.

He was a tall, big-boned man who had once been goodlooking. But now his face was blotched and swollen with drink, the veins on his nose red and broken, his eyes puffy and his hair now turning grey had receded from his forehead.

His hands were unsteady as he raised a glass of brandy to his lips, and Karina saw that the decanter beside him was already half empty.

"Do listen to me, Papa, before you have any more to drink," she begged. "Lord Droxford is anxious to renew his acquaintance with you and he is calling here tomorrow morning. Do please receive him pleasantly. It will be nice for you to see someone of importance for a change."

41

"What do you mean, for a change?" Sir John growled truculently.

"You used to have so many distinguished persons here when you were a Member of Parliament," Karina said. "I can remember them coming to dinner. You used to make them laugh, Papa, and they always used to tell me how brilliant you were."

"And what is wrong with me now?" Sir John exclaimed.

"You have not been well, Papa, and your gout has been troublesome. You know as well as I do you should not be drinking so much—it will only make your foot hurt worse than ever."

"I can do as I like and if I want a drink I will have a drink," Sir John retorted. "That is, so long as I can pay for it. What the hell happens to all the money I give you, I cannot think."

"You have not given me any for a long time," Karina demurred. "I am afraid, Papa, the tradesmen will not serve us anymore unless we can pay them a little of the vast sums they are owed."

"Damned impertinence!" Sir John snarled. "I will teach those swine to dictate to me!"

"Now, Papa, do not get angry," Karina pleaded. "We will just have to sell something. There is not much left except the pictures and furniture in Mama's room. Those I know could contribute quite a considerable amount towards payment of our bills!"

"How dare you!" Sir John shouted in a sudden fury. "How dare you suggest that I should dispose of your mother's things? They are hers and no one shall touch them, do you hear me? Not you—you greedy, grasping brat, always trying to extort money from me.

"You are like all women, never satisfied unless you are given gold. Blast your eyes, but I will not sell what was your mother's if I have to watch you starve in front of my very eyes!"

"That is what I am afraid we shall do, Papa."

Karina stood calm, quite unperturbed by his fury, and this seemed to annoy him more than if she had cringed or cried.

He reached out suddenly and slapped her hard across the face. The blow made her stagger because she was not expecting it. She half fell beside him, saving herself only by holding onto his chair.

He bent forward and gripped her bare arm.

"You will sell nothing of your mother's—do you hear me?—nothing! And if I catch you trying to do so behind my back I will make you sorry that you have ever been born. Do you understand?"

He shook her furiously, his fingers digging into her soft skin.

"Of course I understand, Papa," Karina said quietly, "and I would not do anything without telling you. But I am afraid that is the last bottle of brandy the wine-merchant will deliver. He told me so when he came here today."

"The last bottle!" Sir John released Karina's arm and put his hands up to his face.

"I cannot do without wine. You know—Karina that I cannot do without—it."

She got slowly to her feet. Her cheek was burning where he had struck her, but her eyes were sad and almost tender as she looked at her father, who had begun to snivel into his hands.

"Sell something," he muttered. "Sell anything you like—but do not let me know—do not tell me about it—I cannot bear it—I cannot bear it! Your mother's treasures, and now I have to drink them away!"

He seized the glass of brandy as he spoke and poured half of it down his throat.

Karina knew he would soon be hopelessly drunk and she had gone in search of old James. If they did not get her father to bed soon, he would be incapable of helping himself upstairs and then he would have to stay where he was all night!

She rubbed her arm where he had gripped her. It hurt her and there would doubtless be a bruise there in the morning; but at least he had not hit her as hard as he often did, sometimes almost to render her unconscious!

She had learnt to keep sticks and whips out of his reach when he got very drunk, which had become an everyday occurrence.

This morning, nevertheless, Sir John was comparatively sober and looked quite presentable. Karina prayed that the Earl, if he were coming, would not be long in arriving.

As she turned from the kitchen towards the Study she had one more look out of the open front door, and her heart gave a suddenly leap.

Turning into the gates were a pair of horseflesh she would have given anything in the world to posses and, tooling his High Perch Phaeton with his high hat at a rakish angle, a yellow carnation in his buttonhole to match his yellow waistcoat, there appeared Lord Droxford.

"He is coming! He is coming! James!" Karina called. "Quick, get to the door, I will go down the steps to meet him. Just stand at the door."

She realised that although she was shouting, the old man had not heard her. She ran hastily towards the passage, pulling him into the Hall.

"Lord Droxford!" she bellowed in his ear.

"I hears you—Miss Karina—I hears you the first time—I'm a-coming—I can't move faster with these 'ere feet of mine! Painful they be today—very painful—kept me awake all th'night."

"Yes, I know. James, I know," Karina said. "But just stand at the door holding it open. You do not have to do anything else."

She pushed him into place just as the Earl drew his horses to a standstill outside the door.

44

She hurried to meet him, her face alight, her green eyes shining, and he thought as he stepped down from the Phaeton that she was even lovelier than she had seemed yesterday.

She was again wearing a gown that she had outgrown but at least it was clean, freshly pressed, and the green sash round her waist seemed to match the green of her eyes.

But it was her hair at which the Earl looked, finding it impossible to believe that it was the amazing colour he had remembered it to be. Now neatly and skilfully dressed it seemed to frame her small face with a halo of gold.

As she ran down the steps into the sunshine he thought almost poetically that she might have taken a sunbeam and wound it around her head.

"You have come!" she said, and it was almost a cry of joy. "I did so hope you had not forgotten!"

"If I make a promise I do not forget it," the Earl answered loftily.

"I felt that was true about you," she smiled, "and yet I was afraid."

"Afraid?" he questioned.

"Papa has been looking forward to your visit," she said quickly, "and it would have been a tremendous disappointment to him and very much an anticlimax if you had not appeared."

She saw him glance at the front door as if he expected to see Sir John standing there.

"I am afraid that Papa's gout does not allow him to greet Your Lordship as he should. Will you be obliging enough to come into his Study?"

"Yes, of course," the Earl agreed.

He entered the house, saw old James standing almost to attention by the door, and noted automatically the lack of furniture in the Hall, the spaces on the wall where pictures and mirrors must have once hung, and where the wallpaper was less faded.

Karina led him down a corridor on which the carpet was full of holes, and opened the door of the Study.

It would have been a pleasant room were it not extremely bare. It contained only a few chairs—Sir John was sitting in one—a writing-desk that was so old as virtually to be unsaleable, and one plain oak table on which there was a huge vase of flowers.

"Lord Droxford—Papa," Karina said from the door.

Sir John held out his hand.

"Forgive me, Droxford, but I cannot rise to meet you," he said. "This gout of mine is making life peculiarly unpleasant, as you can well imagine, and it is also corrupting my good manners."

If the Earl was surprised to see the wreck of a man who he once knew as alert, good-looking and intelligent, he showed no signs of it. His smile was friendly as he took Sir John's hand.

"Would you like some coffee, My Lord?" Karina asked.

"Coffee!" Sir John roared. "Is that the hospitality you offer to an old friend? Wine, Karina, or brandy. That is what you would like, is it not, Droxford?"

The Earl was well aware that Karina's eyes had a look of pleading in them.

"No, indeed, Sir John," he replied. "It is too early for me to drink strong liquor. Coffee is what I would prefer, and I am sure you will join me."

Sir John would have ejaculated a denial had not Karina laid her hand on his arm and checked the word on his lips.

"Very well, a cup of coffee," he growled somewhat ungraciously. "I have been waiting for one as it happens."

"I am sure it is ready by now, Papa."

Karina turned towards the door and as she did so the Earl saw the bruises on the whiteness of her arm.

They revealed the brutal imprint of three fingers,

46

and he knew as he saw them that Masters had not exaggerated the stories he had heard.

It was some time before Karina could get the coffee ready. She had cleaned the coffee-pot earlier that morning, and also the tray.

But Mrs. James had somehow mislaid the sugar and when finally she returned to the Study she was frightened lest she might hear her father's voice querulous and disagreeable or, worse still, raised in anger.

To her delight he was laughing at something that Lord Droxford had said and when she had set the coffee down on the writing-desk and poured it out, Sir John took the cup from her and drank it without comment.

Karina was not certain whether she should leave the two men alone together. The decision was made for her when, as his coffee was finished, the Earl rose to his feet.

"It has been a great pleasure to meet you again, Rendell," he said. "I hope it will not be too long before you are back in public life."

"The House of Commons will never see me again," Sir John replied gloomily. "I cannot afford to fight an election these days—I cannot afford even to live if it comes to that!"

"I am sorry to hear that," the Earl answered. "I hope when you are better you will accept an invitation to dine with me. I intend to be in the County more often in the future than I have been in the past."

"You will be taking over the Lord Lieutenancy, I presume, now Handley is dead?" Sir John said unexpectedly.

It was so like him to have a sudden flash of intuition or intelligence, Karina thought, when one least expected it.

She supposed that she must have told him that Lord

47

Handley was dead, or perhaps it was one of his old cronies. He had not forgotten that it was a tradition that the Earl of Droxford should be Lord Lieutenant of the County!

Karina waited for the Earl's reply.

"You are right, Sir John," he said steadily. "It will not be long before His Majesty appoints me as Lord Lieutenant."

He followed Karina through the door and into the passage.

"I wish to speak with you," he said.

She led the way into the Salon and the Earl saw that the room was almost completely bare. There was only a carpet on the floor, a sofa by the fireplace, and curtains to suggest that the room had ever been in use.

Everything else had gone—furniture, pictures, the carved mirror which had once stood over the mantel-shelf; the china, the small walnut secretaire at which Lady Rendell had written her letters, and the inlaid marquetry chairs which had been handed down from father to son for five generations.

Karina made no apologies for the emptiness of the room. She only stood waiting for the Earl to speak to her, her fingers clasped together, her eyes looking enquiringly up into his.

"Have you no relations with whom you could live?" the Earl asked unexpectedly.

"Why?" Karina asked.

He looked at the purple bruises on her arm.

"Does that happen often?"

"Whenever he thinks of my mother," she answered dispassionately. "He loved her so desperately that it is intolerable for him to be alive when she is dead. He resents me because I must try to take her place."

"And what would happen if you left him?"

Karina's eyes flickered for a moment and the colour rose in her checks.

"Papa has a . . . friend," she answered, "who

manages him far better than I do, but she will not move into the house while I am here.

"I think she would come if he were alone. She is a kind woman and she has a little money of her own. That is one of the reasons why I would like to be . . . married."

There was a sudden silence.

"Dammit all!" the Earl said harshly. "You are the best of a bad bunch! At least you should be grateful to me for saving you from being knocked about!"

Do you mean . . . that . . . you will . . .marry me?" Karina asked breathlessly.

"Yes," he answered. "But remember I do it with no feeling of pleasure. I loathe and detest the circumstances which oblige me to take a wife when I have no wish for one.

"I shall not be a particularly pleasant husband, Karina, so do not complain afterwards. You know why I am marrying you and there is no pretence about it!"

"No, there is no pretence," Karina agreed. "But I would like to marry you, My Lord, and not only because I shall escape from . . . this. In fact I think we might deal very well together!"

Despite his irritation, the Earl could not help his eyes twinkling at her tone.

"God knows what I am letting myself in for with you!" he exclaimed. "It seems to me I might be better advised to offer for one of those cabbage-heads I met yesterday afternoon!"

A dimple appeared at the side of Karina's mouth.

"I told you they would say: "Yes, My Lord," and "No, My Lord," she said. "I wager they cast their eyes down as they spoke—they always do!"

"I do not suppose I should have noticed such defects if you had not so spitefully pointed them out to me," he said.

"Can you blame me for using every method possible to win the race?" she asked.

"Is that how you look at it?" he enquired.

"The equivalent to winning the Gold Cup at Ascot!" she replied.

He could not prevent himself from laughing.

"You are incorrigible!" he said. "But as my wife you will have to learn not only to behave yourself, but to curb your tongue!"

"I hope to be known as the 'amusing Countess of Droxford!' " Karina replied. "And at least we shall have something to talk about when we do meet. I promise you that I shall never say: 'Yes, My Lord,' and 'No, My Lord.' "

"I suppose that I must break the news to your father," the Earl said. "I believe if I am correct that I have to request his permission to address you."

"It is too late for that," Karina answered. "You had best let me tell him. How soon do you think we should be married?"

"I had not thought about it," the Earl answered.

"May I make a suggestion?" Karina asked.

"But of course," he replied.

"Then I think that we should be married very quickly," she said. "Just in case His Majesty will not wait and appoints the Duke of Severn."

"Are you afraid that if that happens I should withdraw my offer?" the Earl asked.

"Of course you would," Karina replied frankly. "So I want to be sure of you, and you want to be sure of the Lord Lieutenancy!"

She hesitated and added slowly:

"Could we not be married quietly in your private Chapel at Droxford Park without anyone outside being told what is happening? Later you could explain the haste was due to illness in the Bride's family. After all, Papa would not be very presentable at a fashionable wedding!"

"I see your point," the Earl said.

"And when it is over we could go straight to London," Karina continued. "It would save people in the County calling on us. Let them just wake up and find it announced in the *Gazette* after we have gone! You need not even say on what date the ceremony took place!"

"You seem to have everything worked out," the Earl answered. "I must admit to feeling somewhat bewildered!"

"If you think about it," Karina said, "you will see that it is really the wisest course."

"I believe you are right," the Earl admitted. "My private Chaplain can perform the ceremony; we can leave for London when it is over, and there will be no speculation, gossip or arguments until it is too late for anyone to do anything about it."

He was thinking as he spoke of Lady Sibley. He had a feeling that when she saw the Bride he had chosen for himself she would not be over-pleased. Whatever anyone might say about Karina, they would have to admit that she was extremely pretty.

She was looking away from him now and her tiny straight aristocratic nose was etched against the bare walls of the Salon.

"She is lovely," he told himself and knew that many people would find it hard to believe that he was not genuinely enamoured of his wife.

"We will do exactly as you suggest," he said "I will post to London immediately for a Special Licence and return tomorrow morning. My carriage will call for you in the afternoon. Will three o'clock suit you? We could be married and be in London for dinner!"

"I will be ready," Karina said. "If I can persuade Papa to come with me, he will give me away; if not presumably you can find another witness?"

"That will not be difficult," the Earl replied.

He looked at Karina curiously. He had never

imagined that a young woman could speak so calmly and dispassionately about her own wedding.

Karina looked up at him. Her eyes were bright, otherwise her expression revealed nothing of her inner feelings.

"I must thank you, My Lord, for your kind offer," she said formally. "I promise to make you a complacent and conformable wife and I will not interfere with your other . . . interests. It is a bargain which I hope you will never regret."

"I hope so too, Karina," the Earl replied.

He raised her hand perfunctorily to his lips and as there seemed nothing more to say, he went to the door and waited for her to precede him across the Hall.

He climbed in his Phaeton and she stood on the steps to wave him good-bye. She raised her bare arm as he lifted his reins and he thought she looked like some very young Goddess in a mythical legend. But he was scowling as he steadied his horses. He had a sudden uncanny apprehension for the future.

"God damn the King!" he muttered beneath his breath. "I have no wish to saddle myself with her as my wife or any other unfledged female!"

3

Karina stepped into the carriage which had been waiting for over quarter of an hour. She had been unable to get away sooner, having so many things to see to in the house at the last moment.

As she walked down the steps she took an appreciative glance at the perfectly matched pair of bays which were drawing His Lordship's most elegant and up-to-date landau.

She only wished she could drive them herself rather than sit in state on the cushioned seat behind the panelled doors emblazoned with the Earl's colourful coat of arms.

Then with a smile she thought how astonished the Earl would be if his bride arrived for her wedding tooling the landau with his coachmen sitting inside.

She felt, however, it would be the sort of joke that he would not appreciate.

At the same time, she hoped she would soon be brave enough to ask him for a curricle or a Phaeton which she might drive herself. Yet it might be difficult, she realised, to explain to him how she had become so proficient with the reins.

After her mother had died and her father had gone to London, leaving her with no money to pay the servants or to buy food, she had found she could earn what seemed a quite considerable sum by breaking in horses for a Livery Stable which was only two miles away from Blake Hall.

It was an up-to-date establishment which not only provided customers and other stables with riding-horses, but also sold or hired out carriage-teams of superior quality.

One of the difficulties the proprietor encountered was to find in the country men or women experienced enough to help him break in the animals for which his stable was becoming famous.

He was a middle-aged man who had gained a reputation for being a good judge of horseflesh and who travelled around the countryside attending local fairs. At the same time he had to keep in touch with the Establishment and customers he supplied in London.

When Karina offered him her services he was delighted to accept them, and she had spent many tiring but to her enjoyable hours every day accustoming horses to carry a lady's saddle, and driving Phaetons and curricles drawn by two, three or sometimes four horses, round and round the riding-school or along the country roads.

"How shocked Mama would have been," Karina had thought, "if she had known I was accepting money for doing what she would consider a menial job."

Yet during those months while her father was away it was the guineas she brought back from the Livery Stable which ensured they did not starve.

Leaning back in the carriage, Karina thought with a little throb of pleasure of the horses she would be able to ride once she was the Earl's wife.

She had always been told that he was the best judge of a horse in the County. Because he was a near neighbour she had followed the Earl's successes on the turf and knew that he had in training several animals which were fancied for the classic races of the year.

She found that, in thinking of the horses which were pulling her towards Droxford Park, she had almost forgotten the reason for her going there.

Was it true? Could it really be happening? Was she really driving to her wedding?

There had been so much to do since the Earl had left her the preceding day, that she had hardly time to think what marrying him would entail.

Immediately the Earl left she had prepared luncheon for her father, and then hurrying to the stables she had found Jim there—a young boy who helped her groom her father's two horses in exchange for permission to ride them.

Sir John would have been infuriated had he known that any village yokel had the effrontery to mount his hunters. But after his groom had left, having received no wages for six months, Karina had found it impossible to look after both horses as well as do all that was required in the house. The help Jim gave her was a Godsend.

"Saddle Kingfisher for me, Jim," she said now, "and will you ride over to Mr. Abbott, the furniture dealer, who lives in Severn, and ask him to call on me either tonight or first thing tomorrow. Explain it is very urgent."

"Yer mean 'im that lives in th' house next th' Church, Miss?"

"Yes, that is Mr. Abbott's place," Karina answered, "and make sure that he promises to call, Jim, it is of the utmost import!"

"Oi'll tell he, Miss," Jim answered.

He put Karina's side-saddle on Kingfisher's back, tightened the girths, slipped a bridle over the horse's head and cupping his hands on his knee, helped Karina onto the saddle.

She arranged her gown carefully for fear she should tear it and then, taking up the reins, she rode from the stable across the fields, taking her usual short route from Blake Hall to the Duke's Castle.

Instead of leaving her horse as she usually did at the boundary fence, she entered the Park by a farm gate and rode towards the Castle, making a detour so as to approach it at the back entrance.

Fortunately when she dismounted she saw a groom standing about with apparently nothing to do.

"Will you look after my horse for me?" she asked, "or if you are busy, take him to the stables. I can collect him from there later on."

"Ay, Oi'll do that, Miss Rendell," the groom answered, who knew her by sight.

"Thank you very much. It is very obliging of you," Karina told him.

She gave him a smile which made him tell the other grooms when he reached the stables:

"T'was a bleeding pity 'Is Grace's daughter be not

near as flash as that Miss Rendell from Blake Hall or her'd 'ave more chance o' finding 'erself an 'usband."

Inside the Castle Karina wound her way along the flagged passages of the servants quarters until she reached an unimportant staircase which led to the second floor.

She found Elizabeth as she had expected, sitting in the Schoolroom stitching her tapestry, at which she was exceedingly proficient. Fortunately there was no one else with her, the Governess having taken the younger children for a walk.

Elizabeth looked up as the door opened and sprang to her feet.

"Karina!" she exclaimed. "I was hoping that you would come today. I expected you yesterday. I am longing to hear what you thought of the garden party."

"Did you enjoy it?" Karina asked.

"No! It was ghastly!" Elizabeth said frankly. "Mamma never stopped introducing me to young men and the moment I looked at them everything I had thought of to say went out of my head.

"When they had drifted away, which was inevitable as I was so tongue-tied, Mama was furious with me. 'Talk, Elizabeth!' she kept saying, 'it does not matter what you say, but you must talk!' "

Karina laughed.

"Poor Elizabeth! You must get over being so shy."

"I cannot help it," Elizabeth said miserably. "And you know I hate crowds. I longed to be with you. Could you see everything from our lookout? And did Lady Sibley come to the arbour? I am sure that if she did it was with Lord Droxford. They were walking about together on the lawn."

Karina suddenly knew she could not bear to tell Elizabeth what had occurred. She was not sure whether it was embarrassment or that she felt she must be loyal to her future husband.

She only knew she could not relate the manner in

which the Earl had made love to Lady Sibley or how she had learnt of his desire to be Lord Lieutenant.

She looked away from Elizabeth's eager and curious eyes, and because she seldom lied she felt the blood rise in her cheeks since she must now be evasive.

"I did not . . . stay long," she said hesitatingly. "It was no . . . fun without you being . . . with me."

"How disappointing!" Elizabeth exclaimed. "I thought you would have a deal to tell me. Lady Sibley introduced me to Lord Droxford. He is handsome—very handsome, Karina—but he frightens me. I simply could not think of anything to say to him and that made Mama angrier than anything else!"

"I want your help, Elizabeth," Karina said.

"In what way?" Elizabeth asked. "Have you trouble at home? Your father is not ill again, is he?"

Karina shook her head.

"No, it is something quite different. Papa has been asked by Lord Droxford to visit him tomorrow afternoon. I am to accompany him—and, Elizabeth, I have nothing to wear!"

"You have been invited to Droxford Park!" Elizabeth exclaimed. "Oh, how exciting, Karina! Is it a party? I wonder if Lady Sibley will be there."

"I do not think so," Karina answered vaguely. "But, Elizabeth, could you lend me a gown? I promise to be very careful of it."

"Of course," Elizabeth answered, "but Mama must not find out. She would be incensed, as you well know."

"Yes, I am sure she would," Karina replied. "But you are as aware as I am that I could not arrive at Droxford Park looking like this."

She glanced down as she spoke at the outgrown cotton dress she was wearing. She had been just fifteen when her mother had died, three years ago, and since then she had never had the money to buy herself anything new.

She bitterly regretted now that she had not kept her mother's clothes, for although they would have been slightly out of fashion, all of her mother's gowns had been elegant and in perfect taste.

Many of them had been expensive, which Lady Rendell required for the functions she must attend as the wife of a Member of Parliament.

But during those desperate days when Sir John, having gambled away every penny piece he possessed, had returned from London so ill that his life had been despaired of, Karina had sold her mother's clothes.

Even now as she thought about it her cheeks burned with embarrassment. But at the time it had seemed a piece of wonderful good fortune when an impecunious neighbour, who had sometimes borrowed gowns and pelises from her mother for special occasions, had told Karina that she was to be married and was leaving the country within two weeks.

"I have so little time to buy myself a trousseau," she said. "Your mother's clothes have always fitted me. Please, Karina, let me purchase from you anything that you can spare. I have saved twenty pounds over the years and I will pay you for everything that you will let me have of your mother's."

It had seemed a sacrilege, but Karina could no longer go to the Livery Stable and she was faced with large bills for her father's illness.

There was the nurse, the doctor, and the apothecary to be paid. There was the expense of special food which had been required to tempt his appetite; and most important of all, fuel to keep him warm.

It was a hard winter and coal was expensive. The coalman had made it very clear that not one bag would be left at Blake House unless he was paid what he was owed.

Twenty pounds had tided them over the winter and

Karina had never dared to confess to her father what she had done. Now, she thought regretfully of all the lovely gowns she could have altered for herself.

Then she remembered that the Earl was a very rich man. Once she was his wife he would obviously expect her to be dressed in a manner which fitted her position. But she could hardly ask him to pay for her wedding-gown.

"Let us go and look at my gowns," Elizabeth said, taking Karina by the hand. "Mama has grumbled at the expense of every one of them but I know that she hopes they will turn me from an ugly duckling into a swan! Poor Mama, I long to tell her that she is over-optimistic!"

It was Elizabeth's sense of humour about herself that always delighted Karina. She only wished that her friend's overwhelming shyness would allow her to shine in Society.

"When I am married," she thought to herself, "I will ask her to stay with me in London. Perhaps I can find her a kind, understanding husband."

Immediately she thought of it she wondered if that was not what every woman required. Someone like Lord Droxford would undoubtedly terrify Elizabeth. Karina had an uneasy feeling that he might easily frighten her also.

She had, however, no time for introspection at the moment. Elizabeth opened her wardrobe doors and she saw a profusion of attractive gowns, most of them in white, as was correct for a débutante, and all in the latest fashion.

The new vogue was for a tiny pulled-in waist and full skirts over innumerable silk petticoats. The long, boatshaped *décolleté* revealed the wearer's elegant sloping shoulders while puff-sleeves of gauze or tulle accentuated the tightly fitting bodice.

The dresses were graceful and elegant but most of

them, Karina thought, were over-ornamented with ribbons, feathers, flowers, bows and frills.

"Mama always liked plain dresses best," she murmured; almost to herself.

"So do I," Elizabeth answered, "and personally I
think in many of these I look like an over-decorated
cold salmon on a silver dish."

"Which will you lend me?" Karina asked.

"It had better not be this one, trimmed with real
lace," Elizabeth answered, "because I have not worn it
yet, and this with the satin bows and rosebuds is
Mama's favourite."

She took a dress from the cupboard.

"But here is one," she said, "Which Mama thought
was a mistake, so she is not likely to ask me to wear
it, not at any rate before you bring it back."

She held out a gown as she spoke which was made
of vestal white, jacoret muslin. The skirt was very full
over three silk petticoats, but unornamented, and there
was only a small amount of lace set flat round the
boat-shaped neck, and the softly puffed sleeves were
not exaggerated.

"It is lovely!" Karina exclaimed, "much prettier than
the others."

"That is what I thought," Elizabeth agreed. "But
Mama says it is too austere."

"May I really wear it tomorrow?" Karina begged.

"But of course," Elizabeth answered. "Let us pack
it carefully. I expect you have come here on your
horse."

"Yes, of course," Karina replied. "But you know I
can manage a parcel. Kingfisher goes carefully, he is
getting old."

"What about a bonnet?" Elizabeth enquired.

"I had forgotten I should want one," Karina replied.

"Well, I have plenty!"

Elizabeth pulled open a deep drawer of the wardrobe in which there were at least a dozen bonnets, and pulled them out one by one.

The high-crowned bonnets so popular during the Regency had given way to small shapes worn on the back of the head and ornamented with feathers and flowers.

Elizabeth's headgear was all in the Duchess's taste—ornate—and to Karina's eyes far too overwhelming for someone so small and insignificant.

But there was one she liked, made only of muslin and lace, and which she was sure was intended to go with the very gown which Elizabeth had offered to lend her.

Attached to white lace were muslin ribbons edged with a tiny row of the same lace to tie under the chin.

When Karina tried it on it haloed the front of her hair and her tiny face. It made her appear very young and at the same time arrestingly attractive.

"May I really borrow this one?" she asked.

"How will you get it home?" Elizabeth enquired.

"On my head," Karina replied. "I will slip down the back stairs and no one will see me."

She kissed Elizabeth gently.

"Thank you, Elizabeth dearest. I will pay you back some day for your kindness and that is a promise."

"I do not want to be paid back," Elizabeth protested. "You know your friendship means more to me, Karina, than I can ever say. The only fun I ever have is with you!

"I hate being a débutante and having to go to these terrible parties. Mama scolds me all the time. I feel gauche and ugly, and of course that makes me completely tongue-tied!"

"One day that will change," Karina promised. "In the meantime, Elizabeth, think of me at Droxford Park tomorrow and wish me well."

"Of course I will," Elizabeth said in surprise. "But you are not nervous of going there, are you? You are never frightened of anything, Karina. I do not believe that even the formidable Lord Droxford could frighten you!"

"I would not be too sure about that," Karina answered.

She kissed her friend again and ran down the back stairs, her wedding-gown parcelled up under her arm, her wedding-bonnet on her head.

But when she had looked at herself this morning in the mirror in her bedroom she had known that she appeared very different from the untidy, ill-dressed girl who had scrambled down the tree to propose marriage to the Earl of Droxford!

Elizabeth's dress showed off her tiny waist—she had been forced to take it in several inches—to perfection. It also revealed the soft curves of her breasts more subtly than her outgrown cotton dresses had.

The long skirt which just cleared the floor gave her height and the dead white of the muslin and the bonnet on her golden hair seemed to accentuate the clear transparency of her skin. Her green eyes looked enormous and seemed, because she was nervous, to furnish the only touch of colour in her whole ensemble.

She gave a little sigh of satisfaction at her appearance and then had gone downstairs to find chaos.

Mr. Abbott had called to see her immediately on receiving Jim's urgent message. She sold him almost the entire contents of her mother's bedroom and, making Jim her messenger, had sent the monies at once to the local tradesfolk, paying them back everything they were owed.

Unfortunately the wine merchant, delighted to be clear of a debt which he had feared would never be honoured, had instantly delivered to the house a case of brandy.

Old James, also overwhelmed at receiving his long overdue wages, had taken a bottle into his master's room, feeling that it was a moment to celebrate.

By the time Karina had realised what was happening her father was completely disguised and it was quite impossible for her to get him up to bed.

This morning Sir John was in a truculent mood, and when she had gone downstairs to see if there was any chance of his attending her wedding, he had accused her of every crime under the sun, and particularly of spending on herself the money she had obtained from the sale of her mother's furniture.

She could only prevent him from hitting her or indeed from beating her with the stick which he used to walk with, by giving him more brandy. By lunchtime he was incapable of speaking or even moving.

When she came downstairs to await the arrival of the carriage which was to take her to Droxford Park, it was to find that her father had slipped forward in his chair and was sprawling on the floor.

It had taken every effort on her part and that of old James to get him back into his chair again, and because she had to strain every muscle to help move him she was frightened that she might split Elizabeth's dress.

However, finally they had pushed and pulled Sir John into his place. But he was only semi-conscious and when Karina, having rearranged her bonnet tried to say good-bye to him, she knew that he did not even realise who was speaking.

There was one last errand for Jim to do, and as she left the house she handed him a note for her father's friend, Mrs. Arbuthnot, who lived about a mile away.

In it she explained that she was being married and begged Mrs. Arbuthnot to move into Blake Hall as soon as possible. Karina was sure that the lady in question would oblige, for an ardent worker in his Constitutency, she had loved Sir John hopelessly but devotedly for over ten years.

He was attached to her in his own way and, until his gout had become too bad for him to leave the house, he had been in the habit of riding over to see her three or four times a week.

"I hope I have not forgotten anything," Karina thought.

She gave a little sigh, as if, in leaving Blake Hall, she relinquished the responsibilities which had lain so heavily on her shoulders these past three years since her mother's death.

But when the landau turned down the drive at Droxford Park she had a sudden fear of what lay ahead. She had forgotten that the house—which she had only seen once or twice in her life while out hunting—was so enormous.

The sun was not shining and the clouds were mirrored in the lake. With the black swans gliding over its dull surface, it had a somewhat sombre appearance.

"Will I really live here? How can I possibly find my way around a place so vast, let alone give orders to the servants and entertain," Karina asked herself.

She had, in asking the Earl to marry her, thought only of the man himself. She had in all truth forgotten his exalted position, his great wealth and his enormous possessions, of which she had heard gossip and speculation ever since she was a child:

There was Droxford Park, where George IV had stayed many times; Droxford House in London where it was said a ball given by the Earl three years ago had rivalled the most lavish and extravagant entertainment at Carlton House!

There were other houses of his which Karina remembered being talked about—a hunting lodge in Leicestershire, a Castle in Scotland, a place in Ireland. There were the Earl's horses, his yacht, and dozens of other possessions which now came crowding in on her memory, like a swarm of bees.

How could she have been so impertinent as to ask such a man to be her husband? How could she have

64

thought for a moment that she was qualified to play the part he would require of her as his wife?

She had an insane impulse to stop the carriage, to drive home, to send a message to say that she could not marry him, that it had all been a mistake.

But then she remembered that he was in fact loathing the idea of the ceremony that lay ahead of them; that he was marrying her only to suit his own convenience; and if she did not measure up to the standard expected of her it would be his fault just as much as hers!

She felt the idea steady her and assuage some of her fear. Before her mood could change, the carriage arrived at the front door and she saw a long line of liveried footmen and the Butler standing in the open doorway. She walked up the steps, realising, without raising her own eyes, that she was being closely scrutinised.

"His Lordship is waiting for you in the Chapel, Miss," the Butler said respectfully, "and he asked me to proffer you these with his compliments."

He handed her as he spoke a bouquet of white orchids. Karina took them and felt that in some way they were a gesture of friendship.

Nevertheless she knew she was trembling as she followed the Butler across the great Hall and down what seemed to her enormous and lofty corridors, hung with valuable pictures, furnished with priceless examples of French and English workmanship.

They walked for a long way. Her heart was thumping so violently that it seemed to Karina louder than the silken swish of the petticoats beneath her gown.

She clutched her bouquet as if it were a life-line, and at last, when they seemed to have walked the whole length of the great house, she heard the soft music of an organ and saw in front of her the huge carved doors of the private Chapel. They were open, the Butler moved to one side and she entered alone.

Outside the sunshine had broken through the clouds and a shaft of light came through the stained glass window above the altar. It illuminated the carved pews and seemed to give the massed white flowers which decorated the whole Chapel an almost unearthly beauty.

Karina did not realise that she looked like a flower herself. As she stood very still between the great doors, her gown made her appear like a white rose. Her eyes were very wide and frightened beneath the white bonnet which haloed the golden brilliance of her hair.

Then she saw the Earl was waiting for her, standing at the altar-steps, extremely elegant in a coat of dark blue whip-cord; his intricately tied cravat was high against his chin. His expression was stern and rather grim so that for a moment Karina felt it was impossible to move towards him.

As if he realised that fear had frozen her into immobility, the Earl walked down the aisle. As he reached her he smiled.

"Your father could not accompany you?" he asked in a conversational tone.

It was because he seemed so at ease that Karina felt some of her fear leave her.

"He was not well enough."

Her green eyes looked up at the Earl as she spoke and then almost beneath her breath, so that the Chaplain standing at the altar-steps could not hear, she said:

"You are sure . . . quite sure that you . . . want me to . . . marry you?"

"It is too late now to be anything but sure," the Earl replied. "Do not be frightened, Karina, I am sure that it will not be as bad as either of us anticipate."

She was surprised that he should be perceptive enough to realise what she was feeling. Then he offered her his arm and she took it automatically. He led her

66

up to the Chancel steps and the Chaplain began the marriage service.

Driving to London, Karina found it difficult to remember much of the service. She had heard the Earl's voice steady but grave, making his marriage vows. She had heard herself repeat them and thought it was the voice of a stranger.

When the ceremony was over they had repaired to a large and very impressive Salon to drink a glass of champagne.

"Is there anything you would like to do before we leave for London?" the Earl enquired.

"Would it be possible for me to see your horses?" Karina asked.

He looked surprised. Most people who came to Droxford Park asked if they could inspect the long Picture Gallery, the great Banqueting Hall, the oval Music Room, the huge Library, the tropical Orangery or other of the special treasures in which the house abounded.

But no one on first acquaintance, before they had seen the house itself, had asked to visit the stables.

"If that is your wish," the Earl replied. "I should be delighted to show you some of my horseflesh."

He noted that Karina not only set down her bouquet before she left the house, but pulled off her gloves. He was then amazed to see how her whole face seemed to light up with excitement as she inspected the animals he prized and to which he gave a great deal of his personal attention.

He had certainly not expected her to be so knowledgeable, or indeed to be able to handle a difficult horse in a quite exceptional manner.

She insisted on going into the stall of a stallion who had maimed two stable-boys and who even the Head-Groom admitted was a devil when aroused.

"He will behave like a gentleman with me," she had said reassuringly, and it was true.

She talked to the stallion quietly until he allowed her to pat his neck and finally his nose.

"How did you learn to soothe an animal who is usually out-of-hand?" the Earl asked.

"I think I have always been able to do it," Karina answered. "Horses behave badly when they think someone is frightened of them. They know when one loves them. They sense it instinctively."

She glanced at the Head-Groom as she spoke as if for confirmation.

"That's right, M'Lady," he said. "But there's few as have th'touch."

"You must have handled a lot of horses in your life!" the Earl exclaimed.

She knew he was wondering how she could have done so, considering Sir John even when he was a Member of Parliament, had not the wealth to afford a large stable.

She felt guilty when she thought of the many wild and unbroken horses she had ridden. But she felt this was not the moment for confession, and she diverted Lord Droxford's attention by complementing him on his latest purchase.

It was far later than the Earl had intended when finally they set off for London. Because he was now in a hurry they travelled in his High Perch Phaeton, lightly built, five feet high off the ground, and drawn by a team of four spirited horses. The landau was left to follow more sedately.

Karina felt the wind blowing her hair untidily around her face, but she did not care. It was so exciting to move at such speed, to know that she was sitting beside the Earl and that she was, though she could hardly believe it herself, his wife.

It was only when the Butler came forward as they

left to wish them every happiness that she had become tinglingly aware that she was now "Her Ladyship—the Countess of Droxford," the future chatelaine of Droxford Park and the wife of one of the richest and most important men in the country.

"How could it have happened?" she asked herself.

She could hardly believe that she was not in a dream from which she would all too quickly awake.

Droxford House in Park Lane was in its own way almost as impressive as the Earl's home in the country.

It had stood, overlooking the green trees of Hyde Park, for a hundred years and had been modernised by the present Earl immediately after his succession.

It was a magnificent and awe-inspiring mansion, and at the same time because he lived there so much it had a homeliness which Karina had felt was rather lacking at Droxford Park.

She went upstairs to tidy herself. It took a little time and when she came down she found that the Earl had already changed from the clothes in which he had driven to London into evening dress.

His coat of olive green satin fitted him superbly; there was an emerald glittering in the front of his cravat and another on the fob which fell from his pocket of his brocade waistcoat.

"I think what we both need is a glass of champagne," the Earl suggested as Karina entered the big Salon with its crystal chandeliers glittering with hundreds of lighted candles and bowls of hot-house flowers scenting the atmosphere.

"I have already drunk champagne once today," Karina smiled. "It seems very dashing to be drinking it again!"

"One does not get married everyday of the week," the Earl replied.

"No, indeed," she agreed.

His words made her slightly embarrassed and for

a moment she could think of nothing more to say. Then, as there was a silence between them, the Butler announced:

"Captain Frederick Farrington!"

The Earl gave an exclamation.

"Good heavens, Freddie, I had forgotten about you! Had we planned to dine together?"

"Is not that like you, Alton!" Captain Farrington exclaimed.

He was an extremely elegant and good-looking young man.

"You agreed last week that we should have a look at the new doves the Abbess has procured from France . . ."

He stopped, suddenly noticing that Karina was present.

As he looked towards her the Earl said:

"Karina, may I present Freddie Farrington, a very old friend of mine? Freddie—my wife."

"Your what?" Captain Farrington's mouth seemed to fall open, his eyes almost to protrude from his sunburnt face.

"Are you roasting me?" he managed to ask after a moment.

"No, indeed," the Earl replied. "We were married this afternoon."

"So you really meant what you said before you left London—I thought it a hum and that you could not in fact intend . . ."

Captain Farrington stopped short as he realised that he was being rude, and moving towards Karina, he raised her hand to his lips.

"Your servant, Lady Droxford. Forgive my boorish behaviour, but your husband has taken me by surprise. As his oldest friend I rather expected to be invited to his wedding."

"No one was invited," Karina told him.

"And it was therefore far more pleasant," the Earl

interposed, "than one of those social squashes that you and I have attended far too often at St. George's, Hanover Square!"

"Married!" Freedie Farrington ejaculated. "Well, Alton, I would never have believed it if you had not told me so with your own lips! But indeed I do not blame you!"

He smiled flatteringly at Karina as he spoke and she smiled back. There was something very engaging about Captain Farrington.

"Will you have a glass of champagne?" the Earl suggested.

"Indeed, I am only too willing to drink your health," Captain Farrington replied, "and then I must leave you. I quite understand why you forgot our dinner engagement, Alton. So you must excuse me for barging in upon you and being very much *de trop*!"

"You are nothing of the sort," the Earl said firmly. "Stay and dine with us. We would be gratified by your company."

Captain Farrington glanced at Karina.

"Yes, please stay," she said, "and if you and . . . my . my husband . . . were going somewhere entertaining, could I not accompany you?"

She saw by the expression on Captain Farrington's face that wherever they had intended to go it was certainly not the place for her.

"No, no," he said quickly. "But London is full of gaiety for those who wish to be amused. Are you certain that you would not rather I left you two alone?"

"Quite certain," the Earl replied before Karina could speak.

"Now where shall we go?" Captain Farrington ruminated.

"I must tell you at once that I cannot change into an evening gown," Karina interrupted, "so perhaps you had best leave me behind. This is the only dress I have, and I have but . . . borrowed it."

She realised as she was speaking that Captain Farrington was staring at her in astonishment and that there was a frown on the Earl's face as he said:

"My apologies, Karina, it is something I should not have overlooked."

"Luckily Elizabeth and I are about the same size," she told him. "I could not have asked you to pay for a new gown before we were married."

"No, I realise that would have been most improper," he said, and there was a twinkle in his eye. "However, this lack of apparel is something you must remedy tomorrow. You will find it easy to buy a very comprehensive trousseau, I do not doubt, in Bond Street."

"That will be thrilling," Karina said with a sudden lilt in her voice.

"Some more champagne, Freddie?" the Earl suggested, taking the bottle from the crested silver ice-cooler, and pouring the sparkling liquid into his glass.

"I need it," Captain Farrington said, "for I assure you, Alton, that I have no idea whether I am on my head or on my heels."

"It is all a trifle puzzling," the Earl admitted, "but I will explain it to you in good time. Let us now decide where we can take Karina this evening."

"I can tell you what might be amusing," Captain Farington said, "and it will not matter if Lady Droxford is not changed. We could go to the Royal Cremorne Gardens."

"Good Heavens!" the Earl exclaimed. "Is that place still open?"

"It has just been reopened by Baron Random de Berenger," Captain Farrington explained. "He has built a Stadium there where he endeavours to teach the manly sports to anyone who desires lessons. As it happens he has a number of female pupils as well."

"What do they do?" Karina asked excitedly.

"There are all sorts of entertainments, such as archery, and artificial pigeon shooting. There is a special new method of teaching people to swim. Beside all this there is a concert every night followed by a dance."

"It sounds very gay," Karina exclaimed.

"Can we really take Karina there?" the Earl asked doubtfully.

"Yes indeed, quite a number of your friends have visited the Gardens and my sister says it is most amusing," Freddie Farrington assured him. "There is a gypsy tent where they all had their fortunes told, and apparently the Baron is adding all sorts of sideshows.

"Of course it will end up as a vulgar amusement park and it will doubtless soon be too rough for the Quality, but it is worth seeing now before it becomes overwhelmingly popular."

"Oh, do let us go—please," Karina begged, and Lord Droxford good-humouredly agreed that they might drop in for a short while when dinner was finished.

The meal was somewhat drawn out as the chef had determined to excel himself on such an auspicious occasion as His Lordship's wedding, but finally they reached the Cremorne Gardens.

Lit by twinkling coloured lights, it bordered onto the Thames and had a number of naughty little arbours discreetly arranged under the secluded shade of the trees.

The Earl and Captain Farrington hurried Karina past these and she was soon entranced by trying her skill at archery, quoits, and watching the pigeon shooting contests.

Karina's excitement and enthusiasm, for everything was new and original to her, infected her escorts. Captain Farrington challenged the Earl at each sport suggesting large wagers on the winner, and they scoffed at each other's efforts and teased Karina.

She was so gay and unaffected and so ingenuous

in her remarks that the Earl found himself laughing and quite unexpectedly enjoying himself.

"When he forgets to be stiff on his dignity," Karina thought, "he is fun!"

The concert was to Karina an entertainment as she had never known before but the Earl thought some of the turns vulgar and the audience rather rough. Much to her disappointment he would not permit her to stay for the dancing.

When they arrived back at Droxford House, it was after midnight.

"Thank you for thinking of such an exceptional evening," Karina said to Captain Farrington in the Hall.

"I enjoyed it enormously," he said, bowing over her hand. "We shall, My Lady, meet again very shortly, I hope.

"I hope so too," Karina answered.

She glanced at the Earl as if for confirmation.

"I will see you at Whites' tomorrow, Freddie," he said briefly.

"Good," Captain Farrington answered, "and congratulations, old boy! There is no need for me to wish you happiness. You could not help being happy with anyone so lovely.

He spoke with a sincerity which made the Earl become suddenly interested in the letters on a side table. As soon as their guest had left Karina curtsied to her husband.

"It has been a wonderful day," she said softly. "I cannot really believe it is all true."

"I am glad you have enjoyed yourself," the Earl replied formally.

Feeling a little deflated, she started to climb the stairs to her bedroom.

It was a large, impressive room, very expensively furnished. From a gold corolla above the big bed

74

there hung draped folds of pale blue silk which was held on either side by angels carved and gilded in Italy. The furniture was French and the Aubusson carpet was a riot of pink roses and blue ribbon.

Karina wanted to examine everything, but she was so tired that she felt that on the morrow there would be time to inspect the whole house.

She had no idea, as she took off her gown, that she was expected to ring for a maid to assist her. She had looked after herself for so many years that it never occurred to her that some tired female would be sitting up listening for her bell.

She put Elizabeth's dress in the wardrobe and then slipped on the old cotton wrapper she had worn for over five years and started to brush her hair. It took a little time because it was so long, and then, feeling that that too could wait until tomorrow, she turned towards the bed.

Laid out on it was her nighgown, worn, patched and darned—it was a garment she had worn for so many years that it was now rather tight and uncomfortable and also, she felt, very out of keeping with the beauty and elegance of the room.

On an impulse she picked it up and threw it on a chair. Then with only her hair to cover her nakedness she slipped into bed.

It was delightful to feel the coolness of the fine lace-edged linen sheets against her naked skin; to feel herself sinking into the cloud-like softness of the mattress and to lie back against the feather-filled pillows.

She had left one candle alight on the bedside-table but for a moment she did not blow it out. She looked around the room, feeling a kind of ecstatic joy she had never known before because everything was so elegant.

She knew now how much she had hated the emptiness of Blake Hall—the worn carpets, faded wall-

75

papers, threadbare curtains. She was starting a new life and everything was so beautiful that she felt beautiful too.

She gave a little sigh of contentment and as she did so there was a knock on the door and without waiting for an answer someone came into the room.

She looked up, expecting to see a housemaid, but to her utter astonishment she saw it was the Earl. He shut the door behind him and carrying a candle he crossed the room to her bed to set it down beside the one she had left alight.

She stared at him speechless, realising as he approached that he was wearing a brocade robe which almost touched the floor. It had a high velvet collar and there was a touch of white at his throat which was the frill of his nightshirt.

"Why are you . . . here? What do you . . . want?" she asked and even to herself her voice sounded frightened.

"Do not look so shocked. We are married, Karina," the Earl replied.

She sat up suddenly, forgetting that she had gone to bed naked and for a moment he had a glimpse of two exquisite rose-tipped breasts, before with a little cry she snatched up the sheet with both hands and pulled it close to her chest.

"Do you . . . mean," she asked, "that you intend to . . . sleep . . . here with . . . me?"

"That is one way of putting it," the Earl answered with a twist of his lips.

"But you cannot . . . I mean . . . I will . . . not let . . . you," Karina stammered.

The Earl sat down on the edge of the bed and looked at his wife. With her golden hair falling over her naked shoulders and onto the pillows, she was in the candlelight very lovely. Her green eyes seemed enormous, but they were darkening with fear and her lips trembled a little as she said:

76

"You must . . . go away . . . this was . . . not part of our . . . bargain."

"But you married me," the Earl insisted 'You are my wife."

"A wife you have . . . taken because it . . . suited you," Karina retorted. "You said yourself . . . there was no . . . pretence between . . . us."

"As your husband, Karina, I have certain privileges," the Earl replied.

"Then you should have . . . told me what you . . . intended to . . . do," Karina said, "for if I had known . . . I would not have . . . married you. Why should you want . . . me? You have Lady Sibley! You met her secretly the night after the garden party and for all I know you were . . . with her last . . . night. Do you imagine that . . . I would let you . . . touch me knowing that you would much . . . rather be with . . . her?"

"I think that is beside the point," the Earl said coldly. "We have agreed that we would not discuss Lady Sibley nor any other women who engages my attention. But I need an heir, Karina, and that is something only my wife can give me."

"Do you really think that we could have . . . a baby . . . together when we do not . . . love . . . each other," Karina asked incredulously. "Have you thought what sort of . . . child we would . . . produce?"

She drew a deep breath.

"Your father and mother loved one another . . . I have always heard how happy . . . they were . . . and that is why you are as you are. My father worshipped my mother and she him . . . so they produced . . . me."

The Earl would have spoken but Karina went on quickly.

"I am convinced that girls who are ugly and nit-witted, men who are chinless and turnip-brained, were

77

all born to parents who had no interest in one another except perhaps that of worldly advantage."

"A very interesting contention," the Earl said, "but one which I hardly think would be acceptable to the medical fraternity!"

"But it is what . . . I believe," Karina cried, "and I swear to you, My Lord, that I will not bear . . . a child of your . . . unless I . . . love you."

The Earl was still for a moment. Then with a queer glint in his eyes he said in a deep voice:

"Shall I make you love me, Karina?"

"No . . . no . . ." she answered quickly, then added: "Have you thought what would happen if you did?"

"What would happen?" he enquired curiously.

"I should cease to be a complacent wife," she answered. "If I loved you then I should be jealous and unhappy about the other women in your life. I should make scenes, I should cling to you. That would upset all your carefully thought out arrangements, My Lord, as you well know!"

Her voice was scornful.

"Stop talking nonsense, Karina," the Earl commanded, "and let me show you that it is not so very unpleasant to be married to me."

He bent forward as if he would put his arms around her.

"If you touch me," Karina cried, pressing herself back against the pillows, "I swear to you . . . I will leave this house . . . tonight and I will . . . never come back. You will be . . . married but without a . . . wife. What is more it will cause a scandal and you will certainly not be appointed Lord Lieutenant of the County!"

She spoke angrily, the words spilling over themselves.

The Earl's lips tightened before he said:

"I see that I made a regrettable mistake in marrying you."

"It is a mistake in that you are breaking the rules," Karina said. "Stop cheating, My Lord!"

"How dare you accuse me of cheating!" the Earl said, and although he spoke slowly and did not raise his voice, Karina knew there was suppressed fury behind his words.

"It is dishonourable to cheat at cards," she answered, "but I think it is even more dishonourable to cheat someone who trusts you. I believed . . . if nothing else . . . that I could trust . . . your word."

"I never promised not to touch you," the Earl protested.

"I did not . . . think you would . . . wish to do . . . so . . . considering that you are . . . infatuated with L . . . another woman, that you confess to . . . loving her, that you are in fact . . . her lover! I think that to . . . want me . . . too is . . . disgusting!"

The Earl rose from the bed.

"You are very voluble, Karina. I might have guessed, after your eavesdropping on things which should not have concerned you, what your attitude would be."

He stared down into her eyes and she thought there was a fire smouldering in his.

"I would not force myself upon any woman who had a distaste for me. So I apologise, My Lady, for disturbing you. I hope you enjoy your wedding-night—alone!"

He gave her a formal bow which, like his voice, was so ironic as to be insulting. Then he moved with a dignity across the room and shut the door sharply behind him.

Karina stared after him as if she could hardly believe she had won the battle. Her heart was beating, her lips felt dry.

After a long time, she blew out the candle, but she did not sleep. She only stared wide-eyed into the darkness until it was almost dawn.

4

The new Countess of Droxford came downstairs at what seemed to her a disgracefully late hour. Having not fallen asleep until after dawn she had been horrified, when finally she awoke, to see the time.

She had rung for her maid, who, used to the late hours of the Quality, assured her that no one had expected her bell to peal any earlier.

"But His Lordship . . . " Karina questioned.

"His Lordship has already left the house, M'Lady."

Karina guessed that as soon as it was possible the Earl would be calling at 10 Downing Street to inform the Prime Minister he was married. It was therefore obvious she would not be seeing him this morning, but she thought with a little thrill of excitement that she had plenty to do.

When she reached the Hall, Newman, the Butler, came forward to say:

"His Lordship's compliments, M'Lady, and before leaving the house would you speak with Mr. Wade."

He saw by Karina's face that she did not know who this was, and added:

"Mr. Wade is His Lordship's secretary, M'Lady."

He led her down a passage and opened a door into a somewhat austerely furnished office. There was a man sitting at the desk, who rose as Newman announced:

"Her Ladyship—Mr. Wade."

Karina had somehow expected that a secretary would be elderly, perhaps grey-haired, but the man facing her across the desk was young and pleasant-looking and obviously a Gentleman. She wondered why he had taken such a dull position until he crossed the room towards her and she saw that he limped badly, one leg being stiff and unwieldly.

"May I introduce myself?" he asked. "I am Robert Wade, a cousin of Alton's, and I have the privilege of acting for him in a secretarial capacity."

"How do you do," Karina smiled. "I am delighted to make your acquaintance, Mr. Wade. I feel you will be able to enlighten me about so many things of which I am sadly ignorant."

"Will you sit down, My Lady?" Mr. Wade asked.

He indicated a leather armchair beside the fireplace. Karina seated herself and he took a chair opposite.

"I think you are surprised that I look so young," Mr. Wade began. "I am in fact two years older than Alton, but he took pity on me after I was wounded and obliged to leave my Regiment. I enjoy working for him, and the family—when you get to know them—will tell you that besides having an unaccountable head for figures, I have always been a bookworm!"

"Then you will be able to help me," Karina said, "for I have become this past year or two deplorably out of touch on what I should be reading."

Robert Wade made a gesture with his hand towards the large bookcases which covered two walls of the office.

"My Library, such as it is, is at your service, but you will be far better served with the books that Alton has in abundance at Droxford Park."

"I hope you will tell me what I should read to be up-to-date," Karina said.

"I wonder if you will have much time for reading," Robert Wade replied with a twinkle in his eye. "Having

81

seen you, Lady Droxford, I have a feeling that you are about to be a social success."

"I hope so," Karina answered earnestly. "But first I must have something to wear."

Robert Wade nodded.

"Alton told me that is what you would require. His credit is good, as you can well imagine, at every shop in London and I have also a number of sovereigns here for you to carry in your purse, for it is, as I well know, very uncomfortable to be without money."

"It is indeed," Karina answered.

He walked to his desk.

"Would ten sovereigns be enough for today, do you think," he asked.

"But I shall not want all that!" Karina exclaimed involuntarily. Then she laughed. "It seems to me now an enormous amount of money but I have no idea of what I shall require."

"Do not pay for anything in cash unless it is absolutely necessary," Robert Wade admonished her. "Tell the shops to send their accounts here and I will deal with them."

"Thank you," Karina said, but with a little frown between her eyes she added:

"Can you help me as to where I should go? You see I have never been in London before."

"Never been in London before?" Robert Wade repeated incredulously. "Then I do see that Your Ladyship will find it difficult to know how to get started!"

"I want a large number of elegant gowns very quickly!" Karina told him. "The one I am wearing is the only one I possess! It belongs to my friend and I must return it soon in case her Mama finds out she has lent it to me!"

She paused, then asked:

"Who is the best dressmaker in Bond Street?"

"I suppose most people would say Madame Bertin,"

Robert Wade replied, thinking of the large sums the Earl had paid to that extremely expensive Couturière.

Then looking at Karina's green eyes turned trustingly up to his, he wondered if in patronising shops where the Earl was well-known, she might inadvertently learn too much of her husband's past.

"I was thinking," he said slowly, "that you would receive better service from one of the establishments that have not been so spoilt by a too fashionable a clientèle.

He looked in the drawer of his desk and drew out a card.

"I learnt recently, that Madame Bertin's chief designer has left to start on her own. I am sure she would be deeply honoured by your patronage and make every possible effort to please you."

He glanced down at the card as he spoke and remembered how Yvette—who had been born Elsie Tomkins—had said to him only a month ago:

"I have brought you this bill, Mr. Wade, personally because I wondered if you could do me a favour."

"How can I do that?" Robert Wade asked.

"I'm leaving Madame," Yvette answered. "I've had enough of her tantrums and her meanness! I've run that workroom these last five years without a word of thanks! I've designed half the gowns, I've contrived to make some of the most slippery customers pay their bills, and all I ever get is a command to do more!"

She paused, a suspicion of tears in her eyes.

"I can't stand another week of it, Mr. Wade, and that's a fact."

"But how can I help you?" Robert Wade asked.

"Well, I shan't entice Lady Sibley away from Madame, but when His Lordship takes a fancy to someone else—and I hope for his sake it's soon, for that Lady Sibley is a real termagant—put in a word for me, will you?"

"I will certainly try," Robert Wade replied, "But I am afraid the Ladies to whom you are referring seldom seek my advice as to where they should shop."

"Perhaps you could drop His Lordship a hint?" Yvette suggested. "It may be impossible; if so, I quite understand."

"If I get the chance I will certainly mention your name," Robert Wade answered.

Here, he thought, as he carried Yvette's card across the room to Karina, was the opportunity she had hoped might occur. No designer could fail to be thrilled to dress a Lady as entrancing as the new Countess of Droxford, especially when she was supported by her husband's vast fortune.

"Oh, thank you!" Karina said, taking the card. "I would much rather go to someone who will not look down her nose at me or bully me into buying vulgar garments which are not suitable."

"I am sure you have very good taste," Robert Wade said reassuringly.

"I have always hoped so!" Karina replied. "But I am not very sure where fashionable clothing is concerned. You see, I have never yet bought a gown for myself."

She saw the surprise in his face, but rising to her feet she said:

"I must not weary you with the story of my life the first time we meet, Mr. Wade. May I please come again? It would be nice to know I have someone to talk to in this big house, which rather frightens me."

"I would be very honoured if you Ladyship would do so," Robert Wade answered.

She smiled at him.

"We are cousins by marriage, are we not? My name is Karina!"

"We are indeed," he replied. "And any time you want me, Karina, I am at your service. I live in the house, as it happens."

"I am so glad, Robert," Karina smiled, and he felt she spoke sincerely.

Two hours later Karina emerged from Madame Yvette's shop in the less fashionable end of Bond Street with flushed cheeks and sparkling eyes.

She was wearing a new creation which, with only a few tiny alterations here and there had fortunately fitted her.

She had a quick glimpse of herself reflected in the glass window of the shop and in the shining silver of the carriage lamp.

In a gown of pale green batiste she looked the embodiment of early spring. The bonnet of Leghorn straw which framed her excited face was trimmed with tiny pink rosebuds and wide green ribbons which tied under her small chin.

The footman held open the door of the landau, but Karina hesitated. She had a desire to show off her gown by walking down Bond Street where she could see a number of fashionably dressed Ladies and Gentlemen perambulating in the the sunshine.

"Please wait for me at the end of the street," she said to the flunkey. "I wish to walk."

She did not see the expression of surprise on the servant's face as she turned away and started moving along the pavement, staring first in this window, and then in the next.

Never had she seen such a marvellous display of goods, such variety, such a delectable choice for anyone who was able to spend money for the first time in her life!

She stopped outside a jeweller's window to stare almost open-mouthed at the brooches, rings and necklaces. She was woman enough to be fascinated by the sparkle of them and to wonder how they would look against her white skin.

She was certain, for she had heard people speak of

them, that the Droxford jewels were famous, and she wondered if it would seem very pushing if she asked Robert Wade about them.

Sapphires would look fabulous against the pale pink gown which she had just ordered from Madame Yvette's. It was one of the most beautiful dresses she had seen, but then everything had seemed so desirable that she had wanted to buy almost every model that she had shown.

Madame Yvette had not only been obliging about gowns. While Karina was being fitted she had sent for other more intimate garments for a Lady of Fashion.

Night apparel had been brought to Karina for her approval—so thin and transparent that it appeared to have been woven by fairy fingers—fabulously expensive silk stockings; frilled petticoats; lace-edged chemises; boned corsets; and an exquisite wrapper of white Chinese silk trimmed with Venetian lace.

"There are many other articles Your Ladyship will need, Madame Yvette said. "I will have them all here later this afternoon."

Staring in the jeweller's window Karina wondered if anyone had ever been as fortunate as she was.

Then, almost like a cloud passing across the sun, she remembered the Earl's ironic voice as he left her bedroom last night.

He had been very angry, and yet she told herself optimistically that, when he thought on it this morning, he would realise she was right. If she had to be a Complacent Wife, it would be impossible if . . .

Her thoughts were arrested by a silky voice saying in her ear:

"Entrancing! Lovely! The prettiest little filly I have ever beheld!"

She looked round in astonishment to see a middle-aged Dandy standing beside her. His top-hat was at an angle, his cravat fashionably high, the points of his collar over his chin. But his face was lined and he had heavy bags of dissipation under his half-closed eyes.

There was something about him that made Karina feel instantly revolted and almost instinctively she took a step backwards.

"What attracts you in this window, my pretty dove?" he asked, "for whatever it may be you must allow me to purchase it for you. Can it be diamonds which take your fancy, or perhaps sapphires would become you better? Tell me what you desire and it is yours."

"I think . . . y . you have made a . . . m. mistake . . . Sir," Karina stammered.

Then something in the Gentleman's eyes or perhaps the smile on his thick lips made her realise with a sudden sense of horror that she was being accosted by a stranger—a stranger who thought that she was the type of woman to whom he could speak with impunity.

"There is no mistake," the Gentelman replied. "Let me introudce myself. I am Lord Wyman and I cannot tell you, my beautiful little Phryne how delighted I am that we have met."

"But we have not . . . I mean . . . you have no right to . . . speak to me," Karina said.

He put out his hand as if he knew that she was poised for flight and he would prevent it. As he touched her arm she wrenched herself free of him and in a moment of sheer panic started running.

She thought she heard him laugh and it made her run all the faster until suddenly she collided with a Gentleman coming the other way.

"I am . . . sorry," she gasped and heard him say in astonishment:

"Why, it is Lady Droxford! What is happening? Why are you in such a hurry?"

"Oh, Captain Farrington!" she exclaimed breathlessly but thankfully, "I am indeed . . . glad that you

are . . . here. Please walk with me. It was a man . . .
he frightened me!"

"A man!" Captain Farrington exclaimed. "Who?
Where is he?"

"Oh, let us go . . . away," Karina begged. "It was
my fault . . . I did not realise at first why he was
speaking to me. He said he was . . . Lord Wyman."

"Wyman!" Captain Farrington ejaculated. "That
outsider! A most unpleasant fellow! You should have
nothing to do with him!"

"I have no wish to," Karina said. "Please, let us
move on in case he has followed me."

"He will not speak to you while you are with me,"
Captain Farrington said fiercely. "But why are you
alone? Surely you know you should not walk unattended in Bond Street?"

"Is it not correct?" Karina asked.

"But of course it is not!" he replied emphatically.
"No Lady perambulates here without a friend or a
maid to accompany her. Where is your carriage?"

"I told the carriage to wait at the end of the street,"
Karina answered. "I wanted to look at the shops. I see
now that it was foolish of me."

"Very foolish," Captain Farrington agreed with a
smile. "But you were not to know, having just come
to London."

"Are there many rules of that sort?" Karina asked.

"I am afraid there are," he answered. "Alton should
have informed you of them."

"No, no, he is too occupied," Karina said quickly.
"And please, you will not tell him that I have been so
bird-brained will you?"

"Do you really think that I am a snip-sneak?"
Freddie Farrington asked, and Karina, seeing a smile
on his lips and the twinkle in his eyes, laughed.

"No, indeed! I feel quite sure you would not give
me away!"

"You can be quite certain of that," he answered.

"And now let me escort you. If you wish to look in a shop window, cry halt! I am well trained to the insatiable taste of frail females for the frivolities of Bond Street."

"How is that?" Karina asked.

"I have a sister!" he answered. "And that gives me an idea! Shall I take you to meet Harriet, Lady Droxford? She is married but she was very much the crack for several seasons before she fell in love with a brother officer of mine. She could bring you slap up to the mark, and what is more she would enjoy doing it."

"I would not want to be a burden to your sister," Karina said a little anxiously.

"I am quite certain you could never be that," Captain Farrington declared gallantly, "and Harriet could, I am convinced, be of service to you."

"Then please take me to her," Karina pleaded, "if you are indeed certain that she will not find me an emcumbrance on her hands!"

"I have a feeling," Captain Farrington said reflectively, "that Harriet is going to be as grateful to you as you are to her. She is in much need of something to occupy her thoughts at this moment."

Karina was just going to ask Captain Farrington what he meant by that when, as they approached the narrower end of Bond Street, she saw just ahead of them a closed landau draw up. A Gentleman stepped out and was turning to assist a Lady to alight.

"Oh look!" she exclaimed. "There is His Lordship! We must speak to him! I am sure that he has just come from 10 Downing Street, and I also want to show him my new gown."

She quickened her pace, only to feel to her astonishment Captain Farrington's hand reach out to hold her back.

"No, Lady Droxford," he said, in a strange voice. "I should not speak to Alton at the moment, he . . . he is engaged.

Karina was watching the Earl cross the pavement. There was a very attractive woman walking beside him. She was dark, exquisitely dressed, with an exceedingly large, but to Karina's eyes, somewhat overbefeathered, hat.

"Not to speak to my husband?" she exclaimed. "But why not? He has only entered a shop as you can well see."

"I cannot explain," Captain Farrington said in an embarrassed voice. "Please take my advice and pretend you have not seen him."

"I do not understand," Karina said in perplexity.

Then as the Earl and the Lady he was escourting disappeared she stood still and looked up at Captain Farrington.

"You mean that I should not . . . meet the . . . person who is . . . with His Lordship?"

He avoided her eyes.

"Do not try to comprehend, Lady Droxford, that it has nothing to do with me. I am but giving you advice to the best of my ability."

"Is the woman with him . . . his . . . mistress?" Karina asked in a low voice.

"You must not ask me such questions," Freddie Farrington replied, "and I certainly should not answer them. Let me say she is an —old friend."

"What is her name?" Karina demanded.

"I . . . I do not remember."

"But I wish to know," Karina insisted, "and if you do not tell me, I shall go straight into the shop and ask my husband to introduce me to her."

There was a pause before Captain Farrington, in a tone of a man who is goaded almost beyond endurance, muttered:

"Mrs. Felicité Corwin."

"Thank you!" Karina said. "And thank you for preventing me from making what would obviously have been a social solecism. Shall we walk on now to find my carriage?"

They walked a little way in silence and then Freddie Farrington said gruffly:

"I am sorry about this."

"Please do not be," Karina answered in level tones. "I was just surprised for the moment. I thought His Lordship was . . . interested in someone else."

"As I have told you, Mrs. Corwin is a very old friend," Freddie Farrington said. "But she is beneath your condescension, you understand that?"

"I supposed it would be quite wrong to mention her to His Lordship?"

"Of course it would," Captain Farrington replied firmly. "It would only irritate him, and he would be furious with me for having told you her name."

"I will not sneak on you," Karina said, but this time she did not smile. "It is just that I would rather know about such things, because . . ."

"You ought not to know about them," Freddie Farrington interrupted, "that is the whole point."

"It is best that I should," Karina contradicted. "You see, if I have to be a complacent wife it is far better for me to know what I am to be complacent about than risk making mistakes as I would have done just now if you had not prevented me."

"Well, I suppose . . ." Freddie Farrington began, then added: "Dammit, that is just the sort of thing you should not be saying! A "complacent wife," indeed! What is Alton thinking about?"

" . . . being Lord Lieutenant," Karina interposed. "I am not giving away any secrets, for I know from what you said last night, that he had told you he intended to find himself a wife. Well, I am the wife he found!"

"Good God!" Freddie Farrington ejaculated.

They passed the shop which the Earl had entered with Mrs. Corwin. Karina noted that it was a jeweller's shop while at the same time making every effort to look straight ahead and not try to peer inside the glass window.

They almost reached the carriage when Freddie Farrington said uncomfortably:

"Listen, Lady Droxford. I do not want you to get this wrong. Alton is one of the best chaps I have ever known. He is honourable, straight as a die and he would never do anything crooked or underhand. He is a sportsman, and if ever I was in a tight spot I would rather turn to Alton than to anyone I know."

"His Lordship has been straight with me," Karina answered. "There have been no pretensions between us."

"I can see that," Freddie Farrington said, "but at the same time it does not seem natural. I would wish both Alton and you to be—happy!"

"I am happy," Karina answered. "Very happy. How could I be anything else after all he has given me, and seeing the position I hold as his wife?"

Captain Farrington opened his mouth as if he would say something but as by this time they had reached the carriage, he merely helped her into it and directed the Coachman to drive to 25 Curzon Street.

The Honourable Mrs. Joselyn Courtney was an extremely attractive young woman who was however quite obviously increasing. She sprang to her feet when her brother was announced and ran across the room towards him, her arms outstretched.

"Oh, Freddie, Freddie, I am so glad you have come!" she said. "I have been boring myself to distraction wondering how I can disguise my figure so that I can attend Ascot. My mother-in-law says it is quite disgusting that I should wish to appear in public, but I am determined to see Joselyn's horse run, whatever she may say."

Freddie Farrington kissed his sister's cheek and disentangling himself from her embrace, put his hand up to his cravat to reassure himself it had not been disarranged by such demonstration of affection.

"I have brought someone to visit you, Harriet."

As he spoke, Karina, who had been hesitating rather nervously in the doorway, came further into the room.

"Lady Droxford, this is my sister, Harriet Courtney," he said. "Harriet, Droxford's new wife."

"The Earl married!" Harriet Courtney exclaimed. "Good heavens, why did no one tell me!"

She swept Karina a little curtsey, who curtsied in return feeling unaccountably shy.

"You are lovely! Harriet exclaimed impulsively. "Is not that just like Lord Droxford to spring a wife on us, and someone so beautiful that we will all be eclipsed into insignificance!"

Karina laughed. She could not help it.

"I promise you will not," she said, "and please forgive your brother for bringing me here so unceremoniously, but I have come to ask for your advice."

"My advice?" Harriet exclaimed. "Well, that is the one thing I could proffer you in plenty, and at no expense. Freddie, pull the bell, we must all have some refreshment while Lady Droxford tells me what she wishes me to do. Do you prefer raffia or marsala, My Lady?"

"If it is not too much trouble," Karina replied, "I would so much prefer a cup of chocloate. I was too excited to eat much breakfast this morning, and I have been trying on gowns for hours, I am really very hungry."

"Have you anything sensible to eat in this house?" Freddie Farrington asked.

"But of course," his sister replied. "Luncheon will be ready in about a quarter of an hour. You must both stay. I was going to partake alone and very dismal I find it."

Turning to Karina she went on:

"I do not wish to bother you with my troubles, My

Lady, but never under any circumstances have a baby in the summer."

Karina blushed but Harriet continued blithely:

"In the winter one can cover oneself—the new fashion in pelises with huge taffeta sleeves is a perfect disguise. But in the summer what can one do?"

There was so much tragedy in her voice that Karina gave a little laugh.

"I am sure you can contrive something," she said. "Your brother tells me you know the answer to every social problem. That is why I am here."

Harriet Courtney looked at her wide-eyed.

"You mean . . ." she began.

"I am from the country," Karina said, "and I have been looking after my father for the last three years. He . . . he has been ill. I know nothing about social occasions and how I should behave or what I should do. Captain Farrington thought you could help me."

"It is the most exciting thing I have ever been asked to do!" Harriet exclaimed. "It makes me feel like a Dowager launching a débutante! But at the moment I welcome anything so long as I do not have to think about my appearance or listen to my mother-in-law nagging me. You have no idea how lucky you are that Lord Droxford's mother is dead."

Even as she spoke she put her fingers up to her mouth and looked up to her brother.

"That is the sort of thing I should not say, is it not?"

"It is indeed," Freddie Farrington agreed.

"Do not apologise," Karina laughed. "I spout far worse. I am so used to being alone or with people who do not listen to me that I say just what comes into my head. I am convinced one day I will find myself in a quagmire.

"I will save you from that," Harriet said impulsively.

Karina and Mrs. Courtney went shopping in the

afternoon and she did not return to Droxford House, laden with purchases until nearly five o'clock. Harriet had given her an invitation to dine at her house that evening.

"I have already invited a number of friends," she said, "It would be delightful if you and Lord Droxford could join us." ·

Karina looked doubtful.

"I have no idea what His Lordship's plans might be," she answered.

"Well, I shall expect you both," Harriet said, "unless you send a flunkey to say that Lord Droxford is taking you elsewhere. Or, of course, he might wish to dine alone with you."

"And if he is . . . dining out?" Karina asked hesitatingly.

Harriet looked a trifle surprised, but she managed to say with a pause:

"Then you must come alone. I always have extra men at my parties. We are going on afterwards to Lady Lumley's, who has rooms set aside for loo and ecarté, and if one is not careful, one stands alone while the men gamble. I have learnt to have a surplus of beaux so at least they can take it in turns to entertain me."

"Are you quite sure that I would not be a nuisance?" Karina enquired.

"You could not be that!" Harriet answered. "Besides if I do not see you at once in that white lace gown we have just bought, I will die of frustration! You will look ravishing in it and I want to be the first to introduce you to the *Beau Monde*. Everybody will be at Lady Lumley's tonight and if I cannot shine myself I can at least bask in your reflected glory."

"You are much too kind," Karina said, but Harriet had only laughed at her.

"Wait until you are in the same position," she smiled.

Karina turned away. There was no chance of her producing the heir which the Earl had asked for her last night. Had she been wrong to refuse him she wondered?

Then she thought of Lady Sibley, and the pretty piquant face she had glimpsed crossing the pavement in Bond Street beside him. Was there no end to his women?

She did not know why, but while she had accepted Lady Sibley, perhaps because she had known about her before her own life became entangled with His Lordship's, she resented the thought of Mrs. Felicité Corwin. She was pretty, smart and as Captain Farrington had said, an old friend—or should the word be favourite?

She had a sudden wish to see the Earl, to be with him. Even if they quarrelled it was better than wondering where he was, what he was doing and who he was with.

"Is His Lordship back?" she asked Newman.

"No, M'Lady. His Lordship sent a message to say that he would not be returning till late this evening."

"He will not be at home for dinner?" Karina inquired in a small voice.

"No, M'Lady."

The Butler's voice was calm and impassive, as if it was quite usual for a bridegroom not to dine at home the second evening of his marriage.

"In which case," Karina said," will you send a message to The Honourable Mrs. Courtney, to say that I shall be delighted to dine with her this evening, but His Lordship regrets he is otherwise engaged."

"I'll do so at once, M'Lady. You will require a carriage?"

"Yes please, at half after seven o'clock."

Karina turned, not towards the staircase, but along the passage which led to Robert Wade's study.

She opened the door and found him as she had

96

expected writing at his desk. Entering the room, she threw wide her arms, her eyes alight.

"Look at the transformation!" she cried. "I cannot begin to tell you how grateful I am to you, Robert. I am going to be smart, the talk of the town, and it will be all due to you!"

At the same time as Karina was speaking to Robert Wade, Captain Farrington was entering Whites Club in St. James's Street. He found the Earl lying back in a leather armchair in the Coffee Room, with a decanter of port beside him which was already severely depleted of its contents.

"Are you deranged Alton?" Captain Farrington asked, sitting down in an adjacent chair.

"Not that I am aware of!" The Earl replied.

"Then what the hell were you doing in Bond Street about noon and in such company?" Freddie Farrington enquired.

"Any reason why I should not patronise Bond Street?" the Earl replied.

"Only that your wife saw you," Freddie Farrington answered, "and I had the devil of a job preventing her rushing up to ask how you had fared with the Prime Minister and whether you admired her new gown."

"Karina saw me!" the Earl ejaculated. "I had no idea—in fact I had forgotten that she might be shopping."

"She brought a trousseau as you told her to do last night," Freddie told him. "Good God, Alton, now you are a married man you might consider the propriety of flaunting a ladybird in public, especially in front of someone so obviously just out of the egg as Karina."

"Who gave you permission to call my wife by her Christian name?" the Earl asked truculently.

"You, as it happens," Freddie Farrington answered.

"You told me to do so at the Cremorne Gardens last night, but as a matter of fact I have been keeping things somewhat conventional until Her Ladyship and I are better acquainted."

"You seem to be taking a lot of things on yourself," the Earl said sourly.

"Don't rattle me off with that high-nosed tone," his friend replied. "You are in the wrong, Alton, and you damn well know it. I have never felt so embarrassed in my life trying to explain to Karina why she should not speak to you.

"What explanation did you give her?"

"I told her the truth," Freddie answered. "I tried to get away with the fact that you were with an old friend, but she asked me point blank if the Corwin was your mistress. She is sharp-witted, that wife of yours, and do not forget it!"

"I wish you would mind your own business!"

The Earl picked up his glass and drank from it as if he felt in need of something to fortify him.

"I have done you a good turn, as it happens," Freddie told. "I have introduced Her Ladyship to my sister. She will try and prevent Karina from falling in the most obvious society quicksands, which is apparently more than you are prepared to do."

"I have told you, Freddie, this is none of your business," the Earl said in a voice of thunder.

"Well, if you are not prepared to look after that attractive creature with the most beguiling green eyes I have ever seen," Freddie said, "you will find plenty of people only too ready to play escort."

The Earl glared ferociously at his friend. Captain Farrington quite unperturbed sauntered away to talk to a man he had seen on the other side of the room.

By the time dinner was finished at Harriet Courtney's, Karina had begun to enjoy herself as she had never enjoyed herself before.

98

They had sat down ten to dinner with two extra men, and Karina, seated on the right of her host with an elegantly garbed, witty young Corinthian on her other side, found herself laughing and talking away without embarrassment after the first course was finished.

Her gown—as Harriet had predicted—was a sensation, and Robert Wade, without being asked, had produced from the safe a selection of jewels which had made Karina's eyes almost drop out of her head.

There were parures of every type of precious gem, but she had chosen diamonds as being the most suitable to the white lace of her dress. A necklace of them fashioned as tiny stars glittered round her neck, and there were six stars set on tortoiseshell hairpins, which her maid had arranged in her hair.

She wore a wide bracelet over her long gloves and though there had been also ear-rings and a brooch to match, she had left them in their velvet cases, remembering her mother had said it was vulgar to wear too much jewellery.

"You look like a fairy princess!" Harriet exclaimed when Karina had arrived alone, and a little nervous, at 25 Curzon Street.

"I always admired Droxford's good taste," Major Joselyn Courtney said as Karina sat next to him at dinner, "and now having seen Your Ladyship, I have to admit he is Non-pareil."

Karina dimpled at him and Harriet noted appreciately that she had plenty to say. She was not like so many beauties—prepared to sit dumb with a supercilious expression on their faces waiting to be admired!

When dinner was finished and the men had joined the Ladies in the Salon, Harriet announced as the clock struck eleven o'clock, that it was time to repair to Lady Lumley's large house in Grosvenor Square.

Though Karina did not know it, her parties, while extensively popular, were not particularly select.

There was a band playing when they arrived, and the Reception Rooms were ablaze with hundreds of lighted candles. There were flowers everywhere to scent the atmosphere, and two Salons were filled with green baize tables.

There was a Supper Room and a Buffet piled high with delectable dishes. The garden was lit by Chinese lanterns and although it was not very large, it had many sheltered corners where couples could sit in comparative seclusion.

Lady Lumley, who was large, fat and literally covered with diamonds and pearls, greeted Harriet effusively. She immediately announced she was extremely delighted to welcome the new Countess of Droxford as a guest, although she was considerably surprised to hear that the Earl was married!

After about an hour Karina found herself bemused by the chatter of tongues, the music of the band, the elegant, glittering men and women to whom Harriet introduced her one after another and whose names in the confusion she hardly heard.

Feeling a little bewildered by it all she sat down on a sofa and listened to Harriet chattering like a gaily-plumed humming-bird to a crowd of friends who surrounded her.

Then she perceived a tall, good-looking Gentleman walk up to Harriet. He was a person, she thought, that one would notice however crowded the company he was in. It was not only that he was extremely well-dressed, not only that he was handsome in a rather unusual manner. There was something rakish and debonair about him.

He had the look, Karina thought, of a pirate or buccaneer and she guessed, inexperienced though she was, that the bored expression on his face and the cynical twist to his lips, made him irresistible to women.

He was clearly asking something of Harriet who was expostulating with him refusing to do what he wished, until as if he forced his will upon her, she capitulated and brought him over to Karina.

"I am sure I am making a mistake," she said, "but Sir Guy Merrick insists on meeting Your Ladyship. I have told him I do not think he is a fit person to make your acquaintance when you are so new in London. But he has threatened me that if I will not perform the introduction he will find someone who will."

She looked at Sir Guy definatly, then finished:

"And so with a pistol at my head, Lady Droxford, allow me to introduce Sir Guy Merrick—a rake, a gamester, a most undesirable Gentleman for you to meet, but one who, for a number of years, I have found invariably gets his own way!"

"Thank you, Harriet," Sir Guy said, making her a mocking bow. "At least you do not damn me with faint praise."

"Do not believe anything he tells you, My Lady," Harriet said and went back to her friends.

Sir Guy seated himself beside Karina on the sofa and taking her hand raised it to his lips.

"I am delighted to make your acquaintance, Lady Droxford."

"Why did you wish to meet me?" Karina asked.

"Will you believe me if I reply that you are the most beautiful person I have ever seen in my life."

"No!" she answered. "I would not believe you, but I am delighted to hear you say it."

She saw his look of surprise, and added:

"I have never had any compliments paid to me until tonight, and although I do not credit a word of what is said, I cannot tell you how enjoyable it is to listen to them."

"You have never—had—any—compliments?" Sir Guy repeated incredulously. "Where have you been?"

"In the country," Karina answered.

"And that, I suppose, is where Droxford found you," he queried. "Curse him! But his good fortune is so prodigious that I cannot even be surprised."

"Are you acquainted with my husband?" Karina enquired.

"I have known him since I was in my cradle," Sir Guy answered. "He is, let my tell you, a very old enemy."

"An enemy?" Karina asked.

"Yes, indeed," Sir Guy answered. "We hate each other with considerable bitterness, and now I have a greater aversion for him than ever!"

"Why?" Karina asked innocently.

"Because he discovered you first," Sir Guy explained.

Karina dimpled.

"Is this what they call flirting?"

After a moment's astonishment at her naive question, Sir Guy laughed.

"It is perhaps a pale imitation of it."

"Then you must tell me what I am supposed to answer to your last remark. You see I am very green."

"It is my favourite colour, especially in beguilingly, beautiful eyes," Sir Guy said.

"That is what I mean," Karina cried, "you always have the right reply. It makes me feel so cabbage-headed not knowing what to say."

"Just say what comes into your entrancing little head," Sir Guy suggested.

"I generally do," Karina replied, "but as I've told Mrs. Courtney, I am well aware it may get me into a lot of trouble."

"Then I hope it is with me," he said.

She chuckled delightfully.

"Why do you and my husband hate each other?" she asked.

"It is a long story," Sir Guy said evasively. "One day I am sure he will tell you his version of it. In the meantime let me warn you, Lady Droxford, that he will disapprove of your ever knowing me and he would certainly be extremely incensed if he thought we were to become more closely acquainted."

"Does he disapprove of you as much as all that?" Karina asked.

"Even more so," Sir Guy replied, "and maybe he has reason to do so! At the same time, I want, as I have never wanted anything in my life before, to get to know you better—to be your friend."

Karina looked up at him, a question in her green eyes.

"Are you really offering me your friendship?" she asked and emphasised the last word.

There was a smile on Sir Guy's lips.

"To start with—but I make no promise about what might happen in the future."

"You are at least frank."

"Will you be my friend, beautiful, alluring, little Lady Droxford?" he asked, "at least until our friendship is forbidden to us, as I am quite sure it will be."

Karina felt a little tremor of fear that she might be doing something wrong and that the Earl would be angry with her.

Then she remembered Lady Sibley's pouting red mouth raised to his; she saw the attractive face with the dark hair she had glimpsed accompanying him into a jeweller's in Bond Street.

What was he buying Mrs. Felicité Corwin, she wondered? His Lordship had his friends and she had promised not to interfere. Very well, but it was only fair that she should have hers!

She turned and smiled at Sir Guy Merrick.

"I would like very much to be your friend, Sir Guy, if that is what you really want."

He lifted her hand to his lips.

"It will take some time to explain how much I want it," he said. "I am only hoping that you will be gracious enough to listen to my somewhat longwinded pleas."

"But of course I will," she answered, feeling a little shy because of the expression in his eyes, and because he had not relinquished her hand.

"You are lovely," he said in a deep voice, "so incredibly, absurdly lovely, that I half expect you to disappear!"

Karina drew in her breath, but at that moment they were interrupted.

"Are you coming to play, Merrick?" a man's voice asked. "They are keeping a chair for you at the high table."

Karina drew her hand from Sir Guy's.

"If you are going to gamble," she said, "perhaps I could come and watch?"

"You must come and play!" Sir Guy said firmly.

"But I do not know how to," Karina replied.

"Then I must teach you," he said, and added softly: "Among other things."

5

The Earl finished a substantial breakfast, and, picking up *The Times* which had been propped in front of him on a silver frame, he rose to his feet.

As he did so, the door opened and a small voice asked:

"Could I speak with Your Lordship?"

He looked up to see his wife standing in the doorway. His experienced eye realised that she was wearing an extremely elegant and expensive gown in daffodil yellow and that she appeared to be in the very height of fashion.

At the same time he noitced that her eyes were worried and she seemed unaccountably pale.

"But of course, Karina," he answered. "Shall we repair to the Library. I expect you have already breakfasted."

"Please let us go into . . . the Library . . . My Lord," Karina answered, and he had an idea that she trembled.

He followed her across the Hall, a footman opened the big mahogany doors, and they entered the Library where the Earl habitually sat.

It was a delightful room furnished with Chippendale bookcases and with long windows overlooking a small formal garden at the back of the house. A fountain was playing in the sunshine and there was a profusion of flowers bedded out amongst stone-paved paths.

The Earl walked across the Persian carpet to stand in front of the ornate marble chimney-piece and Karina stood facing him, her eyes raised to his.

She said nothing, and after a moment he remarked in a kinder voice:

"You are very silent! Will you not be seated?"

"Thank you, M . my Lord," Karina murmured and sat down on the extreme edge of one of the big velvet armchairs.

"What have you to tell me?" the Earl asked.

"I am afraid . . . you will be very . . . angry," Karina faltered.

He raised his eyebrows.

"Very angry . . . indeed!" Karina continued in a miserable tone. "In fact . . . I should not be surprised if Your Lordship . . . beat me or sent me . . . back to the . . . country!"

"It would have to be something extraordinarily bad for me to wish to do either of those things!" the Earl exclaimed. "What can have occurred? You have not been long in London!"

Karina clenched her fingers together until, with what was obviously a trememdous effort, she said:

"I have . . . lost money . . . gaming, My Lord."

"Gaming! the Earl ejaculated. "And when did this happen?"

"Last night," Karina answered, "and I . . . lost such an . . . enormous sum that I . . . hardly dare to tell . . . you the . . . amount."

Her voice broke on the words, but at the same time she looked up at him courageously, her little chin held high, her green eyes fixed on his.

"How much?" the Earl enquired.

"Two . . . thousand . . . pounds!" Karina whispered.

She felt as if her voice echoed and re-echoed round the room. Her fingers, laced together, tightened until they were bloodless, but still she did not turn away or drop her eyes.

The Earl slowly and deliberately sat down in the chair opposite her, lent back and crossed his legs.

"Suppose you tell me exactly what happened," he suggested.

Karina drew a deep breath.

"Mrs. Courtney asked us . . . both to dine, but when I returned . . . home to tell you . . . about it, Newman informed me that Your Lordship would not be . . . back for . . . dinner."

She paused for a moment.

"You were . . . punishing me, My Lord, were

you not? That was why you meant me to dine . . . alone."

For a moment there was no reply. Then the corners of the Earl's mouth twitched as he answered:

"Possibly."

"It has proved a very . . . expensive . . . punishment, My Lord," Karina said in a miserable voice.

"Continue with your story," the Earl commanded.

"Harriet Courtney had said it would not perturb her if I came to her party without you as she had extra men. It was very gay and amusing and I wished . . . Your Lordship had been present. After dinner we went on to Lady Lumley's."

"In Grosvenor Square?" the Earl questioned.

"Yes. It was a huge party and Her Ladyship deeply regretted that you could not attend it.

"I am familiar with Lady Lumley's entertainments," the Earl remarked dryly.

"There were a great many people there," Karina went on, "but of course I only knew those to whom Mrs. Courtney introduced me. And then . . . one of the . . . guests said he would . . . teach me how to . . . gamble."

"Who was it?" the Earl asked.

He was aware that Karina hesitated before she replied:

"Sir Guy . . . Merrick."

There was no mistaking the sudden change of expression on the Earl's face.

"He told me frankly that you and he were enemies," Karina said quickly, "but he was very . . . pleasant to . . . me and I thought that if Your Lordship had your friends . . . there is no reason why I should not have . . . mine."

There was a perceptible note of defiance in her voice and she appeared to stiffen as if she expected her husband to rage at her. Instead the Earl said in level tones:

"Tell me the rest."

"At first it was very exciting!" Karina said with a sparkle in her voice. "I have never seen so much money before in my whole life! They were playing very high, I think! Sir Guy tried to explain it to me and he said he would be my . . . banker!"

She could remember as she spoke feeling nervous as Sir Guy made her sit down at a table and she saw the piles of golden guineas in front of every player.

"I have no money with me," she had said to him in a low voice."

"I will be your banker," he promised.

"You mean that I can pay you later, that is if I lose?" she questioned.

"Exactly," he had answered. "But do not think of losing! It is a tradition that a lovely woman always wins the first time she plays."

It appeared he was right because very soon Karina had a pile of guineas in front of her. Sir Guy advised her how many cards to draw, which to discard, and after a little while it seemed that she began to comprehend a little of what was happening.

Then her luck had changed. The guineas in front of her dwindled away.

"I ought to stop now," she said to Sir Guy in a frightened whisper.

"Let us try another table," he suggested and brought her a new pile of sovereigns.

They moved from table to table until Karina became bewildered as to whether she had lost or won. Sir Guy collected her winnings if there were any and gave her at least ten or twenty guineas with which to stake her bets.

When she had tried her luck at almost every game he had suggested that they should play piquet together. Karina had been taught by her father and she knew she was a good player. But she soon found that she had met her match.

Sir Guy was a faultless player. Finally Karina threw down her cards with a little sigh of exasperation.

"I cannot beat you!" she exclaimed.

"Do you mind losing?" he enquired.

"Not really," she replied. "It is only somewhat mortifying when one meets an expert at a game and realises how sadly inefficient one is."

"You need to be proficient at nothing except at looking breathtakingly beautiful."

She dimpled at him.

"Compliments are no compensation for hard cash! You must tell me, Sir Guy, how much I owe you."

As she spoke she had thought with satisfaction of the ten guineas that Robert Wade had given her that morning which were still intact in her purse at Droxford House.

"Do you really want to know?" Sir Guy asked. "Let me make you a present of your losses—whatever they may be—as a wedding gift. A gift, of course, not only to your Ladyship—but also to your husband."

His voice hardened on the words and Karina said, remembering that he had told her that he and the Earl were enemies—

"No, no, it is a debt of honour! I am well aware that gaming debts take precedence over everything!"

"I see you are well-versed in the gamblers' code," Sir Guy said mockingly.

"My father was a gamester and I suffered greatly because of it," Karina explained. "But I would not have had him anything but honourable in discharging his debts."

"And so you wish to discharge yours?"

"But of course. Tell me what I owe you and I will send the monies to you tomorrow morning with a note thanking you for your kindness to me this evening."

"I shall look forward to receiving a note from you, Lady Droxford," Sir Guy replied. "I only wonder after this evening how you will think of me?"

"As someone who has been both kind and . . . friendly.

"And how do you imagine I shall think of you?"

There was something in the way Sir Guy looked at her which Karina drop her eyes.

"I have no . . . idea," she answered shyly. "May I know the extent of my debt?"

He looked down at the score card which lay beside him on the green baize table. Then, after a perceptible pause he said:

"I make it about two thousand pounds, Your Ladyship!"

For a moment Karina thought she must have misunderstood him. Then she felt as if the roof caved in and the room swam dizzily around her! She managed to rise from the table in what she hoped was a dignified manner as she said:

"I will send you . . . the money tomorrow, Sir Guy . . . I think now I must find . . . Mrs. Courtney."

She had turned blindly away from him, unaware that he had not risen but sat staring after her, a very strange expression on his face.

"I have lain awake . . . all night," Karina told the Earl unhappily, "puzzling how I could have lost so . . . much. I seem to remember Sir Guy saying as we sat down to play piquet . . .

" 'Usual stakes I suppose?'

"I agreed because . . . I did not wish to show . . . my ignorance by asking . . . what they were."

Her voice died away and then with a pathetic little gesture of her hands she said:

"I am sorry . . . more sorry than I can possibly . . . tell you. Please, please . . . forgive me . . . I do not know how I can ever make it up to . . . you except by not buying any more . . . gowns and by promising . . . you I will . . . never . . . never gamble . . . again."

The Earl did not answer. Instead he rose to his feet and pulled the bell.

The door opened almost immediately.

"A card table and several packs of cards," he said to the footman.

Karina looked at him in wide-eyed astonishment.

He did not speak again until the table was set up and new packs of cards were placed in the centre of it together with score-cards.

"Come and sit down, Karina," the Earl said. "I am going to teach you the fundamental principles of the games you will find being played in private houses."

Karina was too astonished to speak until, seated opposite her husband and listening intently, she began to learn how to play faro, basset and loo.

She was quick to pick up the points as the Earl showed them to her. She soon learnt on what numbers one drew a card and when one should discard.

It was nearly two hours later before the Earl threw down the cards he held in his hands and asked:

"Now do you understand?"

Karina nodded, her eyes shining.

"I see there is a lot more skill in it than I thought!" she exclaimed. "Are you a very, very good player, My Lord?"

"I do not often lose," the Earl replied.

"Then you are obviously a master, and I hope as your pupil I shall never shame you again."

"There is something you have to promise me," the Earl said sharply.

Karina waited. She almost guessed what was about to be said.

"First, you will never again play with Sir Guy Merrick, and secondly when you have lost a hundred pounds you will leave the table."

He looked at her sternly.

"Will you give me your word on that, Karina?"

"Yes, of course," she answered, "And I hope never to be so cockle-headed as to lose a hundred pounds."

"I trust you," the Earl said.

"And . . . the debt to . . . Sir Guy?" Karina asked in a low voice.

"I will deal with it," the Earl replied. "Merrick will receive my cheque within a few hours."

"I am sorry . . . deeply sorry," Karina said again and the sparkle which had been in her eyes as she began to grasp her husband's teaching dimmed to a sudden dullness.

"Forget what happened," the Earl commanded her. "The Duke of Richmond has asked us both to attend his Ball this evening. The Duchess is not aware of our marriage or she would have sent you a formal invitation. Would it amuse you if we went?"

"Together?" Karina enquired. "I would like it above all things!"

"I have already, as it happens, asked some friends to dine here," the Earl said. "It will give you a chance to wear one of the family tiaras which I suspect Robert has already displayed to you."

"He has indeed! I have never seen such wonderful jewels."

"Then mind you are dazzling tonight," the Earl smiled. "All the *Beau Ton* will be there but it will be a very much smarter party than you enjoyed at Lady Lumley's.

There was a touch of scorn in his voice and Karina wondered whether he thought Lady Lumley was not up to his touch, or whether he was just annoyed she had attended the party without him.

She was so relieved that he was obviously not so incensed with her but she was still troubled at the thought of her losses.

She also found it difficult to know what to think about Sir Guy Merrick. Why had he let her in her

112

ignorance plunge so deeply? Why had his professed friendship ended so disastrously?

When Karina came into the Salon before dinner to await the arrival of their guests, she found the Earl already there and looked at him enquiringly to see if he approved of her appearance.

She was wearing the pale pink gown that she had bought the day before from Madame Yvette. It was the colour of a moss-rose and had an expensive simplicity about it.

It was the perfect frame for the enormous sapphire necklace which made her skin seem in contrast almost dazzlingly white. On her golden hair, dressed high on her head, she wore a large tiara of sapphires set with hugh diamonds, which glittered in the light from the tapers in the crystal chandeliers.

For a moment the Earl stared at her, his face quite expressionless. Then in a quiet voice, as if he spoke to himself, he said:

"I thought that sapphires would become you!"

"Do you think I look . . . nice?" Karina asked. "I would not want to shame Your Lordship the first time we appear . . . together."

She came nearer to him as she spoke and looked up at him anxiously.

"You will not do that," he replied.

Their eyes met. It seemed to Karina that something passed between them, something strange, something she did not understand, and then as she wondered, longing for him to say more, yearning for him to praise her appearance, Newman announced their first guests.

It was very hot at Richmond House. It seemed as if the Duchess was determined to crowd the whole of the *Beau Ton* into her big Reception Rooms!

It took a long time to ascend the wide staircase.

When Karina and the Earl had been received by their host and hostess, they proceeded into the Ballroom which appeared already full to the point of suffocation.

"Do you dance?" Karina asked.

"I do not," the Earl replied. "If you wish to find me during the evening, Karina, I shall be in the Card Room."

She was just about to say nervously that she hoped he would not leave her as she did not know anyone, when she saw coming towards them a well-known figure!

It was Lady Sibley! She was wearing a red gown matched by a tiara of rubies and diamonds, and looking, Karina had to admit reluctantly, extremely beautiful.

She felt herself stiffen and was wondering if the Earl would introduce her, when someone said:

"May I have the pleasure of this dance, Lady Droxford?"

She turned to see the Corinthian who had been on her right at dinner the previous evening.

"Thank you, I would like to dance," she said gratefully.

As she moved away she saw Lady Sibley gliding with hands outstretched towards her husband.

It was nearly two hours later that Karina, finding herself for the first time without a partner, walked down the Grand Staircase in search of the Card Room.

She felt it would be embarrassing to disturb the Earl at his game, but it was impossible for her to stand alone in the Ballroom like a wilting wallflower.

She guessed the Card Room would be somewhere on the ground floor, and she was not mistaken. However, when she looked inside, the tables were all occupied, but there was no sign of the Earl.

She moved a little further along the passage, having no idea of where she might be going. Then glancing into a small Ante Room she saw her husband. Lady

Sibley was with him and they were seated side by side on a sofa at the far end of the room.

She turned away abruptly, knowing she could not interrupt them, and walking back along the passage she saw a door leading into the garden. It was open and she welcomed the feeling of fresh air on her cheeks after the overpowering heat of the Ballroom.

The garden was lit by fairy lights which seemed to twinkle beguilingly amongst the shrubs and trees and which lined the paths so that unwary guests did not stumble into the water-lily ponds or trip over the flower-beds.

Chairs were arranged in shadowy arbors or set under the overhanging branches of the trees. Karina, being alone, did not like to wander but stood quietly in the shade of the house and thought perhaps no one would notice her.

Then as she stood there, hearing the distant music of the band and aware of the beauty of the stars shining high above the trees, she heard a man say:

"So we meet again, Lady Droxford!"

She felt herself start, knowing even before she turned her head that it was Lord Wyman speaking. It was somehow impossible to forget the silky, unpleasant voice which had frightened her in Bond Street.

"We have not been . . . introduced, Sir," she said frigidly in what she hoped was a crushing manner, but which actually sounded only frightened, like a child playing at being grown-up.

"Does that perturb Your Ladyship?" he asked. "Then I will go immediately and find someone competent to perform such a ceremony. Shall it be our host or hostess? It will not be difficult to compel one of them to oblige me."

He spoke so positively that Karina knew it would only seem ridiculous for her to insist on such a formality.

"You know my name, and I know yours," Lord Wyman said "I assure you, my pretty one, that that is sufficient! Come and dance with me; for I have a great desire to partner you in the waltz so that I may put my arm around your tantalising little waist and hold you close."

"I must find . . . my husband," Karina said quickly.

"His Lordship is engaged at the moment," Lord Wyman replied, and she knew by the hateful note of insinuation in his voice that he had seen the Earl and Lady Sibley together.

"And I am also . . . engaged for the . . . next dance."

"You are trying to run away from me," Lord Wyman accused, "and I assure Your Ladyship that is something you will never be able to do! Yet it excites me to see you fluttering like a small bird caught in a net! I promise you there is no escape, for I think you look even lovelier tonight than the first time I saw you! Come, let us dance."

"I have told Your Lordship . . . I have a . . . partner," Karina faltered, and turning as she spoke she moved away from him.

There were some steps leading onto a balcony opening out of the Ballroom. As Karina climbed them Lord Wyman accompanied her. In the light from the windows she could see his narrow eyes, dark and lustful, looking at her in a manner which made her feel as if her gown was transparent.

"You are enchanting!" he said. "Quite enchanting! It is a pity that we cannot sit and talk in the garden, for I have much to say to you."

"No . . . no," Karina cried. "I must find my . . . partner."

Then as she reached the balcony with the wide French windows opening into the Ballroom, she saw to her utter relief Sir Guy Merrick walk out alone to stand staring down into the garden beneath him.

116

Karina hurried to his side.

"I am sorry . . . so sorry that I am . . . late and that I have kept you . . . waiting for our . . . dance," she said breathlessly, her eyes looking up at him pleadingly, feeling that he must understand what she was trying to convey to him.

"I was searching for Your Ladyship," Sir Guy replied with only an infinitesimal pause.

Karina turned to Lord Wyman.

"You see, My Lord, I have found my partner!"

"Then I must claim the next dance," Lord Wyman said.

He took her hand and raised it to his lips, squeezing her fingers as he did so.

"I am . . . engaged," Karina answered.

"Then I shall wait until you are free," he replied. She dragged her hand from his and said to Sir Guy: "Shall we dance?"

"But naturally," he replied.

Karina moved ahead of him into the Ballroom. Without looking back she was aware that Lord Wyman was watching her and she could imagine the expression on his face which made her even more afraid.

The band was playing a waltz and the Ballroom was still very crowded.

"Can we escape?" Karina asked.

"Let us do that," Sir Guy answered. "I want to talk with you."

They went down the Grand Staircase and Sir Guy led her out into the garden by another door. They found an empty arbour. Karina sat down and gave a sigh of relief.

"What were you doing with Lord Wyman and why are you frightened?" Sir Guy asked.

"I was alone," Karina answered. "I was . . . looking for . . . His Lordship and Lord Wyman came up and spoke to me! I do not know why . . . it is foolish of me, but he terrifies me! There is something

117

horrible about him . . . something which makes 'my flesh creep', as my Nurse used to say!"

"You are quite right, he is unspeakable," Sir Guy agreed. "You must have nothing to do with him."

"You cannot think I wish to know him?" Karina asked. "He spoke to me in Bond Street . . . when I was walking alone and then again . . . tonight."

"You were alone in Bond Street?" Sir Guy questioned.

Karina put her fingers to her lips.

"I ought not to have said that! Captain Farrington, whom I met there, told me I should not have been unattended. It was perhaps my own fault that Lord Wyman spoke to me then—but I feel now as if I cannot . . . escape him!"

"You are safe with me," Sir Guy told her.

As if she suddenly remembered what had happened the night before, Karina stiffened.

"Have you forgiven me?" Sir Guy asked.

He put his arm round the back of the seat behind her and half turned so he could look closely at her.

She stared across the garden.

"No!"

"I was sure that you had made up your mind not to speak to me again," Sir Guy said, "and I have been wondering all evening how I could contrive a moment alone with you to say how contrite I am and—to beg your forgiveness."

"I did not mean to speak with you," Karina admitted, "But I was so frightened of Lord Wyman that when you appeared I could only remember that for a . . . short while you had seemed a . . . friend."

"Forgive me, Karina," Sir Guy said, using her christian name for the first time. "I did not mean to hurt you."

"You were striking at His Lordship, were you not?" Karina enquired.

"So you realised that?" Sir Guy exclaimed. "Yes,

118

that is the truth, Karina, I meant to insult Alton and instead I lay awake all night remembering a stricken look in a pair of innocent green eyes. They have haunted me ever since!"

Karina said nothing and after a moment he asked:

"Was His Lordship very incensed with you?"

"No, he was kind—extremely kind about it! He said he would pay you! I hope, Sir Guy, that you have received his cheque."

"I have received and torn it up."

Karina started and looked at Sir Guy for the first time.

"You must not do that . . . it was a debt of honour."

"It was nothing of the sort," he said roughly. "It was the action of a cad, a man with whom you should not associate, my dear. Besides, surely you realised that it was impossible for you to lose such a sum in so short a time?"

"You mean that you . . . merely . . . invented . . . my losses?"

"But of course!" he answered. "And Alton would also have realised it was false! I meant him to do so!"

"I do not understand," Karina said a little piteously.

"What would you think if someone you knew had found a treasure—a pearl of great price, and then did not trouble to safeguard it?"

"Do you think . . . His Lordship understood what you were trying to convey to him?" Karina asked.

"I am certain he did," Sir Guy answered. "Alton and I were more or less brought up together. We were like brothers for twenty years of our lives. I know exactly how his mind works and he is conversant with mine!"

"Then why do you hate each other?" Karina asked.

There was a pause before Sir Guy deliberately parried the question.

"Have you been forbidden to speak to me again?"

"No, but I have promised not to game with you."

"That is generous of him!" Sir Guy exclaimed, then added with a twist of his lips: "I wonder if he thinks me not sufficiently dangerous or whether he just does not care?"

Karina did not answer and suddenly Sir Guy said violently:

"Curse it! But we should not be using you as a pawn in our games! I hate Alton and he hates me, but it has nothing to do with you—it all happened long ago when you were only a child!

"Forgive me, Karina! I have behaved abominably to you, and all I can beg is that you will not only be merciful to a very humble sinner, but to a man who has never had you out of his thoughts since the first moment he set eyes on you."

"I have a . . . feeling," Karina said shyly, "that you should not be talking to me like . . . this."

"We talked together quite easily last night," Sir Guy replied. "We cannot go backwards and pretend I am not bemused and enchanted with your beauty; that you have not already crept into my heart so that I have found myself thinking of you every second of the day; wanting to see you again, longing to hear your voice, and cursing myself for being such a fool as to hurt you when you had offered me your friendship."

His voice was passionate with sincerity. Then he asked:

"I did hurt you, did I not, Karina?"

"Y . yes," she answered. "I had trusted . . . you!"

"And that is the cruellest thing you could say to me," Sir Guy vowed, "a punishment which my behaviour deserves but which makes me feel so ashamed that there is nothing I can plead in my favour."

"I too stayed awake . . . last night," Karina whispered, "so now . . . I am very tired . . . I would like to go . . . home."

"I understand!" Sir Guy said. "It is too much on top of everything else to have some fool being emotional."

"No, it is not that," Karina said hastily. "It is just that it is all extremely bewildering! I thought that I really had lost all that money and that . . . His Lordship would be . . . very angry with me, and that you had only . . . pretended to be my friend! I felt lost . . . unhappy and afraid!"

She made a little sound that was almost a sob.

"Now I do not know what to think! His Lordship was kind and brought me here tonight and you are sorry! I want to go on being friends with . . . you because I have so few friends . . . and men like . . . Lord Wyman . . . terrify me!"

"Oh, Karina!—Karina!" Sir Guy said in a low voice she hardly recognised.

He took her left hand and drew her glove from it very gently. Then while she wondered what he was about to do, he kissed her fingers one by one and finally pressed his lips into the softness of her palm.

"You are so young, so unspoilt, so unbelievably innocent!" he said hoarsely.

"I think . . . I ought to . . . go," Karina murmured.

She felt that she could not allow him to kiss her hand, but she was aware at the same time that the feel of his lips on her skin was exciting and she liked the strength of his fingers holding hers. There was also a throb in his voice which told her that he was deeply moved.

"You poor little thing, you are tired out!" he said gently and the kindness in his tone made her suddenly feel like tears. "Let me find your husband for you and if he does not want to leave, I will take you back safely to Droxford House."

As Sir Guy spoke Karina remembered where her husband was.

"His Lordship may indeed desire to . . . stay on . . . he is . . . enjoying himself."

121

Sir Guy glanced at her.

"I will find him for you," he said. "Come, let me take you into the house; for I would not like to leave you here alone—you are far too alluring and will draw men to your side, like moths to a candle."

"You called me that last night."

"I meant it!" he said. "Do you doubt for a moment that I have not meant every word I have just said?"

He waited for her reply, his eyes on her face, as if he compelled her to answer him. Finally, Karina said in a very low voice:

"I . . . believe you."

"Then forget my treachery," he pleaded. "Let us go back to the moment when we first met and I told you you were the most beautiful person I had ever met in my whole life! That is true, Karina, and, what is more you are someone I have been searching for years but now when I find you it is—too late!"

He saw the startled expression on her face.

"No, I am not flirting. I know that is what you are trying to tell yourself. This is the truth, but I should not have revealed it to you so quickly."

"What do you . . . mean?" Karina asked.

"I mean that I have fallen in love with you," he answered. "You may be innocent, my darling, but not as innocent as all that! When a man at last sees the woman who is his ideal, whose image he has always held hidden in his heart, then the barriers of reserve and doubt fall away at the touch of her hand!"

His fingers tightened sharply on hers.

"I love you, Karina, and because I know that I am going to be crucified by loving you, I should go away and never see you again! But instead I shall stay and torture myself because you are the wife of the man I hate most in all the world and because I know only too well that I am not worthy even to touch your hand—let alone kiss it."

Again he pressed his lips passionately and lingeringly against her palm! Then he relinquished her and said sharply:

"Put on your glove—I am taking you to your husband!"

Bewildered and a little afraid, at the same time unable to suppress a tiny thrill of delight because she could move him so deeply, Karina pulled on her glove, buttoned it, and followed Sir Guy meekly from the arbour up onto the terrace and into the house.

He did not look at her or speak to her until as they reached the Hall he said:

"Have you any idea where Alton might be?"

"His Lordship said he would be in the Card Room," Karina answered, "But when I saw him last he was in an Ante Room beyond it with . . . a friend."

"Then wait here," Sir Guy said, "but I would not leave you alone because of Lord Wyman."

He glanced around and saw a number of young men talking together at the bottom of the stairs. He walked across to one of them—a young, fresh-faced youth—and said:

"Lovelace, would you be obliging enough to look after Lady Droxford while I seek her husband?"

"Yes, of course, Sir," Mr. Lovelace replied.

He might have been expecting a Dowager or some unattractive female because his eyes lit up when he saw Karina.

"Lady Droxford, let me present Ian Lovelace, whose father is an old friend," Sir Guy said. "If you will both wait here I will be as swift as possible."

"Thank you," Karina answered.

She was amused at the trouble Mr. Lovelace took in finding her a chair and the manner in which he strove eagerly to entertain her with the social chatter which he thought appropriate for the occasion.

Sir Guy glanced in at the Card Room, saw that the Earl was not playing, and then proceeded to the Ante Room beyond it. There he found His Lordship and

Lady Sibley seated on the sofa where Karina had last seen them.

They did not notice him enter the room, and watching them he perceived that they were in the midst of an altercation. Lady Sibley was pouting and her dark eyes were stormy, while the Earl's chin was set square and there was a frown between his eyes.

As Sir Guy approached them, they both looked up as if to question an intrusion.

"Your servant, My Lady," Sir Guy said, bowing over Lady Sibley's hand. "May I venture to say that you are in great good looks this evening?"

"Thank you, Sir Guy," Lady Sibley replied. "It is a long time since you have called on me. As I am now back in London I hope that is a neglect you will remedy very shortly."

"Your Ladyship can be assured that I shall pay you my most humble respects at the first opportunity," Sir Guy said with a mocking note in his voice.

Lady Sibley looked at him coquettishly. She had for a long time wished to enslave Sir Guy but he had always avoided her. There was something about him, she thought, that was irresistible, and yet he was one of the few men she had desired who had ignored her blandishments, however blatantly she proffered them.

She would have said more, but Sir Guy had turned to the Earl.

"Have I your permission, Alton, to escort your wife home?" he asked. "She is tired and wishes to leave."

The Earl sprang to his feet.

"If my wife is tired, I will take her home myself," he said angrily, "And I will thank you, Guy, to leave my wife alone."

The two men moved away from the sofa.

"That is the whole point," Sir Guy said in a low voice, "she is—alone, so alone, Alton, that a swine like Wyman can frighten her."

"Wyman! That lecher!" the Earl exclaimed.

"Exactly," Sir Guy said. "I have just rescued her from his quite intolerable advances. Does that mean anything to you?"

"Damn it! Will you not interfere with my private life," the Earl demanded fiercely.

"Your private life is of no interest to me whatsoever," Sir Guy replied. "It is your wife that concerns me."

"Have you not done enough damage already?" the Earl asked. "You received my cheque, I presume?"

"I was most grateful for your promptness," Sir Guy said. "I tore it up—as you expected me to do."

"Your behavior is extremely provocative, even for a blackguard such as you!" the Earl sneered. "If you are not careful, Guy, I shall call you out."

"You will not do that," Sir Guy said mockingly, "for I might kill you, Alton. That is something I have wished to do for a long time, but never so much as at this moment."

"Why particularly at this moment?" the Earl asked, as if his curiosity could not prevent him from asking the question.

"You will find the answer lies in your latest acquisition," Sir Guy replied, "Which, like all your possessions, appears to be of little consequence to you once you own it.

"But doubtless you will learn that a wife is not like a racehorse to be sent away to your stables, or a picture to be hung on your wall. And if you are not particularly interested in her—other men might be!"

"God damn you for your impertinence!" the Earl thundered. "Is there no end to the insinuations you imagine you can make with impunity? If we were not in a private house, I swear I would knock you down!"

Sir Guy smiled infuriatingly.

"We used to be well-matched, Alton, if you remember. I wonder if it came to fisticuffs who would be the winner?"

"If you say one more word I will challenge you," the Earl replied, "but not with fists, Guy, with pistols!"

"In the meantime," Sir Guy drawled in a manner which contrived to be particularly insulting, "your wife is waiting to be conveyed back to that mausoleum in Park Lane. Am I to be her escort, or are you?"

"I will take her, and you can go to hell before I despatch you there!" the Earl snarled.

"Then you must allow me to take your place with the charming Lady you are abandoning for your duties," Sir Guy said, seating himself beside Lady Sibley on the sofa.

She smiled at him but there was an insolent look in his eyes which only the Earl understood.

"You will find Lady Droxford," he added casually, "in the Hall."

The Earl muttered farewell to the Beauty who had entertained him for the past two hours, and scowling prodigiously he walked away down the corridor to where Karina was waiting.

He strode up to her and she saw at once that he was incensed.

"You wish to go home, I understand?"

"Not . . . if it is . . . inconvenient . . . My Lord," Karina faltered.

"I will call the carriage," he said, turning towards the door.

Karina thanked Mr. Lovelace for his attentions. While they were waiting she had sent a footman to fetch her wrap and now, pulling it round her shoulders, she went to stand beside her husband.

She wondered what Sir Guy had said to put him in such a rage, and she wished that, instead of allowing a man who she knew was an enemy to go and fetch the Earl, she had been brave enough to seek him out

126

herself. Yet she knew she shrank from coming face to face with Lady Sibley.

It had been one thing to watch the Earl, with whom she was not yet entangled, kiss Her Ladyship at the Duke's garden party, but quite another thing to meet socially a very beautiful woman with whom her husband was enamoured.

She wondered if Lady Sibley had chattered about the reason for the Earl's hasty marriage. She thought that if she were indeed as fond of him as she pretended, she would say nothing. And yet it was almost to much to hope that any woman could keep such a delicious morsel of gossip to herself.

In the carriage the Earl threw himself into his corner without speaking. After a moment, as the horses started off down Piccadilly, Karina said hesitatingly:

"I am s . sorry if you did not . . . wish to leave so . . . early."

"Merrick told me that Wyman had upset you," the Earl stated. "What happened?"

"Lord Wyman spoke to . . . me," Karina said. "He insisted that I should . . . dance with him! It was an excuse to . . . touch me . . . he said so! It was foolish of me, but I was . . . frightened!"

"You seem to have a penchant for consorting with the most undesirable men," the Earl said crushingly.

His tone somehow swept away Karina's humbleness and made her defiant. Why should her husband speak to her in such a tone when he had spent the whole evening with Lady Sibley and not worried in the least whether she had a partner or stood alone?

"Perhaps you would be obliging enough, My Lord," she replied, "to introduce me to some pleasant ones! After all, my acquaintance in London is very limited!"

There was no gainsaying the truth of this, and after a moment the Earl said more kindly:

"I will certainly introduce you to some of my

friends, Karina. We must entertain! I will tell Robert to send out invitations."

"That would be delightful, I should like it so much."

"I have, unfortunately, already a number of engagements which I cannot change," the Earl went on, "but I dare say I could fit in two dinner parties this week and perhaps a visit to the opera, if that is what you would like."

"I do not wish to . . . bore you . . . My Lord," Karina said humbly.

"That is another matter!" he replied. "But now I have a wife I quite see that it is of import that she should meet the right people and not be involved with outsiders like Wyman or indeed—Merrick."

They travelled a little way in silence, and then the Earl asked:

"What did Merrick say to you tonight?"

"He told me that he had torn up the cheque you had sent him! He had asked for that sum only because he wished to . . . insult you."

"I had realised that perfectly!"

"Then you might have told me so!" Karina said sharply, "or did it please you to deliberately make me humble myself before you, to apologise for something which you knew I had not really done?"

"I had not thought of that," the Earl admitted.

"Nor did Sir Guy. I do not know what it is which makes you hate each other, but you have both contrived to use me as an instrument in expressing your emnity."

She gave an exasperated sigh.

"Do you realise that I lay awake nearly all last night, terrified as to what you would say in the face of such losses; dismayed by my ignorance; and desperately trying to find a way in which I could repay the monies which I now learn I had not in fact expended!"

"You must blame Guy for that—not me," the Earl said quickly.

128

"But Your Lordship could have reassured me this morning, could you not?" Karina asked. "You were not disagreeable about it, I grant you that, but you left me feeling that I was deeply at fault; that I should try to behave better in future, that I was an ignorant turnip-head from the country in that I could become involved in such a disaster!"

"You are right, Karina," the Earl admitted. "Guy and I should not use you as a weapon against each other. I apologise and I hope that he will do so."

"Sir Guy has apologised and I have . . . forgiven him!"

"You sound as though you intend to extend to him a friendship of which I shall not approve," the Earl said accusingly.

"I have told you," Karina answered, "that while you have your friends I am entitled to mine! You may dislike Sir Guy, but he has in fact shown me a kindness which no one else has done since I came to London!"

As she spoke the carriage drew up outside Droxford House in Park Lane. A footman opened the door and the red carpet was run across the pavement.

Karina stepped into the brightly lit Hall.

She felt a suddenly pang of disappointment that she had spent the time she had been alone with the Earl in quarrelling with him instead of trying to ensure that what exchange they had with one another should be pleasant—or at least courteous.

She looked up at him and realised how exceedingly handsome he was in his satin evening coat with its long tails, his knee breeches, and meticulously tied cravat in which glittered one large diamond.

She took a little step towards him. She was ready to say she was sorry, to coax if possible a smile to his lips and the kind look to his eyes which she felt had been there when he had invited her to go with him to Richmond House.

Then before she could speak she heard him say to Newman:

"Keep the carriage!"

He was going back to Lady Sibley, she thought, and without looking at him again she dropped a curtsey.

"Good night, My Lord," she said in a muffled voice and went up the stairs feeling forlorn, lonely and for no reason she could explain, on the verge of tears.

6

The Earl of Droxford walked into White's Club, and avoiding several members who might have wished to converse with him, sat at a table in a corner of the Dining Room where he hoped he would not be disturbed.

He held a number of papers in his hand which he set beside him preparatory to reading them while he enjoyed his meal. They concerned the Reform Bill, which had occupied His Lordship's mind considerably for the past two months.

He had in fact been attending yet another lengthy meeting of his fellow peers that very morning. It was one of dozens at which his presence was expected and which he had begun to find were of increasing boredom.

The Reform Bill, which aimed to reduce the power of the Crown and transfer political power from the upper to the middle classes, had inflamed the country.

It was not only that the reform of the electoral system was sadly overdue, it was that the people themselves felt that a new style of administration would benefit the poor and the workers who had become increasingly restless during the reign of George IV.

"Damn it, if we are not careful we shall have a revolution on our hands," one of the older peers had ejaculated that very morning to the Earl.

There had been riots in all the major cities; in the country ricks had been burnt down; farm labourers had marched menacingly on their employers, and in London Sir Robert Peel's new Police Force, which had only been operating for two years, was finding it hard to keep the mobs in check outside Buckingham House and around the Houses of Parliament.

"Peel's Bloody Gaing," were very unpopular. "Raw Lobsters' and "Blue Devils" were two of the names they were called. Yet the cry: "The Peelers are coming!" usually dispersed a mob hooting and window-breaking.

Independently-minded peers like the Earl were lobbied almost day and night by enthusiasts for or against the Bill.

The Prime Minister, Earl Grey, represented those who favoured reform, while the opposition was led by the greatly revered but ageing Duke of Wellington.

"How are you going to vote, Droxford?" one of his contempories had asked the Earl as they left the meeting.

"I have not yet made up my mind," the Earl had replied. "I am prepared to admit that the redistribution of Parliamentary seats is urgent, but at the same time I feel that Lord John Russell's proposals for a new Constitution go too far."

His Lordship was obviously expressing the feelings of a great number of his fellow peers. But he thought as he listened to the interminable speeches made either in the House or at private meetings that the reactions to the Bill were so inflammatory that a compromise would have to be reached quickly.

So insistent was the pressure brought upon the Earl

that he found it almost impossible to find time for any other activity.

Meetings, discussions and conversations took place daily: there were invitations to breakfast, to luncheon, dinner and supper in the various strongholds of those in favour of Reform and those equally obdurately against it.

The Earl had not thought to tell Karina why he was so preoccupied and she had imagined, when he said he was engaged, that he was enjoying the company of the beautiful and possessive Lady Sibley or of the fascinating Mrs. Corwin.

In actual fact, the Earl had not seen Lady Sibley since the Duke of Richmond's Party, and he would have been considerably surprised if he had known that Karina's feelings concerning his mistress amounted to an almost violent dislike.

The Earl finished a generous helping of lamb and had just decided to partake of some succulent roast pigeons for which the Club Chef was famous, when he realised someone was standing at his table.

He looked up, an expression of irritation on his face, for he had no wish to be disturbed, and saw it was Lord Barnaby, a very stout and aged member of the Club who had been a close friend of his father's.

"Good day, My Lord," the Earl said with an effort at affability.

"Do not get up, my boy," Lord Barnaby told him, "I just wanted to congratulate you on your appointment as Lord Lieutenant. I saw it in the *Gazette* last week."

"Thank you, My Lord," the Earl replied. "Will you not sit down?"

"No, no! Go on with your luncheon!" Lord Barnaby insisted. "I am just leaving, as it happens, and have no time to gossip. Besides, I expect you are hurrying to see the race!"

As His Lordship's mouth was full with pigeon he did not answer and Lord Barnaby continued:

"The betting is against Her Ladyship, of course. She is an unknown quality, no one having seen her drive. At the same time, Alton, I should be shirking my duty if I did not suggest to you that it would be best if such a wager did not reach the ears of the Court. It was very different in the last reign, as you well know!"

Lord Barnaby gave a fat chuckle. It seemed to make his enormous stomach shake like a jelly.

"By jove, Prinny would have thought it a great jest and would, I should not wonder, have insisted on being present. But it is not the sort of thing that appeals to our Sailor King, let alone his most respectable, Lutheran Queen. No, Alton, my advice is keep mum and do not let it happen again!"

The Earl put down his knife and fork.

"Forgive me, My Lord, but I have not the least conception of what you are saying. To what race are you referring?"

Lord Barnaby's eyes, enclosed as they were in layers of fat, managed to open wide, so he looked not unlike a surprised goldfish.

"Not know what I am talking about, my lad? Good Heavens, you must be roasting me!"

"No, indeed, My Lord," the Earl replied, but his expression had darkened and there was a frown between his eyes.

"So that pretty wife of your is playing truant," Lord Barnaby chuckled. "Well, I do not blame her. 'Tis likely she suspects that, if she had told you what she was about, you would have put a stop to it! The right thing to do, as it happens!"

The Earl rose slowly to his feet.

"Will you be kind enough, My Lord, to explain to me exactly what is occurring?" he asked with a note in his voice which drove the smile from Lord Barnaby's lips.

"None of my business, dear boy. I have no wish to be involved in your private affairs, but there is a betting-book on the result—and half White's have set down their wagers—so it is no secret!"

"Wagers—on—what?" the Earl asked slowly and distinctly.

"The race Lady Droxford is driving against the Marchioness of Downshire."

"And where is it taking place?"

"In Regent's Park."

"And the time?"

"Two o'clock, I believe! I must leave you, Droxford. My apologies if I have brought you unwelcome news —but keep it quiet! That is the best way to handle these matters—the less talk the better!"

Lord Barnaby turned to waddle away but already the Earl had passed him and striding across the Dining Room had disappeared into the Hall.

"In a miff!" Lord Barnaby murmured to himself. "Should not have said anything—stupid of me—how was I to know he was ignorant of his wife's escapade?"

Muttering to himself Lord Barnaby reached the Hall, to see through the open door into St. James's Street the Earl of Droxford climbing into his Phaeton and scowling as he took the reins.

As he turned the horses the Earl glanced at the clock on St. James's Palace and saw that it wanted four minutes to two.

Driving through Berkeley Square His Lordship pushed his horses in a manner which made the groom mutter a prayer between his teeth. Even so, four minutes in which to reach Regent's Park from St. James's Street would have been an impossibility for any bloodstock.

The Earl reached the entrance to Regent's Park and hesitated for a moment whether to drive left or right. He chose the left, and found he had been right in his supposition, for half-way down the straight run west of the Park he saw a hastily improvised winning post.

In front of it was assembled a large crowd of top-hatted Bucks and gamesters, the majority of whom His Lordship despised.

The Earl knew by the manner in which they all watched the far distant curve of the soft ridingway that the race must have already started. Sure enough, a few seconds after his arrival there was a sudden shout and in the distance two pairs of galloping horses appeared.

This, the Earl realised, must be the first time round for the competitors. A few moments later he was able to see the Marchioness of Downshire driving a smart black horses with considerable ability.

She was well-known as a Lady Driver and had enjoyed a tremendous popularity during the roistering days of the Regency, when her manner of frank speech and the oaths with which she embellished not only the hunting field but also Rotten Row, were considered both smart and amusing.

She had, however, over the years become not only coarsened in appearance but *declassée*, and a number of London hostesses no longer included her in their invitations.

But there was no doubt she could drive, and as her curricle flashed past the watching crowd there was a general waving of top-hats and a few noisy cheers.

Karina seemed in contrast a lovely child, far too small and weak to control a spirited pair. She was wearing a pale blue driving coat which revealed her slender waist, and a small straw bonnet trimmed only with blue ribbons.

Her golden hair was brushed smoothly away from her forehead and bound tidily in a neat chignon. She looked not only beautiful but a Lady of Quality, something which the Marchioness with her tumbled curls dyed with henna had never looked.

135

As Karina passed the Earl, he saw she was holding her horses well in hand. She was driving a curricle which had been delivered to His Lordship only in the past two weeks. It was specially sprung and pulling it was a matchless pair of chestnuts for which he had paid not less than a thousand guineas the previous month.

He had not considered them as yet sufficiently trained to London usage, and it was with a feeling of frustrated fury that he watched them tear by as he sat frozen to an immobility in his Phaeton.

"Cor, 'er Ladyship handles 'em as well as His Nibs," he heard his groom say in an undertone. "Copied 'im, she 'as, til 'er be the spitting image of 'im!"

The compliment, if it was meant to be one, made the Earl even more enraged than he was already. The fact that Karina was sitting bolt upright and holding the reins and whip in the manner approved by the Corinthian set, increased rather than appeased his anger.

He could hear the odds shortening on the Marchioness and realised that Karina's forbearance in holding her horses back was not understood by the majority of those watching, who thought that women, if they drove at all, must thrust and push to assert their supremacy.

Then, as the minutes ticked by, the Earl found himself torn between a desire that Karina should be humiliated as the loser in a race for which she should never have entered, and the wish that his wife, driving his new pair of chestnuts, should show that loud-mouthed harridan, the Marchioness of Downshire, that she was not the only woman who could handle the ribbons.

"Here they come!" he heard someone shout, and a moment later the horses appeared once again in the far distance.

There was no doubt that neither Lady was going to have an easy victory. It seemed to the Earl that the

136

four animals were moving side by side, neck to neck. Then, about a hundred yards before the winning-post, Karina drew ahead.

By this time the Marchioness was bending forward shouting encouragement to her horses and whipping them violently; and her hair was blowing untidily around her flushed face.

Karina was driving as if she were enjoying a quiet outing in the Park. Holding herself upright, her hands at the correct angle, she was not using her whip.

Her encouragement of her team lay in the movement of her fingers on the reins, and angry though he might be, the Earl could not but approve the style in which she passed the winning-post a length in front of her opponent.

There was not even a smile on her lips to show her satisfaction—no vulgar elation such as the Marchioness would surely have shown. Only, he thought, as she flashed by, her eyes were shining as if lit by a thousand tapers.

There was a loud cheer as, in truly British manner, even those who had backed the wrong driver were prepared to give credit to a sporting winner.

Karina, checking her horses and drawing them in slowly, heard the cheers receding into the distance.

"I have won!" she told herself. "I have won! I knew I could do it!"

Now the race was over she felt deflated. She had wanted so much to beat the Marchioness, and yet now to turn her horses round and return to the winning-post to receive the winner's stakes seemed somehow a little tame.

For the first time since the race started she wondered what the Earl would think when he learnt what had occurred. Then as finally the sweating chestnuts were drawn to a halt and she was ready to turn them, she realised that a Phaeton had drawn up alongside her.

137

She looked up, saw the Earl's face, and felt as if an icy hand compressed her breast.

She wanted to speak, but the words seemed to die on her lips, and she could only sit looking at him, her eyes very large and frightened.

"You will come with me, Karina!" the Earl said, and she knew from the steel in his voice how incensed he was.

"Drive Her Ladyship's curricle home, James," he ordered his groom.

The groom jumped down from the Phaeton, Karina handed him the reins and stepped out of the curricle. It was always difficult for a Lady to climb into a Phaeton, but the Earl showed none of the nicety of stretching down his hand as was usual to assist her. Instead he only just permitted her to seat herself before starting his horses.

"I must apologise . . . if Your Lordship is . . ." Karina began.

"We will speak of this when we reach home," the Earl interrupted chillingly.

She glanced up at him nervously and knew that never before had she seen a man in such a rage. It was not only just the squareness of his chin and the tightness of his lips, but there was a white ring round his mouth as if it was with difficulty he held himself in control.

Karina felt her spirits drop into a bleak despondency. She knew now she should never have accepted the Marchioness's challenge and yet at the time it had been irresistible.

Almost every day for the past week she had gone driving with Sir Guy Merrick. It was strange, she thought, that he always called for her at Droxford House after the Earl had left.

At first she had been afraid that the two men might meet, but then she began to guess that by some means of his own Sir Guy knew when she was alone.

He never entered the house, and if she was occupied she only had to refuse his invitation for him to leave immediately. But as she had so few engagements she was more glad than she could express to drive with Sir Guy in his Phaeton and know that he tooled his horses as expertly as the Earl.

Sir Guy was too wise to invite gossip by taking her into Hyde Park. They journeyed along side streets until they were clear of the more fashionable parts of the City.

They drove in Battersea Park, Chelsea and Bloomsbury Square, and then, becoming more adventurous, visited places outside London. Sir Guy found that above everything else, Karina enjoyed the Horse Fairs which at this time of year took place on the outskirts of the metropolis.

Perhaps unwisely, because Karina was so insistent, he took her to Tattersalls, the famous saleroom in Knightsbridge where all the fashionable owners bought and sold their horses.

It was, Karina and Sir Guy knew, inviting comment for them to be seen together in such a public place. Yet Karina's love of horses and the interest she showed in them overruled caution and Sir Guy promised a trifle reluctantly to be her escort.

"I have heard so much about Tattersalls," Karina said. "Papa bought a horse there once and a very high-stepper it was. I think he paid too much for it but he was a heavy man and it took a very strong animal to carry him."

"I bought a pair of bays there last week." Sir Guy told her. "I am waiting to show them to you."

"You know I am longing to see them," Karina answered.

"What a funny child you are," Sir Guy said with a caressing note in his voice. "I really believe that, unlike most females, you would rather I gave you a good horse than a diamond necklace."

"You cannot give me either. But you are right in your supposition as to which I would rather have! Do you think His Lordship will ever let me set up my own stable?"

"Why do you not ask him?" Sir Guy suggested.

Karina shook her head. She had a feeling that it was not the moment to beg His Lordship for any special favour, and yet when she was at Tattersalls she saw half a dozen horses she would have given all her new gowns to own.

"Look at that stallion!" she cried enthusiastically. "He is almost perfect. Why should anyone be selling him?"

"I suspect his owner's pockets are to let," Sir Guy answered.

"I am sure you are right," Karina said, "for otherwise he could not bear to part with such a splendid animal."

It was while she was inspecting the stallion that she heard a woman's voice, loud and over-hearty, hailing Sir Guy.

"Where the devil have you been, you naughty man?" the Lady exclaimed. "I expected to meet you at Newmarket but there was not a curst sign of your handsome phiz. You know you always give me far better tips than anyone else!"

"Your Ladyship flatters me," Sir Guy replied.

Then as the newcomer looked curiously at Karina, he was obliged to say:

"May I introduce the Countess of Droxford—The Marchioness of Downshire."

"So you are the bride I have been hearing about!" Lady Downshire exclaimed in a manner which made Karina wonder whether it was a compliment or an accusation.

The Marchioness was a plump middle-aged woman, overblown and overdressed. She was accompanied by three some what racy-looking Gentlemen. They all started to talk horses until suddenly the Marchioness exclaimed:

"I have purchased a new pair of cattle to drive my new curricle. I swear they will beat the sneezy horse-flesh any one of you could put up against them!"

"Better throw the gauntlet at Merrick," one of the Gentlemen suggested with a loud laugh. "The bays he bought last week are superb! I would put my blunt on them.

"Don't you insult me!" the Marchioness screamed. "I know my black boys can outrun any damned cattle that Merrick or any other shuttle-headed Tulip of Fashion can produce!"

"Be careful, My Lady," another Gentleman remarked, "you might be taken up on that challenge!"

"By God, that is exactly what is it!" the Marchioness exclaimed. "A challenge, to every one of you! Let us make it worthwhile—what do you say to five hundred guineas as the prize-money? Do you take me on, Trevor?"

"Oh no!" the Gentleman in question answered. "I am not in the running!"

"What about you, Sir Guy," the Marchioness asked. He shook his head.

"I have not handled my bays for long enough to be sure of their prowess."

"Hell, you are all chicken-livered!" the Marchioness shouted. "Not a touch of spunk among you! The trouble is you manly cockle-heads are all afraid of me! Woman though I may be, I can outdrive the cat-crawling lot of you. And do it, I swear, with one hand tied behind my back!"

"You are boasting!" someone accused her.

"And you are gutless," she replied. "Will no one accept my challenge?"

"I will!" Karina heard a voice say, and wondered if indeed it could be hers. "But my wager, My Lady, will only be for a hundred pounds."

141

She had not meant to speak but she had in fact formed a strong distaste for this loud-mouthed, boasting female. The Marchioness might be a good driver, but at the same time Karina was sure that Her Ladyship was the sort of rider she tried to avoid out hunting—the type who would thrust ahead, lead the field, ride too close to the hounds, and yet was surprisingly seldom in at the death.

She had promised His Lordship not to wager more than a hundred pounds! She meant to win the race, but she would not risk breaking her word.

"A hundred pounds!" the Marchioness ejaculated. "Well, I'll take your cheese-paring widow's mite. Maybe Your Ladyship hasn't much confidence in your own driving, and who would be surprised at that!"

She looked Karina up and down insultingly. Then she turned aside with a loud laugh.

"Blancmange!" she sneered. "God knows I'll be an odds-on favourite!"

Karina had not realised exactly what she had agreed to in accepting the Marchioness's challenge until she found that without being consulted the race was arranged for the next day and knew that somehow she had to coax His Lordship into lending her his chestnuts.

She had in fact meant to tell the Earl of the wager, but when she arrived back at Droxford House it was to find yet another of those messages—delivered so frequently by Newman—that His Lordship would not be returning until late.

It was, though Karina did not know it, an urgent meeting at Holland House on the Reform Bill, but she thought that once again His Lordship was with Lady Sibley.

Finally she had gone to bed thinking that if the Earl was not in the house there was no reason to tell him about the race.

The Earl had left in the morning to breakfast with

the Prime Minister before Karina came downstairs and she had salved her conscience, which had begun to prick her, by telling herself that there was little likelihood of his hearing about the wager.

If he did, she would explain how impossible it had been to ask his permission.

But now, driving beside the Earl down Baker Street she knew only too well that he was mad-as-fire and she had little or no defence.

The footman helped her alight at Droxford House and she walked into the Hall very conscious of the Earl behind her.

We will go into the Library," he said in a voice which seemed to Karina like the voice of doom.

Nervously she took off her coat, pulled off her bonnet and handed them to a footman. Then she smoothed back her hair and having reached the Library stood irresolute in the centre of the room waiting to see where the Earl would wish her to sit.

But when she looked up into his face she knew that this was not to be an occasion when he was concerned with her comfort. Instead, towering above her, he glowered down at her making her feel, with his great height and broad shoulders, that he was overpowering and somehow menacing.

She guessed that he was almost too angry to find words with which to begin his condemnation, and nervously clasping her cold hands together she tried to appease him:

"I am . . . very . . . sorry if . . . you are . . . angry!"

Angry!" he exploded. "What do you expect me to be? How could you make such an exhibition of yourself? How could you flaunt all refinement and decency by such an action? Do you think it is pleasant for me to see my wife—bearing my name—being laughed at and joked about by every cit and ruffian who has access to a public Park? Do you imagine that any

143

Lady with any sense or sensibility would expose herself to being the object of Club anecdotes; to have half-drunken fops placing bets on her; to allow herself to compete with a woman whose very name is a byword for vulgarity?"

His Lordship paused for breath, then asked:

"And who gave you permission to drive my horses?"

"I . . . thought . . . you would not . . . mind," Karina murmured.

"Mind!" His Lordship exploded. "Of course I mind! You have no authority to take out a pair that I have hardly broken in to my own touch!"

"They won . . . the race!" Karina said with a flash in her eyes.

"A race that anyone could have won!" he snapped.

"The Marchioness is well-known as a whip," Karina protested.

"She is well-known for a number of other things as well!" the Earl retorted. "God, that I should have to explain to you the mere rudiments of behaviour! I know I took a chance in choosing you as my wife, but I did think at least you were a Lady by birth and that you had some idea of how a Gentlewoman should behave! It seems I am mistaken!"

"That is not . . . fair!" Karina said in a low voice.

"Not fair!" the Earl echoed. "Do you think it is fair for me to be warned in my own Club that if a whisper of this outrageous escapade should reach Court circles I should be severely censored for your misdemeanour!"

"Oh, no!" Karina exclaimed.

"It is true," he answered sharply. "Such manners were not frowned upon during the late King's reign but today they will not be tolerated."

She did not speak and he continued:

"You promised when we married you would behave

144

circumspectly and yet today I am ashamed—ashamed to acknowledge you as my wife! Ashamed that the new Countess of Droxford should act like a common hoyden!"

The Earl spoke with a bitterness and fury which was all the more telling because he did not raise his voice. There was an icy cut to his words, so that Karina went very pale although courageously she still faced him, her eyes on his.

"Damn you!" the Earl ejaculated. "Cannot you understand what I am saying to you!"

He flung out his right hand as he spoke in a gesture to express his frustration, and, as he did so, Karina winced and instinctively threw up her arm in front of her face as if she expected him to hit her.

It was an involuntary action and almost immediately she straightened herself, but he had ceased speaking.

It was if he suddenly realised how small and defenceless she was! She was so fragile, her eyes so large in her tiny pointed face, while her action in cringing from him had reminded him all too forcibly of the life she had lived with her father.

"Good God, you do not imagine I am going to hit you, do you?" he asked abruptly.

As she did not reply he turned and walked away from her towards the window to stand looking out onto the fountain with his back towards the room.

He felt his anger ebb away. After all, she was very young. It must have been an overpowering temptation to show how she could drive; and she had won—won superbly, not only with an expertise which was remarkable but with a style that was unmistakeable.

Then, as the Earl stood looking blindly into the sunshine and seeing instead a white, frightened face cringing away from him, he heard Karina's voice say:

"I would . . . rather you . . . hit me than speak . . . to me as you . . . have."

Her voice broke on the last word. For a moment the Earl fought with the last remnants of his anger. Then he turned.

"I did not mean it, Karina . . ." he began, only to find the room was empty.

He was alone.

It was two hours later that Karina answered a knock on her bedroom door.

"Who is it?" she enquired.

"Excuse me, My Lady, but Sir Guy Merrick has called. He wonders whether Your Ladyship would wish to go driving."

"Tell Sir Guy I will be down in five minutes," Karina answered.

But it was double that time before, dressed in a white gown and wearing a bonnet which was just a mist of muslin, she came running down the front steps.

Sir Guy was having difficulty in controlling the restlessness of his horses but he smiled as he helped her climb up beside him and they set off towards the north of the Park, which was not fashionable at this time of day.

"You have been crying," he said when they had driven a short way in silence.

Karina flushed. She had hoped that witch-hazel and the juice of cucumber had erased the traces of her tears.

"Why did you not . . . stop me from accepting that . . . stupid challenge?" she asked miserably.

"So Alton was angry!" Sir Guy exclaimed. "I was afraid he would be!"

"You did not . . . warn me."

"My dear, what could I do?" Sir Guy asked. "It would have been difficult for you once you had spoken—to back down. I just hoped—like you—that he would not hear of it."

"Yes, that was what I . . . hoped," Karina answered. "But he was there . . . someone had told him at the Club what was . . . happening."

She gave a deep sigh.

"Why was I so foolish? I can see now how wrong it was, but at the time I just resented the fact that a woman could boast so bombastically about herself."

Sir Guy did not answer, he merely drove on until they reached the north bank of the Serpentine. Then he drew his horses to a standstill beneath the overhanging branches of a tree, and turned his head to look down at the woe-begone little face beside him.

"Will you come away with me, Karina?"

She looked up at him, wide-eyed in astonishment.

"What do . . . you . . . mean?"

"What I say!" he replied. "You can race my horses from John o'Groats to Land's End for all I care! You can dance on top of St. Paul's Cathedral! Everything you did, Karina would be a joy and a delight to me if we were together."

"How could you . . . ask me to do . . . such a thing?"

"Is it so surprising?" he asked. "I have told you that I love you! I have wooed you very gently, Karina, because I did not wish to frighten you, but I cannot stand by and watch you unhappy."

Karina did not speak, but her face was troubled and Sir Guy added quietly:

"Let me take you away and teach you what love means. You are so young, so vulnerable, and unprotected! Besides, I want you! Dear God how I want you!"

Sir Guy's words were suddenly deep with passion.

"But if I went away with . . . you, we would . . . be living . . . in sin!"

Karina's voice was low and shocked.

"Would that worry you, my sweet?"

"Yes . . . it would," she replied. "I should always

be . . . aware that Mama would have . . . disapproved."

"I do not think your mother would have wanted you to be unhappy. I love you! I love you so desperately that I would devote my whole life to making you happy!"

"You must not . . . speak to me like . . . that," Karina said, "it is . . . wrong! You know full well that I am . . . married and even if we . . . ran away I do not think that . . . His Lordship would face . . . the scandal of a . . . divorce."

"What does it matter if he does or does not?" Sir Guy asked. "Come with me, Karina, we shall leave nothing behind that is worthwhile. We will go abroad, we will live anywhere you wish. But let me take care of you! Alton does not deserve you."

Karina was still for a moment, looking onto the silvery water of the Serpentine, her expression very grave. Then she said:

"There would be . . . no happiness for . . . either of us, Guy, if I did anything so . . . dishonourable! I made a bargain with His Lordship . . . he has not broken his part of it . . . I have broken . . . mine!"

"What do you mean?"

"I promised to be a complacent and comformable wife. I am complacent but I am certainly not . . . comfortable. I see now that His Lordship was right to be . . . angry with me. It was crazy of me to race publicly in Regent's Park so that . . . everyone could see . . . me!"

"What the hell does it matter?" Sir Guy asked violently.

"It matters to His Lordship," Karina replied. "I might have known when I saw Droxford Park that I would not be . . . worthy of such . . . a place . . ."

"That is utter fustian!" Sir Guy interrupted. "Alton

148

is not worthy of having a wife like you simply because he does not look after you. If you had a husband who loved you, Karina, you would not make mistakes. You would never make them with me!"

There was silence for a moment before Karina said:

"I am flattered . . . that you should ask me to . . . run away with you, Guy, but I must stay . . . of course I must stay with His Lordship and keep to my side of the bargain! I shall . . . try to make him a . . . conformable wife. Perhaps one . . . day I shall . . . succeed."

"What can I say?" Sir Guy asked despairingly. "I want you so desperately, Karina. Have you no tenderness for me?"

Karina hesitated.

"Perhaps it is . . . wrong but I want your . . . friendship. I have enjoyed this past week . . . so much, driving with you, talking to you, and even . . . hearing you talk to me of . . . love. I know that is very . . . wrong, but as His Lordship has no fondness for me perhaps he would not mind."

Sir Guy's lips twisted in an ugly sneer.

"He would mind," he answered, "but only because you are his possession! He owns you! You belong to him! You are not a person as far as Alton is concerned, Karina, you are just part of the Droxford inheritance!"

His voice was hard and bitter.

"Why do you hate each other? Karina asked. "Tell me why? It is something I have to understand."

"Very well!" Sir Guy answered. "I think you should know the truth!"

He steadied his horses, although in fact they were standing quite quietly, brushing away the flies with their long tails.

"Alton and I were brought up together," he began, "because my mother and his were close friends. My father was not a rich man and so I spent a great part of my holidays at Droxford Park.

"We went to Eton at the same time; we shared rooms at Oxford. We shared our birthdays, our anxieties, our ambitions—and we were, in fact, inseparable. Each of us was the only child of our parents, and we were even closer than brothers would have been; we were more like twins!"

Sir Guy turned his head towards the water and Karina knew he was looking back into his childhood.

"We rode together, hunted, fenced, boxed," he went on. "In fact, it would have been difficult, I think, to say which of us was the better at any sport, we were so equally matched. And then in my last year at Oxford when I was staying at Droxford Park I met Alton's cousin—Cleone Ward."

Sir Guy paused. It seemed to Karina that his voice altered.

"She was very young, only seventeen, ethereal, graceful, lovely—as lovely as you. And perhaps in a way a little like you, save that her eyes were blue."

Karina heard the pain in his voice and slipped her hand into his.

"Do not tell me . . . if you would rather . . . not," she whispered.

"I want to tell you," he replied. "Cleone was a wild, tempestuous girl, high-spirited, but in an unbalanced way which would have told a man older and wiser than I was that she lived entirely on her nerves."

"She loved . . . you?" Karina asked.

"She told me she did and I believed her. I would never have dared to declare myself had Cleone not sought me out and made it very plain that she wanted me as much as I wanted her."

Sir Guy's fingers tightened on Karina's.

"Before Cleone had been at Droxford Park for a week I was wildly, passionately, insanely head-over-heels in love with her."

Karina drew in her breath. She felt a little jealous of this woman who could still arouse so much feeling in his voice.

"I knew, of course, it was hopeless to approach Cleone's father, Lord Ward," Sir Guy continued. "He was an over-bearing, self-opinionated nobleman who would listen to no one who was not his superior in rank and who had very grandiose plans for his daughter's future.

"About three weeks after we realised we were in love with each other, Cleone told me that her father had given the Duke of Wye permission to announce their engagement."

"You mean that she was told she had to marry him?" Karina asked, thinking of Lady Mary.

"Lord Ward did not even ask Cleone if she was interested in the Duke, she was merely informed that the marriage had been arranged. She came to me frightened and in tears. She detested the man! It was not surprising! He was twenty years older than she was, a dissipated roué who had buried his first wife—a pathetic creature who, public opinion averred, had cried herself into the grave."

"What did you do?" Karina asked breathlessly.

"I asked Cleone to run away with me. She was only too willing to agree. We decided to drive to Gretna Green and be married. Once wed there would be little our two families could have done about it!"

"How romantic!" Karina exclaimed with a little smile.

"It was rather more a matter of desperation," Sir Guy said. "The only difficulty was, of course, that I did not have enough money for the post-chaise, or indeed to pay the Marriage Fee!"

"Then what did you do?"

"I made our plans, waited up till the last moment, and then borrowed the money from Alton."

"He lent it to you?" Karina asked.

"He lent it to me," Sir Guy answered. "He had never refused me a loan and he asked no questions. But because he had always been such a close friend, because I loved him as if in fact he were my twin-brother, I told him why I needed it."

There was a little silence.

"Lord Ward, informed by Alton's father what was happening, caught up with us at Baldock! Cleone was dragged screaming from my arms and her father thrashed me insensible."

"Oh no!" Karina cried.

"It was a week before I could move," Sir Guy continued in a dispassionate voice. "When I crawled home still more dead than alive it was to find Cleone's engagement had been announced in the *Gazette*."

"Did she marry the Duke?" Karina asked.

"She broke her neck out riding the day before her marriage," Sir Guy replied, and now there was no mistaking the pain in his tone. "She was so gay, so full of life, it seemed impossible that she should die!"

"It was an accident?"

"That was of course what the world was told, but privately my parents were informed that Cleone was with child."

"Oh no!" Karina's exclamation was one of horror.

"I had no idea of it," Sir Guy said. "Had I known I would have reached her even if a battalion of soldiers had barred the way. As it was, my letters to her were returned unopened. I was informed that if I attempted to see her Lord Ward would horsewhip me as he had done before. But I swear that had I guessed the truth even that threat would not have stopped me!"

"What did you do after—her death?" Karina asked.

"I was mad with hatred," Sir Guy replied. "I no longer wished to live. I went to London; I gambled, I drank, I went in for every vice and excess that was available to a young man in search of dissipation. Of course I plunged into debt. As a result my mother had to sell her jewellery, my father to part with his lands.

"They were desperately unhappy about me, tragically ashamed! When my father died some years later his ill-health was of course attributed entirely to my deplorable behaviour!"

"But what happened to you?" Karina enquired.

"I was on the point of being taken to the Fleet," Sir Guy answered. "The debtor's prison is not a pleasant one, and I dare say it would have proved a salutory lesson. But fate changed everything with one of those strange quirks of fortune no one anticipates. An uncle I had not heard of for years as he lived in Jamaica, died and left me over a million pounds!"

"Too late!" Karina exclaimed.

"Too late as far as Cleone was concerned! It made me laugh bitterly to realise that had the money been there when we loved each other my offer for her hand would at least have been considered. A very wealthy man is almost equal to a dissolute, ageing Duke."

"How very, very sad," Karina murmured.

"Can you understand now," Sir Guy asked, "why I hate Alton and why Alton hates me. Perhaps he was right to put family above friendship, but I have always felt he betrayed my trust, though he may think that in betraying one of his family I betrayed him also!"

Karina gave a deep sigh.

"There is no answer to that . . . is there?"

"No," Sir Guy replied. "Again it is a quirk of fate that the only woman I have wanted to marry since I lost Cleone—is Alton's wife."

"Is that really true?" Karina asked. "You must have . . . loved many women."

"Many, and many have loved me. But as I told you, my lovely, every man has a secret ideal and you are mine. I knew it the moment I saw you. It was as if a streak of lightning flashed across my brain and

153

seared its way into my heart. I saw you sitting on the sofa and something told me—'Here is the woman you have always been seeking.' "

"You would not have thought that if Cleone had been alive."

"I wonder?" Sir Guy replied with a little smile. "Now I sometimes think that perhaps we might not have been as happy as I anticipated. She was very headstrong, very spoilt, wanting everything her own way. Even though she was so young, she could, like her cousin Alton, be decidedly overbearing!"

"I can see in so many ways you are like him," Karina said reflectively.

"Of course," he replied. "The good and the bad! That is the whole story of man, is it not? He has two sides to his nature—he can rise or he can sink. So Alton sits high on a pedestal while I wallow in the dirt!"

"No, it is not true," Karina answered. "You are not as bad as you make yourself out to be."

"My dearest, you know very little about life or men," he said very softly. "I am bad—make no mistake about it! And I enjoy my wickedness! That is why I shall do my damnest to take you away from your husband!"

There was something in his voice which was disturbing. Karina looked up at him and her eyes searched his face. She saw the harsh, cynical lines at his mouth, but his lips were smiling. There was a glitter in his eyes which made her feel he was already sure of her, confident of getting his own way."

"No . . ." she whispered. "No . . . Guy!"

"There is no such word where you and I are concerned," he answered.

She felt suddenly as if the ground opened in front of her and she trembled on the brink of a chasm.

"No . . . please . . . I must go . . . home!"

It was the cry of a child frightened by the dark.

Sir Guy lifted her hand to his lips. Then he looked down at her, a fire smouldering behind his eyes, an expression on his face she dared not translate into words.

"I will take you back," he said softly. "But I shall be waiting for you Karina—waiting until you can stand it no longer! Remember I shall always be there—waiting!"

7

As the Earl walked across the green lawns of the Royal Enclosure at Ascot Races he suddenly thought that Karina should be there!

He had been so occupied up to the very moment of leaving London that automatically he only remembered that three months ago—a perennial bachelor—he had accepted an invitation to stay with Lord Staverley—a party he enjoyed every year.

He did not recall that Ascot was particularly a Social occasion until he saw like a kaleidescope a profusion of taffeta and silks, feathers and flowers, muslins, ribbons and parasols.

With a frown between his eyes he realised that he was at fault, even while he tried to justify his forgetfulness by the manner in which Karina had contrived to avoid him since he had thundered at her so violently for daring to race against the Marchioness of Downshire.

He had regretted his ill-temper ever since and had meant to apologise for it, but somehow the opportunity had never arisen.

It was true that he had seen Karina sitting at the far end of his table at the dinner parties arranged so successfully by Robert Wade. She looked entrancingly lovely and he was forced to admit to himself not once but a dozen times that she certainly graced the Droxford jewels.

She also captivated his friends and acquaintances. The Earl was aware that when they congratulated him on his marriage they did so in all sincerity, and where the men were concerned there was no doubt that there was a note of envy in their voices as they told him what a fortunate fellow he was.

At the same time, looking back over this past week, the Earl knew that Karina must have deliberately planned that they should never be alone.

He had thought he was certain to have the opportunity of speaking to her, if at no other time, when they met before dinner to receive their guests. But at each of their dinner parties Karina had managed to enter the Salon either as the first guest was announced or else a few minutes late, profuse with apologies, but having, it appeared, a most convincing excuse.

At the same time the Earl told himself irritably that he should have remembered that she would wish to attend Ascot Races. He should have driven her down himself every day instead of accepting the hospitality of Charles Staverley.

The Earl had another source of irritation which had indeed kept him awake for the better part of the night.

He had the previous evening not arrived at Lord Staverley's house until nearly seven o'clock, having left London an hour later than he had originally intended. This meant he was forced to change into his evening clothes in haste—something which he most disliked. He actually came downstairs only a few minutes before the Butler was due to announce dinner.

When he entered the large Salon where Lord Staverley's cronies were assembled there was no time

156

for him to be introduced to all those present. Most of the men were old friends and they met year after year, but there were some new faces and the Earl was just going to ask his host to identify them when he heard a young man say:

"Talking of horses, have you seen the new bays that Merrick has acquired? I swear that they are the finest pair of horseflesh one could find anywhere."

"I agree with you," another stranger to the Earl replied. "I drew up alongside them on the Cambridge Road last week. We were both waiting at a toll-gate as it happened, and I was able to inspect them closely. To my mind they are faultless!"

He waited as if he expected someone to contradict him, and then added:

"As faultless in fact as "the Incomparable" who accompanied Merrick."

"Who was that?" the first speaker asked.

"I have no idea of her name," was the reply, "but she was a glorious creature and had the largest green eyes I have ever seen on any female! Trust Merrick to find anything so delectable!"

There was a sudden silence as always falls in a company when someone has said something tactless. Several of the men present glanced at the Earl, then deliberately looked away, and he knew with rising anger that they were all well aware who had accompanied Sir Guy Merrick, and that each of them was wondering if he was ignorant of the gossip circulating about his wife and his avowed enemy.

He was, however, too well-bred and too self-controlled to show that he had even heard the conversation. Instead, he walked across the room to sit down in an armchair and announce in level tones to the man nearest to him that the King was unlikely to attend the Course if it rained.

"He would welcome the excuse," was the bitter reply. "His Majesty thought he must keep up the Royal

157

Stud—expensive though it might be—but he told several members of the Jockey Club that it was only because the Queen liked horses, and he would do anything to please the Queen!"

The Earl had to laugh at this, but he could not forget what had been said about Karina and found it continually recurring to his mind as he tried to sleep after losing a considerable sum of money at écarté.

Now, almost instinctively, he found himself looking amongst the crowd of Gentlemen on the lawns to see if Merrick was amongst them.

If not, was he with Karina? The thought made the Earl scowl and several people who had intended to greet him swerved away as they thought better of the impulse.

The Duke of Richmond, the Senior Steward of the Jockey Club, had asked the Earl and several other noblemen to receive the King and Queen.

The Earl heard a distant cheer—not a particularly enthusiastic one—and saw the Royal Family driving down the Course with a great cortège: there were eight coaches, each drawn by four horses, two Phaetons, pony sociables, and led horses.

The Duke of Richmond was in the King's calèche and the Prime Minister—Lord Grey—in one of the coaches. The King's three illegitimate sons were accompanying their father: the Earl of Munster was riding on horseback behind the King's carriage. Augustus—the Parson—and Frederick were both driving Phaetons.

As they drew nearer to the grandstand the Earl realised that the reception was strikingly cold and indifferent—not half as good as George IV had always received.

He watched their approach and then walked through to the back of the Stand where the Royal Party would disembark.

The King stepped out in a good humour. With his beaming red face, his grey beaver hat, his blue coat and white nankeen trousers, his gold watch-chain attached to the big gold repeater which played tunes, he looked the very embodiment of a jolly sailor.

The Queen was as usual most elegantly gowned and wore an enormous amount of glittering jewellery.

They shook hands most affably with the reception party and were escorted to the Royal Box, to look down at the crowds lining the rails, at the green lawns where social figures fluttered like colourful butterflies; and at the horses already being cantered down to the starting-post.

High hats of silken satin or transparent gauze had suddenly become the vogue for the evening, but a number of fashionable Ladies were sporting them with their elaborate Ascot gowns.

Despite incurring ridicule by their unusual appearance, some of the *Ton* wore them with enormous gigot sleeves and a wide shoulder line. These of course, accentuated their pinched in, tight-laced waists.

The Earl, as he walked through the stand was amused to overhear one woman say:

"Pick up my race-card, love; if I stoop down my stays will burst—with an explosion that will scare the horses!"

In the comfortable Royal Box with its crimson cushioned chairs and refreshment room in the rear, the Earl made polite conversation to the Queen, and then with some relief turned to talk to King William.

He liked the bluff, genial old man with his pineappleshaped head, and wished that there had been a warmer greeting for him at attending this, his first Ascot as King.

There was no doubt that the new Monarch enjoyed his position to the full. He was in ecstasies with his Prime Minister, his people, his glorious new life and everyone concerned in it, except the Duchess of Kent, whom he referred to as "That Person" and who infuriated him every time he thought of her.

The Earl found that the King was eager to visit Droxford Park and he talked with knowledge of the treasures he wished to see there, hardly bothering to watch the first race until the horses thundered past the winning-post just below the Royal Party.

"Who has won? Who has won?" the King asked because he thought it was expected of him.

"The Duke of Devonshire, Sire, with March Hare," the Earl informed him.

"I am glad!" the King replied. "Fine chap! Someone told me the other day he is called 'The glass of fashion'. I should not be surprised! Seems very apt! The Queen says he has much courtesy and grace. She could not say that of me—could she?"

The King gave a noisy laugh, which turned into an asthmatic cough. Then he picked up a race-card.

"Have I any horses running?" he enquired.

"Your Majesty has one in the next race, I believe," the Earl replied.

He opened his own card and as he did so he heard the King say:

"I see your wife is running a horse against yours, Droxford!" he said. "That is unusual! If one of you wins do you share the prize-money?"

Again the King was laughing, but the Earl was staring at the card as if he could not believe his eyes, and yet there it was, printed clearly:

"The Countess of Droxford's Merlin, trained by Nat Tyler, ridden by J. Tyler."

"There must be some mistake . . ." he started to say, but the words seemed to stick in his throat.

One of the Gentleman in attendance approached the King:

"Would you care to visit the Paddock, Sire, as your Majesty has a horse running in the next race?"

"Yes, yes, of course!" the King replied. "Come, Droxford, I will look at my horse and we will see if yours or your wife's is likely to beat him!"

His Majesty chatted away as they proceeded across the lawn, the Ladies curtseying, the Gentlemen raising their hats and bowing as they passed.

"Nice day"—"Nice to see you"—"Thank you"—"Thank you—" the King said again and again, stopping occasionally to shake hands with someone whose face was familiar.

He was shepherded forward by his escort until they reached the Paddock where the horses for the next race were parading round the ring.

It was then, standing by the rail, that the Earl saw Karina! For a moment he could hardly believe his eyes, but there was no mistaking that little pointed face or the shining gold of her hair beneath the pale pink bonnet which, matching her pink gown, made her look like a small rose-bud.

As if she was instinctively aware of his scrutiny, she turned her head and saw him. For a moment it seemed as if she would run away, then she came courageously towards him with an anxious look in her eyes.

She did not seem to realise he was in the Royal Party but as she reached the Earl, the King, who was bowing to right and to left so that he should not miss any of those who wished to salute him, saw her.

"This your wife, Droxford?" he asked.

"Yes, indeed, Sire. May I present her to Your Majesty?"

"Of course—of course!" the King replied, not waiting for a formal presentation but putting out his hand as Karina, suddenly abashed, sank down in a deep curtsey.

"Glad to meet you, Lady Droxford," he exclaimed. "I have known your husband a long time! Heard you were married! The Queen will wish to make your acquaintance. Come now and show me your horse and tell me why you are trying to beat your husband at a sport at which I am told he is extremely proficient."

Karina gave a little frightened glance at the Earl, but as his face seemed inscrutable she could only walk beside the King, answering his question by saying:

"I did not realise when I entered my horse, Sire, that His Lordship would be competing in the same race."

"Well, I hope my animal beats you both!" the King laughed. "Do you think that is possible, My Lady?"

Karina hesitated for a moment and then she answered frankly:

"I do not think so, Sire."

"You do not think so, eh?" the King asked. "Why?"

"I have a feeling, but of course, Sire, I may be wrong," Karina answered, "that Royal Crown is not particularly fit."

"Not fit!" the King exclaimed in astonishment, "and what makes you think that?"

Karina glanced at the Earl, saw the frown on his face and realised she should not have spoken.

"It is only a foolish idea of mine, Sire," she said. "Please do not credit anything I say, I am certain to be mistaken."

"Well let us have a look at him," the King suggested.

They entered the ring where only owners and jockeys were permitted. The horses were circling round and the Earl opening his card saw that Karina's horse was number six. He picked it out and nearly laughed aloud!

A large-boned, long-necked, rather gawky animal, it looked extremely out of place besides the other prime and well-fed horseflesh being led past. He had been prepared to be angry at this unexpected action of independence on the part of his wife, but now he felt sorry for her.

He knew how greatly she loved horses—she had shown him that very clearly on their wedding-day when she had asked him if she might inspect the stables at Droxford Park.

But he thought she would have had more sense than to buy an animal who, as far as he could see, had no attributes of beauty, and less of breeding.

The King was still talking to Karina, but it was obvious to anyone who knew her that she was finding it hard to concentrate on what His Majesty was saying. The Earl was aware that she was worried and apprehensive in case he was incensed with her.

Well, on this occasion he decided he would surprise her! He would not be angry and if she wanted to set up a racing-stable, he would help her to do so.

He would tell his own trainer to pick her out one or two decent horses, not like that ramshackle nag which she must have bought with her pin-money and which looked likely to break down half-way round the Course.

He admitted that he had been extremely negligent in not arranging to bring his wife down to Ascot. He would now make amends by being generous-minded and ready to console Karina when she saw what a fool she had made of herself in putting an animal absurdly like a child's rocking-horse into a race in which the best bloodstock in England was competing.

"Now, where is my horse?" he heard the King say.

"There is Royal Crown, Sire," Karina replied pointing to a restless roan.

The Earl looked at the animal critically. The horse appeared to be up to scratch, and yet there was something about it which with his experienced knowledge of horseflesh made him pause.

Perhaps Karina was right, perhaps the animal was

163

not in perfect trim. But who except Karina would have been so nitwitted as to tell the Royal owner the truth?

The jockey's were mounting. The Earl turned aside to speak to his own trainer and he saw Karina move across towards the big ungainly animal which already had a very small, insignificant-looking jockey in the saddle.

Really, it was too absurd, the Earl thought, that the child had not had the sense to take him into her confidence. He would at least have found her an experienced jockey.

"We was not expectin' to have a competitor in 'er Ladyship," his trainer remarked to the Earl.

"I do not think we need be anxious on that count," the Earl replied.

The trainer smiled.

"No, indeed, M'Lord. At the same time, these Irish horses are often unpredictable.

"Irish?" the Earl enquired with a lift of his eyebrows.

"Yes, M'Lord, Irish, and Nat Tyler . . ."

Whatever he was about to say about Karina's trainer was lost as the Earl realised the King was beckoning to him. He went hastily to the Monarch's side.

"I want to place a bet, Droxford," the King said, "so we will return to the Box."

"Of course, Sire," the Earl replied courteously.

"Are you coming with us, Lady Droxford?" the King asked as Karina, having seen her horse out of the ring, joined them.

"Thank you, Sire. I am deeply honoured," she said with a smile which would have captivated anyone even less vulnerable to female charm than the ever susceptible Royal Billy!

"Now, you must tell me what animal I am to back," the King said. "I do not like losing money, you know!

I have been too often below hatches to enjoy squandering away my blunt on show horses. Shall I wager that Royal Crown is the winner?"

"He is the favourite, Sire," Karina replied, "but that is because everyone wishes to be complimentary to Your Majesty and they are anxious for you to enjoy your first Ascot."

"Do they?" Damn good of them!" the King exclaimed. "Well, if they are backing my horse I must certainly do the same."

"But just as a safeguard, Sire," Karina said hesitatingly, "why not put a trifle each way—on Merlin—that is my horse. It is a long price—about ten to one, I think."

"Ten to one!" the King exclaimed. "A good return for one's money, eh Droxford!"

The Earl did not answer him. He was wondering how he could stop Karina making such a fool of herself. Really, to ask the King—who knew nothing about horses—to back a complete outsider was sheer lunacy!

It was well-known that in some ways the King was very parsimonious. He had been in debt the whole of his life until he came to the throne, and even though he enjoyed his new-found riches like a schoolboy let loose in a tuckshop, he was still inclined to be distinctly cheese-paring when it came to the ready.

"Let me put your bets on for you, Sire," the Earl was just about to say, thinking that he could somehow contrive to see that the King won, whatever horse passed the winning-post first.

But he was too late—Lord Howe, the Queen's Chamberlain, eager to be of service, had already been entrusted with the King's bets, and once again annoyed with his wife the Earl proceeded in silence to the Royal Box.

Karina was presented to the Queen, who was extremely gracious and introduced her to her sister—the

165

Duchess of Saxe-Weimar—who was staying at Windsor Castle.

"I hope, Lady Droxford, that you and your husband will dine with us tonight," the Queen said in her gentle voice.

"We should be very honoured to do so, Ma'am," Karina replied.

She looked at the Earl as she spoke, and doing a quick calculation in his head he realised that if he sent a groom back to Droxford House immediately, Karina's clothes and jewels, accompanied by her maid, could, if they travelled in one of his fast chaises, be at Ascot in plenty of time for her to change and be at the Castle by seven.

He nodded his head slightly showing he had understood the question in Karina's eyes and she smiled at him—an interchange which was not missed by the Queen, who put her hand on Karina's arm and said:

"I can see you are happy! I must congratulate you, My Lady, for I understand you have but recently been married."

"Yes, Ma'am, and thank you for your most gracious congratulations," Karina replied.

"I am happy with my kind husband," the Queen said, "and I like to think that many other people are happy too."

She spoke in her soft, broken English and Karina in some surprise realised that the Queen spoke the truth when she said she was happy.

There was no mistaking the tenderness in her face when she looked at King William, or indeed what amounted almost to adoration in his.

Younger than his illegitimate daughters, the Queen, coming to England without having seen her bridegroom, had managed with her sweetness, her gentleness and

166

her elegance, to inspire an old man with the idealism and at times the ecstasy, of youth.

"They're off!" someone shouted, and everyone on the Course turned to look to where in the distance the bright colours of the jockeys could be seen clearly in the afternoon sunshine.

Karina, almost without realising she was doing so, went to the front of the Box, and the Earl watching her saw that she was suddenly tense, her fingers gripped together, her eyes anxious.

He remembered what he had felt the first time a jockey had carried his colours. It was sad, he thought, that Karina would have to be disappointed in the result even as he had been. But at least he would show her that she had his sympathy and his understanding.

He went to stand beside her.

"I am wishing you luck, Karina," he said in a low voice.

"Thank you," she answered.

Her lips moved but she did not take her eyes from the track.

"You must not be too disappointed if Merlin fails," he said. "And next time let me help you. Although you may not know it, Karina, I am considered a good judge of horseflesh."

"Yes, I do know," she answered. "I think your horse, My Lord, will be in the first three."

"Thank you!" the Earl said with a little twist of his lips. "The odds have shortened on him and despite the crowd's undoubted loyalty to His Majesty, Dragonfly is now the favourite."

"He will not win!" Karina murmured.

The Earl smiled. He was prepared to make every excuse for her optimism, but this was going a little too far.

"Are you really suggesting," he asked, "that you might beat me?"

"I know I will!" she replied.

The Earl smiled again and raised his glasses. The horses were coming round the bend. Already there was a hush over the huge crowd as they reached the straight and everybody craned their necks to see who was leading.

There were two horses clear in front and then there was a cry as it could be seen that a horse had broke down, run out, and was no longer in the race.

"Good God!" the Earl exclaimed. "It is Royal Crown. There must be something wrong!"

"I told you that he was not well," Karina said.

"Then why the devil did they let him run?" the Earl asked almost beneath his breath.

"What is this? What is this?" they heard the King say. "My horse has broken down? I cannot believe it. Who says so?"

"I am afraid it is the truth, Sire," the Duke of Richmond told him. "I need not tell Your Majesty how disappointed we all are. I do not believe there is anyone here who was not hoping that your colours would be first past the post."

"I cannot understand it!" the King exclaimed irritably.

Karina was not listening. She was watching an ugly horse moving with a rhythmic stride, coming up on the outside. She stood very still—so still it seemed as though she was hardly breathing.

Merlin passed Lord Derby's horse, and the Duke of Richmond's. Now he was neck and neck with Dragonfly. Now he was ahead—he was leading the field! There was no doubt about it—the gawky animal with unknown little Jim Tyler perched on top like a small monkey, was within twenty yards of the winning-post!

Then with a roar from the crowd which was combined with gasps of astonishment, Merlin was ahead by a length and half! He had won!

"Good God!" the ejaculation seemed to burst from the Earl's lips.

"I told you, I told you he would win!" Karina said and her voice was alive with excitement. "Come, come quickly! We must see him led in!"

She sped impetuously out of the Royal Box and because he felt he must accompany her, the Earl, muttering a formal apology, followed her.

He had almost to run to catch her up because Karina was slipping through the crowd on the lawn almost as if there were wings on her feet. She reached the gate at the same time as Merlin was being led in by a small, wizened-looking little man whose smile seemed to reach from ear to ear.

"We have done it, Nat! We have done it!" Karina cried.

"Yes, M'Lady, we've done it!" Nat Tyler replied.

There were a few cheers as Karina walked beside the horse. They reached the large crowd waiting to see the jockeys weigh in, and here there was noisier enthusiasm, especially from a number of stable-lads and grooms who had obviously put a few pennies on the unknown horse which the Quality had not fancied.

"Wherever did you get him?" the Earl asked Karina, who was patting Merlin's head.

She gave a start when she heard his voice, not realising he had followed her.

"I bought him at Barnet Horse Fair," she answered. "I knew as soon as I saw him that he was wonderful, did I not, Nat?"

"You did indeed, M'Lady," the trainer answered.

"Congratulations," the Earl said, holding out his hand to the little man.

"Thank you, M'Lord. I hopes there be no hard feelings that we beat Dragonfly?"

"No, indeed," the Earl replied. "He took third place. I actually did not expect him to win."

"I told you the King's horse would never do it," Karina smiled.

She looked so pretty in her excitement that the crowd was as interested in her as in the unknown winner. At the back of those pressing forward to see what was happening, Lord Wyman kept his eyes on Karina.

There was a lustful expression on his face which did not escape the notice of an elegantly-gowned woman who was watching not only the new Countess of Droxford, but her husband.

After a moment Lord Wyman was conscious of the scrutiny of someone standing beside him, and turned to look into a pair of boldly inviting eyes.

"I think we have met—Ma'am," he began hestiatingly, then exclaimed: "Of course—Mrs. Felicité Corwin! I have seen you in the company of Lord Droxford!"

Mrs. Corwin curtsied.

"And you, I am well aware, are the redoubtable Lord Wyman!"

He raised her gloved hand to his lips, his eyes speculative.

"I have the idea, Mrs. Corwin," he said slowly, "that a quiet conversation might be to our mutual advantage!"

Jim Tyler was weighed in and came from the Weighing-Room beaming with satisfaction and impatience.

"I think we should return to the Royal Box," the Earl suggested to Karina. "You left somewhat unceremoniously!"

"I am sorry!" she replied. "Should I have asked permission to retire?"

"It would have been at least polite," the Earl answered.

"I will make my apologies," Karina said humbly.

"Surely you did not come to Ascot alone?" the Earl asked, his voice hard at the thought.

"No, indeed," Karina replied. "I came with Harriet Courtney and her husband. Harriet is sitting in the Stand, her mother-in-law will not let her walk about. Major Courtney escorted me to the Paddock, but he was in such a tizzy about his horse which is entered for the next race that he vanished into thin air!"

"I am relieved that you have, for once, behaved conventionally!" the Earl remarked, but he was smiling and she knew that he teased her.

"I would have walked here alone rather than miss the race," Karina replied.

She turned to her trainer.

"Good-bye, Nat. You know how grateful I am. Arrange for me to see those two horses you told me about. I am willing to buy them."

"I'll do that, M'Lady. But I doubt if either of 'em will be as good as Merlin!"

"No one could be as good!" Karina smiled.

With a final pat on the neck of the big horse, she walked away beside the Earl.

"Stepping out big, are you not, Karina?" he enquired.

"I am buying two more horses," she replied. "But I can afford them, indeed, I can afford a dozen more! It is so exciting! I can still hardly believe Merlin has won!"

"And how much have you won?" the Earl asked with an amused smile. "I hope you went to a reliable Bookmaster?"

"Indeed I did," Karina replied. "I asked Robert with whom you laid your bets."

"That was wise!" the Earl approved. "Most Bookmasters are twisters and have no capital behind them.

171

Mine are backed by several Gentlemen of Quality so they will not default. What odds did you get?"

"Ten to one," Karina replied. "I thought it sensible to take a good price just in case someone got wise to him and the odds dropped."

"Ten to one!" the Earl ejaculated. "And what did you stake?"

Karina started to speak and then suddenly she stopped still and stared up at the Earl, her face very pale. She put one of her hands to her lips.

"I forgot!" she cried. "I swear to you I forgot! I never thought of it until this moment! How terrible! How wrong of me, but you must believe . . . it was a mistake!"

"What did you forget?" the Earl asked in bewilderment.

"That I promised you I would not risk more than a hundred pounds!" Karina said. "I remembered when Lady Downshire wished to wager five hundred on our race in Regent's Park, I insisted the prize was only a hundred, but after I have seen Merlin on the gallops two days ago I knew he was going to win!

"I was determined to make enough money to buy the other horses Nat had told me about. But if I had remembered I would either not have broken my word or asked your permission first. You do believe me?"

It was impossible not to believe the sincerity shining in the worried green eyes.

"I believe you," the Earl said. "How much did you stake?"

Karina looked away from him, her eyelashes fluttering.

"A thousand pounds!" she said and her voice trembled.

"A thousand pounds!" the Earl ejaculated. "Do you mean to tell me, Karina, that you have won ten thousand pounds!"

He was so surprised that for a moment his voice

172

was loud, but when he would have said more, they were interrupted.

"I am deeply in your debt, Lady Droxford," the King said. And taking Karina's hand he raised it to his lips. "You have made me quite a fortune. Ten to one! A good price—a very good price! I have told the Queen and she says that you must advise me in all the races for the rest of the Meeting; for you are a far better tipster than the Duke of Richmond or indeed your husband!"

Karina dimpled at him.

"Thank you, Sire, but I would not want to push my luck."

"Come and look at the horses for the next race," the King said. "I am determined to have another winner and you shall be my guide!"

There was no doubt that Karina had made a great hit with His Majesty. He kept her at his side the whole of the afternoon and when finally the Royal Party drove away down the Course, receiving a few more cheers than when they had arrived, the King's last words were:

"I shall look forward to seeing you tonight, Lady Droxford. You will enjoy the Castle, I am sure of it. I enjoy it myself and so does the Queen!"

Alone with the Earl, Karina looked up at her husband apprehensively. She knew he was waiting to finish their interrupted conversation.

"Who lent you the money?" he enquired.

This was the question she had been dreading and there was a slight hesitation before she answered:

"Sir . . . Guy . . . He . . . offered to do so and I knew that . . . he is very . . . rich."

"And how would you have repaid him had you lost?" the Earl enquired, a harsh note in his voice.

"He said that he was prepared to wait indefinitely," Karina answered, "and I would have contrived it some-

173

how. But I was sure, absolutely sure, that Merlin would win!"

"No one can be sure . . ." the Earl began, only to be stopped by another interruption. This time it was Freddy Farrington.

"Congratulations, Alton," he said, slapping his friend on the back. "And many, many congratulations to you, Karina. It was a very great surprise to see that you are an owner!"

He kissed her hand and continued:

"But what an animal! I have never seen anything like its stride! He hardly seemed to be exerting himself, he won so easily. How did you find him?"

"At Barnet Horse Fair," Karina answered. "I was looking at the horses and I saw Merlin in the corner of the field. And Nat Tyler, who was with him, was on the verge of tears."

"How did you know that?" the Earl asked.

"I suppose I sensed it in a way," Karina replied. "He was petting and fussing over the horse and I knew that he loved him. When we started talking I realised that it was breaking his heart because he had to part with Merlin!"

"Tyler! Was not that the name of one of Prinny's trainers?" Captain Farrington asked.

"Nat's father trained for King George when he was Prince of Wales," Karina answered. "But when he got old and retired, he would bet! He gambled away everything that he had ever saved! And when Nat, who had worked with him, tried to carry on alone, he had bad luck.

"One owner defaulted on his debts, another died, and finally he was only left with Merlin, whom he had bought in Ireland as a foal. He was forced to sell as he could no longer afford to buy feed; but he knew he would have some difficulty in disposing of Merlin."

"I am hardly surprised at that!" the Earl remarked.

"Yes, Merlin, is unattractive to look at," Karina

agreed. "But when you see him move you know there is something exceptional about him."

"I see that now," the Earl said. "But I must be honest and say I did not realise it at the first glance!"

"I did!" Karina answered smiling and without boasting. "And when Nat put him through his paces for me in an adjacent field I knew he was exceptional! I asked him what he wanted for Merlin."

" 'I'm hoping to ge a hundred and fifty guineas,' he replied. 'But I expects in a place like this I'll have to be content with about ninety!' "

"What did you say?" the Earl asked curiously.

"I told him I would give him two hundred," Karina answered. "On one condition."

"What was that?" Freddy Farrington enquired.

"That he and his son Jim would continue to train Merlin."

The two men looked at each other and burst out laughing.

"Why is it funny?" Karina asked, looking from one to the other.

"It is damn funny!" Captain Farrington replied. "Here is the best bloodstock in England costing God knows how many thousands—brought to Ascot to make a show—and you pick up some unprepossessing nag at Barnet, get the horse and the trainer for two hundred guineas, and walk away with one of the best prizes of the Meeting. It is incredible, astonishing! It could only happen to someone who looks like you!"

"What have my looks to do with it?" Karina enquired.

"Because you look like a princess who has walked straight out of *Grimm's Fairy Tales*," Freddy Farrington replied. "And damned if I do not think it is all done by magic!"

"I think we should find Mrs. Courtney and tell her you are leaving with me," the Earl said to Karina.

"Are you staying as usual with Staverley?" Freddy Farrington enquired. "I am dining with him."

"Yes, but I shall go back to London with Karina after dinner," the Earl replied. "Anyway, I had only intended to stay for two nights."

"Where am I to change?" Karina enquired.

"Lord Staverley is delighted for you to use his home," the Earl replied. "It is a bachelor houseparty since Lady Staverley does not care for racing, but you will only be there for an hour or so. We shall have to leave for Windsor at half after six."

"It is a wonderfully exciting day for me," Karina said to Freddy Farrington. "First I win a race, and now I am going to dine with the King! That is something I never thought I would do."

"You will find it very dull and hellishly hot!" Freddy Farrington informed her.

"I refuse to let you depress me," Karina flashed at him.

But he teased her all the way to Staverley House, and only when she had gone upstairs to change did the Earl realise that there were a great many questions he still wanted to ask.

He had no chance, however, of talking alone with Karina when they drove to Windsor Castle. Another member of the houseparty had also been invited to dinner and they travelled there in the Earl's new travelling landau which had brought Karina's gown from London. It was very smart and the two coachman wore their ceremonial livery with powdered wigs.

"I feel exceedingly grand," Karina exclaimed as they set off.

"That is exactly what you look!" Lord Lindhurst said, who was accompanying them.

Karina's appearance was indeed dazzling. She was in a white satin gown trimmed with frill upon frill of delicate lace and ornamented with tiny bunches of diamond-speckled flowers.

There was a great diamond tiara on her head and diamond ear-rings falling from her tiny ears. Her necklace was one of the most spectacular from the whole of the Droxford collection, and her bracelets were so heavy that she thought it was likely her wrists would ache before the end of the evening.

They arrived at the Castle a little before seven but they had to wait for dinner until almost eight. Over forty people sat down at the huge, magnificently dec-orated table and ate off gold plate which Karina was told was the finest in Europe. The gold candelabra each weighed three hundredweight!

But, she thought, the Chef at Droxford House could have provided a better menu, and, as Freddie had warned her, the room was intolerably hot!

The Queen was taken into dinner by the Duke of Richmond, and the King followed with the Duchess of Saxe-Weiner. Once they were seated the King insisted on drinking wine with his guests, six or seven at a time—a custom which Karina had never seen before, and which rather fascinated her, but at the same time continually interrupted the meal!

Karina had Earl Grey on one side which delighted her, for she plied him with questions about the Re-form Bill, to which he replied in detail.

She realised after a little while that what he was telling her was intended to be passed on to the Earl and she thought the Prime Minister would be disap-pointed if he realised how little influence she had with her husband.

Coffee was served in the Drawing Room, and there a band began to play and continued playing after they were joined by the Gentlemen.

But the King soon got bored.

"Come along, come along," he said. "I want to show St. George's Hall and the Ballroom to the Ladies."

He offered the Marchioness of Tavistock his right

arm and Karina his left and, gaily laughing, led them from the room.

A number of the party followed them, and there were three servants carrying lamps to reveal the proportions of the Great Hall.

Then the King showed his guests the shield of Achilles in gold; cups of crystal encrusted with diamonds and rubies; and a huge tiger's head made entirely of pure gold, as large as life, and finely sculptured.

There was also an Uma bird which looked like a peacock, made entirely of diamonds, rubies, emeralds and sapphires. These treasures from India had all belonged to Tippoo Sahib and were taken at Seringapatam, after it was stormed by the British thirty-two years earlier in 1799.

It was all very interesting for Karina. It was only when finally they left the Castle after a most genial good-bye from their host and had set off towards London, that she realised that at last she was alone with the Earl.

She glanced up at him a little apprehensively. Thinking how handsome he looked and hoping that he was in a good humour.

"You have enjoyed yourself?" he asked.

"More than I can tell you," she replied. "The Castle is very impressive. And all those wonderful treasures! No wonder the King is delighted after having lived for so long in that commonplace house in Bushey. Yet sometimes he must feel overwhelmed at the change in circumstances!"

"You obviously impressed him," the Earl said. "He has always had a great partiality for pretty women!"

"Did you think I looked pretty?" she asked in a low voice.

He did not answer and once again she looked searchingly at him in the light of the candle lantern which lit the interior of the landau.

It was difficult to be sure of his expression in the flickering light; but she had a feeling he was looking stern and said quickly:

"Thank you for not being angry about Merlin. I was afraid you would be incensed with me!"

"Why did you not tell me?"

"I thought you might forbid me to enter the race, and Nat was so keen. I did not want to disappoint him!"

"So your trainer's feelings were more important than those of your husband!"

"I did not say that," she answered.

"You were right about Merlin and I was wrong," the Earl said. "I did not think he was a good choice until after I had seen him run. I bow to your superior judgement, Karina."

"Now you are teasing me," she answered. "It was just luck. But you will not mind if I have other horses as long as I can pay for them myself?"

The Earl was silent for a moment and then he said:

"I will allow you to set up a Racing-Stable if it pleases you. But there is one thing you have to promise me, Karina, and on this I am adamant."

"What is it?" she asked.

"You will not see Merrick again."

She gave a little gasp.

"I have been very lenient up until now," he said before she could speak, "but you are being talked about and that is something I will not stomach.

"You will give me your word of honour, Karina, and I shall expect you to keep it, that there will be no more drives, dances, or meetings of any sort with this man, who you know full well is someone I do not count amongst my acquaintance."

"And if I say that I feel I am entitled to my friends . . ." Karina began.

"I have heard that argument from you before," the Earl interrupted. "I want your promise, Karina."

"And if I . . . do not give . . . it . . . ?"

There was a moment's pause.

"Then I shall take steps to make you do what I command," the Earl said.

There was something steely and inflexible in his voice and yet she could not help asking curiously:

"What will you . . . do?"

"I have not thought about it yet," he replied, "but it would not be difficult to make you obey me."

She did not speak and he went on:

"For one thing, I could engage a companion for you who would ensure that you behaved circumspectly when I was not there."

"A companion!" Karina ejaculated. "You mean a spy! Someone who would report all my movements to you. You could not do such a thing!"

"Or alternatively," the Earl continued, as if she had not spoken, "I could send you to Droxford Park. You would doubtless find it somewhat lonely there if there was no one with you, especially if you were having a—child!"

Karina gave a little cry of horror as if it was forced from between her lips.

"How can you . . . say such . . . things to . . . me?" she asked.

"Has Merrick made love to you?" the Earl asked.

"What do . . . you . . . mean?" Karina stammered.

"You know quite well what I mean—do not trouble to lie! I know his methods! Has he kissed you?"

"No! Of course not!" Karina exclaimed indignantly. At least she could answer this question truthfully.

There was silence then unexpectedly the Earl said in a very different voice:

"I have no wish to bully you, Karina. You must obey me in this, but I swear to you I will be kind and

180

generous on other counts. This friendship of yours with Merrick is something which concerns me very deeply. Give me your promise that you will not see him again and we can, I am sure, deal together far better than we are doing at the moment."

Karina was very still, she was no longer angry, no longer afraid—there was something in the Earl's voice—a warmth and an appeal so unlike his previous icy tones—which made her feel that whatever he asked of her she could not refuse.

"I will . . . promise," she said at length in a low voice, "if you will allow me to see Sir Guy just once so that I may explain. He has been kind to me. I would not like him to misunderstand why I suddenly refuse his invitations."

"You may of course explain," the Earl said graciously. "But not in public, not where you will be seen, Karina. There has been too much talk already!"

"Thank . . . you."

He put out his hand towards her.

"Let us put a stop to these stupid misunderstandings," he said. "I do not want to be a tyrant, Karina, or to make you afraid of me. I will try and do better in future!"

Shyly she put her hand into his. She had taken off her glove and she felt the warmth and strength of his fingers.

"Shall we both try?" he asked softly.

She felt herself quiver and for some reason it was hard to speak.

"Yes . . . please," she whispered after a moment.

"And now tell me," the Earl said, "something I have been aching to ask you the past week. How is it that you drive so well? How did you ever learn to tool a Phaeton as I saw you doing so successfully in Regent's Park?"

He was not sneering or being unkind. There was an

interest in his tone and his hand still held hers. Karina hesitated for a moment.

"You will perhaps be shocked if I tell you," she answered. "But when Papa left me without any money I worked in a . . . Livery Stable."

"A Livery Stable!" there was no mistaking the astonishment in the Earl's voice.

"You must not think that I did anything so unconventional as to drive their clients," she said. "I only broke in the horses. Most of them were raw and unused to the saddle and many of them were wild."

The Earl gave a muffled exclamation.

"Wild horses!" he ejaculated. "Is there no end to your surprises, Karina? You drop down out of trees, you win races which no one in their senses would expect you to do, and now you tell me you have broken in wild horses!"

The Earl began to laugh, his laughter echoing round the landau.

"Wild horses!" he choked. "Oh, Karina, you are incorrigible!"

8

Karina walked into the office where Robert Wade was working.

"Good morning, Karina," he said, rising to his feet as soon as he saw who had opened the door.

"Good morning, Robert," Karina replied.

She was holding a letter in her hand and looked entrancingly pretty in a morning muslin sprigged with flowers and trimmed with ribbons of pink and blue intertwined round her small waist, which were echoed by bows which lay flat at the edge of the boat-shaped neck.

"Congratulations on your win at Ascot Races," Robert said, "It must have been exciting!"

"More than that," Karina smiled. "And his Lordship has been so kind in promising to help me find new Stables. I shall have three horses in training next month and I hope to have half a dozen more before the end of the year!"

Robert Wade looked at her animated face with a smile.

"You will find them an expensive hobby!"

"Not if I keep winning!" Karina retorted.

"There speaks the gambler!" Robert remarked in mock dismay, and they both laughed. "Well, I shall look forward to reading the whole dramatic story of your triumph in *The Times*!"

"In *The Times*?" Karina queried.

"There should be a commentary on the race tomorrow," Robert informed her.

"How exciting!" Karina exclaimed then continued: "I hoped to see His Lordship before he left the house, but by the time I came downstairs to breakfast he had already departed."

"He is breakfasting with Sir Robert Peel," Robert explained. "I am astounded, Karina, at the way in which the Reform Bill has reformed the habits of the *Ton's* most fashionable Gentlemen. All the Bucks and Dandies are up by breakfast-time these days, starting their worldly arguments almost before the dew is off the grass.

"I am sure it is good for them," Karina said absently, "but I did want to see His Lordship."

"He told me he would be dining at home tonight."

Karina's eyes lit up.

"That is exactly what I wanted to know. I have here a letter from Harriet Courtney inviting us both to din-

183

ner, but it would be much nicer if we could dine alone."

She glanced at the letter she held in her hand, then said:

"Harriet says it is only a small dinner party and that if His Lordship is otherwise engaged she will ask her brother, Captain Farrington, to escort me. It is kind of her to think of it, but of course I would rather be here."

"Then write Mrs. Courtney a refusal and I will have your note sent to her by groom," Robert suggested.

"I will do that," Karina replied, "and actually her groom is waiting for an answer. Can I use your desk?

"Of course."

Robert held the chair for Karina to sit down, put a piece of impressively thick crested writing-paper in front of her, and handed her the big white quill pen that he habitually used himself.

Karina scribbled a few lines, sanded the note and sealed it with a wafer. As she addressed it, Robert pulled at the bell and a footman took the note to the waiting groom.

"Thank you," Karina said as she rose from the desk. "I shall wear a new gown tonight to dazzle His Lordship, so while I am here perhaps I could choose the jewels to go with it."

"I must congratulate Yvette on your present raiment," Robert said.

"She is so talented," Karina answered. "I cannot begin to thank you for your kindness in sending me to her."

"It has been a great piece of good fortune where she is concerned," Robert replied. "I am told that Ladies of Quality are flocking to her shop, anxious to look exactly like you!"

"Well a large number of them will have to shrink a trifle and take off some extra weight!" Karina said mischievously, "but I am sure you are right—that fat Lady Binghamston who looks like a pink elephant, asked me where I shopped and I could see she was determined to copy my new blue gown! It is infuriating, I do not want too many facsimiles of myself floating about the place."

"I do not think you need be frightened of that," Robert said. "You know without my flattering you, Karina, that there is not one in the *Beau Ton* who can hold a candle to you."

"But you are flattering me," Karina laughed, "and how nicely you do it! Why have you never married?"

Robert looked embarrassed.

"To be quite honest," he replied, "I have never fallen in love with someone with whom I could spend the rest of my life."

Karina sat down on the arm of one of the big leather chairs.

"You know, Robert," she said, "I think you would make an excellent husband. You are kind, sympathetic and understanding. At least, you have been to me!"

"Now you are making me blush," Robert said with a twinkle in his eyes. "The answer is, Karina, that it is very easy to be kind to you."

"There must be dozens of young women who would welcome the same treatment," Karina said reflectively. "Tell me the sort of female you admire."

"I admire you, Karina, but I would have no wish to be married to you," he answered. "You are too clever and unpredictable for my taste. I would like a quiet wife. Someone who would be happy to spend the evening sitting in front of the fire and reading a book. Someone who does not want to attend every Ball or Assembly to which we might be asked. To tell the truth, I would like a girl who is rather shy! But alas they are not made that way these days!"

Karina gave a little cry.

"Robert! I have the very person for you! She is

185

shy, she is sweet, she has a delightful sense of humour once you know her. She would be perfectly happy to sit at home and read a book with someone she loved."

"Does a woman like that really exist?" Robert asked wonderingly.

"You will see!" Karina answered. "I shall ask her to stay, and when you meet Elizabeth you will find she is just the person you have been looking for all your life."

"Was there ever a married woman who did not want to match-make?" Robert exclaimed.

"Why not?" Karina enquired. "I feel like the Queen—if one is happy oneself, one wants other people to be happy too!"

"And are you happy, Karina?" Robert asked quitely.

Her eyes dropped before his. Then she said:

"I am happier, Robert, much happier than I have been before."

"I am glad," he said.

There was a little silence before Karina, jumping to her feet, said:

"I must stop wasting your time! Let me choose some jewels suitable to wear tonight. My gown, which is quite one of the prettiest Yvette has ever designed, is green gauze over silver. It looks as if I am moving through water and it is sprinkled with tiny dewdrops which glisten as I move."

"From what you tell me I definitely think you need emeralds," Robert said.

"Are there any?" Karina enquired.

"A great number," he replied.

He took his keys from a drawer in his desk and opened the big safe. There, reposing on steel shelves, were dozens of boxes fashioned in velvet on coloured leather which held the famous Droxford jewels.

Robert brought several to the desk and when he opened them Karina gazed wide-eyed at their contents.

There was a tiara with large emeralds the size of pigeons eggs. There were two necklaces, one a collet, another much more elaborate with emeralds dropping from a huge centre stone.

There were bracelets, ear-rings, and a brooch, all set with diamonds, displayed on white velvet, and worth a King's ransom, Karina was sure.

"Where did these come from?" she asked in an awed tone.

"The fifth Earl brought them back from the East," Robert explained. "I believe some of them were given to him by a Sultan whom he had befriended. The rest, he purchased at a very low price, having, I understand, a knowledge of jewels which also very considerably increased his fortune.

"They are beautiful!" Karina exclaimed.

"The Earl gave them as a wedding present to his bride when he married her," Robert went on, "And because he was so infatuated he did something which horrifies connoisseurs."

"What was that?" Karina asked.

"He engraved the large emerald in the centre of the brooch with his initials and that of his wife's. Of course, it has depreciated the value of the stone, but at the same time I think it was a loving gesture when you see that the initials are encircled by a heart."

He picked up the brooch as he spoke and walked towards the window. Karina followed him. In the sunlight she could see the entwined initials quite clearly and the outline of the heart.

"It is a charming story," she said. "Please may I wear the brooch tonight?"

"But of course," Robert answered, "and what about the rest of the set?"

"I think the small necklace and the ring will be sufficient," Karina said, "after all we are only dining at home, but I want to look my best."

She said the last sentence almost beneath her

breath and Robert glanced at her speculatively. He left the cases with the jewels she had asked for on his desk and put the others back into the safe.

"What is that?" Karina asked suddenly, making him start, for he had not realised she was just behind him.

He looked to see where her finger was pointing and took from the safe a casket of engraved gold and silver set with amethysts.

"It is so pretty!" Karina exclaimed.

"It is Russian," Robert told her. "Again we have to thank the fifth Earl for such a treasure. He was an inveterate traveller and after he was married he used to take his wife with him round the world. I often wonder what the poor woman suffered in the heavy seas and whether she longed for the peace and quiet of England when she was being carried in a sleigh over the snows to St. Petersburg."

"I expect she enjoyed every moment of it," Karina retorted "especially if on every trip she acquired such wonderful jewels."

"The casket was a present from the Czar. Open it, you will see what is inside."

Karina did as she was told and there, lying in the velvet interior, was not a necklace or bracelet as she had expected, but instead a small pistol fashioned in entwined gold and silver to match the casket, and also set with deep purple Russian amethysts.

"Oh, what an amusing weapon!" Karina exclaimed. "It is too pretty to use!"

"It has been, nevertheless," Robert said "The Earl shot a wolf with it that was pursuing them behind his sleigh! And Alton fired it one day at Droxford Park. He said it was quite the most accurate pistol he had ever used!"

"Then I must try it," Karina said, taking the pistol in her hands and loading it with the tiny bullet made of silver. "Look how easy it is to handle!" she exclaimed, pointing it at the carved crest on the chimney-piece.

"Can you shoot?" Robert enquired.

"You insult me by the question!" Karina retorted with mock severity. "I am a very good shot! I used to go out shooting with my father when I was quite small. At first I only carried his game for him; then I begged and pleaded until he let me try his gun. When he saw how keen I was he gave me a gun of my own—a small one—and later he taught me to fire his duelling pistols!"

Karina laughed.

"I became a dab hand with them and when Papa was away from home I used to sleep with one beside my bed just in case anyone attempted to rob us. Our old butler was so deaf that he would not have heard an army of soldiers breaking into the house—let alone a thief!"

"I see that you are perfectly competent to try the Russian pistol," Robert said. "Tell me when you want it."

He held out the casket for the pistol but Karina said:

"I will keep it with me now. I would like to talk to Alton about it tonight. I do not believe that he knows that I am a marksman. I will surprise him with my knowledge!"

"I should do that," Robert agreed. "After you win at Ascot and the manner in which you defeated Lady Downshire, His Lordship is due for another shock!"

Karina shook her head.

"This will be a pleasant one! I am determined to be good and not to upset his Lordship again."

"I am glad about that," Robert smiled.

Karina went from the room carrying both the emeralds and the casket in her hands. She took them upstairs and gave them to her maid, telling the woman to keep them in a safe place.

She put on the leghorn straw bonnet trimmed with

ribbons which matched her gown. Then with a serious expression on her face she went downstairs.

She had ordered her carriage for half after eleven o'clock and it was already waiting for her. There were two men on the box and the hood was down so she could enjoy the warm sunshine.

As they had said good night the Earl had suggested she should accompany him the next day to Ascot Races. Karina had refused simply because she knew until she could tell Sir Guy of her promise not to see him again the anticipation of what she had to do would hang over her head like a drawn sword.

"I think I had best rest tomorrow," she told the Earl, "but I would love to come with your Lordship on the other three days. I want to watch the Gold Cup on Thursday as I know you have horses running on both Friday and Saturday."

"I believe that you are crying off because your new Beau, the King, said he was not attending tomorrow," the Earl teased her.

"I shall be hard put to find winners on Thursday for His Majesty!" Karina said. "The responsibility of seeing that he does not lose money terrifies me."

"You brought it on yourself," the Earl said unfeelingly, "but if you smile at him as beguilingly as you were doing in the Great Hall tonight, I feel he will forgive you anything!"

"I hope it did not appear that I was attempting to flirt with His Majesty!" Karina said in a worried tone.

"No, of course not," the Earl replied soothingly. "Besides, Silly Billy attempts to flirt with every pretty female he sees, and you looked very pretty indeed Karina!"

There was a note in His Lordship's voice which made Karina blush. She suddenly felt shy. At the same time, a little quiver of excitement went through her.

Although she did not quite understand why, compliments from her husband meant much more to her than those she received from anyone else.

Early this morning, before she left her bedroom Karina had written a letter, and enclosing in the envelope a note of hand for a thousand pounds, sent it by a footman to Sir Guy's house in Curzon Street.

She wondered if he would be surprised at hearing from her because she had told him she would be at Ascot the whole week.

"I shall be there on Thursday and Friday," Sir Guy had said. "I have a horse running on Friday, and I never miss the Gold Cup."

Karina therefore felt sure that he would be in London and she was not mistaken. Within half an hour she received an answer to her note.

It contained only five words:

I will be there—Guy.

It was, however, a very surprised man who walked into the new British Museum just before noon. Built on the site of old Montagu House, it housed the Library of George III presented to the nation by the present King, it was not yet completed. But its enormous pillars and perfectly proportioned Hall had been excessively admired.

There was, however, this morning, a few visitors beyond some earnest-faced students and a conducted party of voluble foreigners.

"Which is the way to the Egyptian Salon?" Sir Guy asked.

In keeping the new building in the tradition of the old private house the rooms were still referred to as Salons.

An official directed Sir Guy in bored tones and he walked up a wide stone stairway until he found a collection of Sarcophagi, broken statues and slabs of stone engraved with hieroglyphics.

191

In the centre of the furthest Salon he found Karina, looking like someone who had strayed from one century of time into another.

"Karina!" his voice seemed to echo round the gloom and silence of the long departed Pharaohs.

He took her hands in his and raised them both to his lips.

"Good morning, darling, why are we meeting in such a strange place? I thought you would be at Ascot."

"I stayed away because I had to see you," Karina answered.

He looked down into her eyes.

"Something has happened! What has gone wrong?"

She was not surprised at this perception, she knew him well enough by now to realise that at times he could read her thoughts and was always aware when she was disturbed or unhappy.

Because she was afraid of what she must tell him, her fingers instinctively tightened on his.

"Come and sit down," he said, "and tell me what is disturbing you!"

He drew her to a marble seat and they sat side by side. The dust of antiquity around them seemed to encroach like a fog.

"Is it Alton?" Sir Guy asked quietly.

Karina nodded.

"What has he said? What has he done to you?" Sir Guy asked fiercely.

"I have promised," Karina answered unhappily, "that I will never see . . . you again!"

She felt as though her words struck at him, wounding him as she had no wish to wound anyone who had shown her such kindness—who had in fact given her his heart.

Sir Guy drew a deep breath.

"So that is it, what I expected! I am only surprised that he had not forbidden us to meet before now."

"People have been . . . gossiping about . . . us."

"Did you imagine they would do anything else?" Sir Guy enquired. "You are too lovely, my sweet, not to be noticed wherever you go, or whoever you may be with. And I, as I have always told you, have an unsavoury reputation."

"I am so . . . sorry," Karina said miserably.

"What do you think I feel?" Sir Guy asked and his voice was raw. "Do you think I can tamely let you leave me without protest?"

"What can we do? His Lordship is adamant and he was kind to me, yes very kind, about my having bought a horse without telling him."

"I hear that Merlin won."

Just for a moment Karina's face lit up.

"Even now I can hardly believe it, it was the most exciting moment in my life when I saw him pass the post. I knew he could do it, but I was afraid up to the very last moment that something or somebody would prevent my running him."

"And Alton was not enraged?"

"No indeed, he has even offered to help me build up my own Stable."

"Very generous of him!" Sir Guy said bitterly. "And in return you have promised to throw me away like an unwanted toy?"

"No, that it is not true," Karina said quickly. "His Lordship insisted that I should see you no more, but I think we both knew in the back of our minds that he was bound to object sooner or later. Let us be honest Guy. I wanted you as a friend but I knew, yes, I always knew that it was . . . wrong for you to make . . . love to me; wrong for us to be so often together unchaperoned and without His Lordship's permission."

Sir Guy released Karina's hands and turned his head away from her. He appeared to be looking intently at a huge half-open Sarcophagus but she saw the pain in his eyes, the tightness of his lips and knew that he was suffering.

"Oh, Guy! Guy!" she said, "I have no wish to hurt you, but I must do what His Lordship wishes. It is not only because he has threatened me with dour punishments if I do not obey him, but rather because I know that what he asks is right!"

Sir Guy jerked round to face her again.

"He has threatened you?"

"Only because at first I defied him," Karina answered. "That was wrong too. He is my husband, he has been exceedingly generous to me ever since I married him. As I told you before, it is I who am breaking the bargain between us."

"It is intolerable!" Sir Guy exclaimed. "Can you not understand, Karina, that I cannot give you up! I want you, I love you, you have become a part of me. Alton may be your husband, but he does not love you as I do! For God's sake, Karina, come away with me!"

He put out his hand and drew her to her feet. He stood looking down at her. He saw the worry in her eyes, the wistfulness of her lips and yet, experienced and sophisticated, he knew full well that what she felt for him was not love!

"You are so young," he muttered almost to himself. "So ridiculously innocent, what can I say to you? How can I make you understand what I feel?"

"I am sorry, Guy."

Karina felt helpless. She longed to say or do something constructive, and yet she was aware that while Sir Guy suffered she had nothing to offer him but empty words.

"How can I make you love me, Karina?" Sir Guy asked, and there was a sudden flicker in his eyes which had frightened her once before.

"I must . . . go," she said nervously.

"And suppose I will not let you? Suppose I tell you

we have gone too far, both of us, for you now to turn away and leave me?"

"I do not understand."

"Suppose I go to Alton and tell him you are mine? Suppose I claim you? Suppose I inform him that you are already my wife in everything but name?"

Karina stepped backwards. She had gone very pale, her eyes were wide and frightened.

"You could not say anything like that, because it would not be true! Oh Guy, we have been such friends and I have so much to thank you for. Do not spoil it now . . please do not spoil the affection that I have for you."

"Affection!" Sir Guy said in a strangled voice. "That is not what I want from you and well you know it!"

He stepped forward and before she realised what he was about to do, he had swept her into his arms. He crushed her against him so that she could not move and as she tried to struggle his lips were on hers, holding her completely captive.

She wanted to be free of him but she could not breathe, she could not even think of anything save that his mouth imprisoned her. . . .

After a long time Sir Guy raised his head and ejaculated hoarsely:

"I love you, Karina! God I love you! You are mine! Mine!"

Again he was kissing her—fiercely, with a forcefulness which was almost brutal—kissing her eyes, her cheeks and again her lips. It was as if she were being battered by a storm so overwhelming that there was no shelter. She could not move, she could not escape. She could only let his passion rage over her. . . .

Suddenly as if he realised her lack of response, he lifted his head again and looked down at the fear in her eyes.

"Now do you understand?" he asked roughly. "I

will make you love me! I will make you want me as I want you!"

His voice was still passionate, but some of the fire seemed to have gone from him.

Karina did not speak, she did not move. Sir Guy slowly took his arms from her. The fear in her eyes faded and instead was replaced with a look of compassion and tenderness.

"Forgive me, Guy," Karina said quietly.

Then she turned and walked away from him, leaving him alone and confounded amongst the Egyptian dead!

It was only as she drove away from the British Museum that Karina realised she was on the verge of swooning. She was not certain how she had found the strength to leave Sir Guy. She only knew that, while she was desperately sorry to have hurt him, she could never give him the love that he wanted from her.

She could still feel the roughness of his lips on hers and she felt as if he had bruised her cheeks and her eyes with his kisses.

She had never been kissed before, and for a moment she thought it was an experience she had no wish to repeat. Then there flashed into her mind a mental picture of the Earl drawing Lady Sibley into his arms and kissing her slowly and deliberately, with self control and at the same time an elegance which had made Karina watch him admiringly.

How different that had been from the roughness with which Sir Guy had embraced her. No wonder the Earl had forbidden her to see him if this was the way his Lordship expected Sir Guy would behave!

She might not love Sir Guy; but as the day passed Karina knew she was going to miss him almost unbearably. Their drives together had been a delight and she had enjoyed talking to him, for he had gone out of his way to interest and amuse her.

She was also honest enough to admit that she would miss his compliments, the manner in which he made love to her—subtly, wittily, and at times compellingly, so that her eyes would meet his shyly and a blush would colour her cheeks.

"I must not think about him," she told herself." I must find other things to do."

But the hours seemed to drag until it was nearly time for dinner. Then Karina ran eagerly upstairs to change into her new gown, to clasp the emerald necklace round her white throat and to pin the emerald brooch with its loving engraving in front of her breast.

She was waiting in the small Salon when the Earl came downstairs.

She rose, to greet him, setting aside as she did so a copy of *Hansard*—the official report of the daily proceedings in the House of Commons and the House of Lords.

"I have been reading your speech, my Lord," she said with a smile. "I wish you had told me, that you intended to speak on Monday—I would have come down to the House of Lords to hear you."

"Would you have enjoyed that?" the Earl asked, advancing across the room. "But of course. I forgot, you are well-versed in political life. I will take you to the Lords next week when there will be another endless debate on the Reform Bill."

"I have been reading the Bill," Karina said, indicating a White Paper which lay on the sofa beside several copies of *Hansard*. "There are many things I wish to ask you about it. But first tell me how you fared at Ascot."

"It was rather a dull day," the Earl answered. "The favourites won and there were no surprises such as you provided yesterday!"

"Then I am glad I stayed away," Karina smiled. "What time will you wish to leave tomorrow?"

"Oh, I should think eleven o'clock will give us plenty of time," the Earl replied.

He glanced at the clock as he spoke.

"What time is Freddie calling for you?"

"Calling for me?" she asked in surprise. "But I am dining here with you!"

"Freddie told me at Ascot that he was taking you to a dinner party at his sister's."

"Robert told me you were dining in, so I refused the invitation!"

"I see! I wish I had known this earlier," the Earl said. "I deeply regret the misunderstanding, Karina, but as Freddie told me you were dining with his sister, I have made other arrangements."

"You are not dining here?" it was almost a cry.

The Earl hesitated before he answered:

"It is all a stupid tangle and I should have made certain what you were doing before changing my plans."

"Can you not change them again?" Karina asked wistfully.

He looked down into her eyes and for a moment it seemed as though they were saying something to each other which had nothing to do with a prosaic discussion about their arrangements for dinner.

The Earl looked again at the clock and frowned.

"I think I must keep the engagement I have made tonight, Karina," he said reluctantly, "but can we not make a definite promise to dine together tomorrow?"

He saw the disappointment in her eyes fade a little.

"We can do that although we have accepted to attend the Ascot Ball given by Lord and Lady Althrop."

"Damn the Ascot Ball!" the Earl said. "We will dine alone, Karina. There are a great many things which I wish to discuss with you."

"I shall look forward to it, My Lord."

"And what will you do tonight?"

198

"I think I shall go to bed with *Hansard!*" Karina replied. "It would be very mortifying to sit alone in the Dining Room with no one at the other end of the table!"

She spoke lightly. Nevertheless he could still sense the disappointment in her voice.

"Forgive me, Karina," he said, and lifted her hands to his lips.

He felt her fingers quiver in his. Once again he looked down into her eyes; then resolutely, as if it was somewhat of an effort, he turned away.

"Good night, Karina."

"Good night, My Lord."

She watched him go and then sat down again on the sofa feeling dreary and low-spirited.

She did not know why, but she had felt that tonight was to be a particular import. Perhaps it was because she had parted with Sir Guy. Perhaps it was because the Earl had asked last night that there should be a new undersanding between them.

She only knew that she wanted to be with him.

She wondered, now he had gone, whether he had noticed her new gown. Then dismally she found herself wondering whether he was dining with Lady Sibley or Mrs. Felicité Corwin. She felt sure it was one or the other, because had the Earl had an engagement with a political leader, or indeed any ordinary friend, he would have revealed their name.

She thought of his kissing Lady Sibley or holding Mrs. Corwin close in his arms . . . of him touching them with his hands . . . loving them . . .

She gave a little cry of despair. She could not hold him! Could not even persuade him to cancel an appointment he had made only at the last moment!

"I hate those women . . . hate them! . . ." Karina murmured beneath her breath and found she was

199

clenching her hands until the nails bit into her soft palms.

Suddenly the door opened and Newman unexpectedly announced:

"Lady Mayhew, M'Lady."

Karina looked up in surprise. A woman of about thirty wearing a crimson taffeta pelisse with exaggerated sleeves, came into the room.

Karina was certain that she had never seen her before as she rose politely to her feet.

"My dear Lady Droxford, pray forgive me for dropping in on you like this," the newcomer said in an effusive voice, "but I have just seen His Lordship. He informed me that you are sadly alone this evening! Always so considerate he thought that you might find it preferable to accompany me to a dinner party. I am dining with a friend who would be enchanted to meet your Ladyship."

"You have just seen His Lordship?" Karina asked in surprise.

"Yes indeed—such a pleasure—I spoke to him from my carriage as his landau was driving away from the door. We are old friends, and when I suggested that you should both dine with me, it was his Lordship's suggestion that I should invite you to be my guest without him.

"It is very kind," Karina said slowly, "but do you really want an unattached female?"

"My hostess, Mrs. Connaught, has extra men," Lady Mayhew replied. "So you need have no anxiety on that score."

"It is very kind . . ." Karina said hesitatingly.

She did not know why, but she did not feel at all drawn to this new acquaintance despite the lady's obvious eagerness to be friendly. There was something hard about the expression of her eyes, something artificial about the colour of her hair, and her pelisse and the gown under it were in bad taste.

Nevertheless Karina had nothing to do and she knew it would seem exceedingly rude to tell the truth and say she would rather go to bed than dine with a number of complete strangers!

"Now do say 'yes' Your Ladyship!" Lady Mayhew was pressing her. "My carriage is at the door, and if we do not leave soon we shall be late for dinner, for my friend lives in Hampstead."

"It is very kind of you to invite me," Karina said, making up her mind. "I will get my wrap."

"I should bring a cloak," Lady Mayhew suggested. "It has turned quite cold this evening."

"Very well then, a cloak!" Karina smiled.

She went from the room and requesting Newman to offer Lady Mayhew a glass of madeira, she climbed the stairs to her bedroom.

Her maid, Martha, was tidying the room and looked up in surprise to see her return.

"My cloak, Martha," Karina said. "I am going out to dinner after all."

"You will find your cloak too hot, M'Lady. The white wrap, edged with swansdown, would be more suitable."

"The Lady who has invited me informs me that it is quite chilly and as we are going as far as Hampstead, I think a cloak would be advisable," Karina replied, "there is one which matches this gown!"

"Hampstead! Oh no, M'Lady, not when you are wearing those precious emeralds! Why, Mr. Newman was telling us only this morning there have been footpads holding up coaches and chaises on Hampstead Heath and threatening the occupants into hysterics! They say that Lady Bougham, wife of the Chancellor, would have been robbed last week if her coachman had not had the foresight to carry a firearm!"

"I cannot believe it is as dangerous as all that," Karina laughed, "And I expect that Lady Mayhew has two men on the box."

"Well, it's frightened I am for those gems and that is a fact," Martha said in the tone of one who prophesies the worst.

"I have no time to change them," Karina said, "and this gown would be too plain without jewels."

As she spoke she suddenly remembered what else she had brought from the safe that morning.

"Give me that casket, Martha," she said. "Where have you put it?"

"It is in the cupboard, M'Lady, where I hide your other jewellery during the day," Martha replied.

"Then bring it to me."

Martha did so and then as she went to the wardrobe Karina swiftly transferred the small jewelled pistol from the casket into her reticule.

She remembered the pistol was loaded but it had a safety catch and she knew it would not go off accidentally.

Martha might be exaggerating and there might be no danger from footpads, but at the same time she was well aware what a commotion there would be if she lost the Droxford heirlooms.

"Good night, Martha," she said as her maid, still muttering about footpads, slipped her cloak round her shoulders.

It was a very attractive garment, of emerald green velvet edged with ermine, but it was not too cumbersome even for a summer's night and Karina went lightly down the stairs to collect Lady Mayhew from the Salon.

Her Ladyship's coach was comfortable and well-sprung. It was drawn by two horses and it did not take them long to drive through Regent's Park and onto Hampstead Heath.

Lady Mayhew chatted away the whole of the drive. For no obvious reason Karina felt there was something nervous and a little strained beneath the tittle-tattle and empty gossip which she obviously relished.

Finally they arrived at quite a pleasant house and found a party of a dozen people waiting in a big Salon which was furnished with expensive vulgarity.

The same description might have been applied to Mrs. Connaught! A middle-aged woman—plump and strained into a dress that was obviously too tight for her—she wore a lot of gaudy jewellery and her hair was as yellow as a guinea.

"This is a real pleasure, My Lady," she said to Karina. "I have been hoping to meet you ever since I heard of your marriage to that handsome blade who sets all our hearts abeating."

Karina felt she wanted to giggle and only wished the Earl was there to hear himself described in such a manner.

Mrs. Connaught introduced her to the other ladies present, but Karina found that, while they were young and pretty, they were certainly not of the *Beau Ton* and she was exceedingly surprised that the Earl should have wished her to join such a party.

The Gentlemen at least were well-bred but she had never heard any of their names before. She thought from what was said that the majority of them belonged to one of the Foot Regiments which were stationed in London.

Dinner was served soon after Karina and Lady Mayhew arrived. The food was good and the wine flowed freely. After the first course the guests seemed to be laughing peculiarly loudly, while the Gentlemen, who had at first been formal and stiff with Karina, now paid her such extravagant compliments that she felt embarrassed.

There was no doubt that by the time dessert was served the Ladies' cheeks were flushed and their laughter too shrill and too frequent, while the Gentlemen's voices became somewhat slurred.

It was with a sensation of relief that Karina saw

Mrs. Connaught rise from the end of the table. As the Ladies left the Dining Room two of the Gentlemen were unable to lift themselves from their chairs.

Outside, as Mrs. Connaught moved towards the Salon, Lady Mayhew said to Karina:

"I feel, My Lady, you would like to slip away. It was not quite the party I expected!"

"I am indeed ready to leave," Karina replied, hoping she was not being too rude, at the same time feeling that the rest of the evening might become quite intolerable.

"I will tell our hostess," Lady Mayhew said.

She went into the Salon, followed by Karina.

"I am afraid, Ivy, that Lady Droxford and I have to depart," she began.

"That's all right dear, 'tis what we arranged!" Mrs. Connaught replied to Karina's surprise.

Karina saw Lady Mayhew frown at Mrs. Connaught who immediately looked shamedfaced. Then the goodbyes where said and thankfully Karina found herself driving homewards.

"I do apologise for taking you to a party which you could not have enjoyed," Lady Mayhew said. "Ivy Connaught is a kind-hearted person, but she lets young people impose on her. I have spoken to her about it time and time again but she will not listen to me."

"I hope Mrs. Connaught did not think I was discourteous," Karina said. "It was kind of her to have a stranger to dinner."

"Oh, Mrs. Connaught would do anything for me." Lady Mayhew replied. "And that reminds me, Lady Droxford, would you mind if I drop a parcel in Park Street before we reach your house. It is, as you know, quite near and it will not take me a moment."

"Of course not!" Karina answered.

"It is a gift for a poor old friend of mine who is crippled with arthritis. She is a rich woman but she lives alone and I often think the days go by without her seeing a soul."

"How sad!" Karina said. "Why does she not find herself a companion?"

"I think she had had one from time to time," Lady Mayhew said vaguely, "but at the moment there is no one. She is just alone in a big house with her servants, and you know that is cold comfort when you are indisposed.

"It is indeed," Karina agreed. "What are you taking her?"

"Oh, just some trifling pieces of nonsense," Lady Mayhew replied. "I have to rack my brains to think what I can give her which she does not possess already! That is the trouble with the rich—they have everything!"

There was a undisguised note of envy in Lady Mayhew's voice.

"I expect what your friend would rather have than anything else is your company," Karina said.

"That is true," Lady Mayhew agreed, "and as you have said that, My Lady, I shall not just hand the parcel in at the door—I will slip in and show her my new gown. She loves pretty things. She has often said to me: "Margaret, it does me good to see you looking so pretty and dressed up like a Christmas pudding!"

Karina laughed, and Lady Mayhew went on:

"Of course that is just her joking way, but as I am wearing one of my best gowns, I know she would like to see it."

"I am sure she would."

"And you must show her yours!" Lady Mayhew said. "It is one of the prettiest dresses I have ever seen, and your jewellery is fantastic. It must be worth a fortune!"

Again there was the note of envy.

"I am sure your friend will not wish to see a stranger at this time of night," Karina expostulated.

"Oh, but she will; it'll give her something to talk about for weeks," Lady Mayhew insisted.

Karina wanted to refuse but at the time she felt it would be unkind. At least she was nearly home. She told herself she would ask His Lordship tomorrow what he meant by introducing her to such strange people. She could not imagine that Lady Mayhew was really to his taste! There was no doubt about it that despite her title there was something intensely common about her!

A few minutes later they drew up outside an imposing house in Park Street.

"Here we are!" Lady Mayhew exclaimed. "Now come in, My Lady, and give my old friend a treat! I promise she'll be really grateful for your kindness."

Patiently Karina followed Lady Mayhew out of the coach and into a large Hall. The old friend certainly did things in style, Karina thought, seeing the smartly liveried footmen, the furniture and the carved staircase leading to the floor above.

"This way, My Lady," the Butler said, leading them not upstairs but along the Hall and down a long passage leading obviously to the back of the house.

Karina wondered why, if Lady Mayhew's friend was arthritic, she troubled to have a sitting-room so far away from the main rooms. The Butler opened a mahogany door at the far end of the corridor.

Karina was not quite certain how it happened, but instead of Lady Mayhew walking in first, she stepped aside and Karina found herself entering a large room with, in the center of it, a table set for supper.

Eight candles in the big silver candelabra were alight and for a moment they seemed to dazzle her eyes. She looked around, finding to her surprise that the room seemed empty.

Then she heard the door shut behind her, and turning, found herself looking straight into the leering, lustful eyes of Lord Wyman.

9

For one moment Karina could only stare at Lord Wyman in astonishment. Then in a voice sounding shrill even to herself, she exclaimed:

"Why are you here? Where am I?"

Lord Wyman locked the door and put the key into his pocket.

"You are in my house, my pretty one."

Before Karina could move or scream, he had put his arms around her and pulling her close against him, attempted to kiss her.

Her cloak made it impossible for her to strike at him with her hands. Instead, she could only turn her face from side to side, struggling fruitlessly against his strength and the desire of his eager lips, until with a superhuman effort she managed to wrench herself free and run from him, leaving her cloak in his hands.

Breathless, her heart thumping, her hair disarranged, she reached the other side of the table to stand watching him with frightened eyes.

Lord Wyman laughed, and placing her cloak on a chair standing against the wall, he said:

"You will not escape me so easily, Lovely Lady, so let us enjoy this moment when we are at last alone together."

"My husband is . . . waiting for . . . me," Karina faltered.

It was difficult for her to speak when Lord Wyman was looking at her with an expression of lust and lechery which terrified her.

He made no movement, and yet she felt as if he reached out across the table to take her in his arms. There was something in the way his eyes flickered over her body which made her feel as if she stood naked before him.

"Your husband, my pretty, fluttering little bird," Lord Wyman replied, "is at the moment in the arms of the most delectable Mrs. Félicité Corwin! She has promised me that she will keep His Lordship happily engaged until dawn."

Frightened though she was, Karina was conscious of a pang of jealousy. She had been unable to make the Earl forgo his dinner engagement, and he in fact had preferred the company of his mistress to that of his wife.

"You have brought me here by a trick!" she said accusingly. "If there is any decency in you, My Lord, you will allow me to leave at once."

"A clever trick, was it not?" Lord Wyman asked in a conversational tone. "Maggie Mayhew is an excellent actress!"

"An actress!" Karina exclaimed. "Then you mean it was a plot—a plot from the very beginning to inveigle me here?"

"But of course, you beautiful creature," Lord Wyman replied. "From the first moment I saw you I knew that you must belong to me and so it was only a question of waiting, planning and plotting until my most ardent wish was fulfilled!"

"And do you think that my husband will let you go unpunished for such an insult?" Karina asked proudly.

She was holding onto the back of a chair because she felt as if her legs were almost incapable of supporting her. But she still carried her chin high and her eyes as they met Lord Wyman's were bright with anger.

"Would it not be more comfortable if we both sat down?" Lord Wyman suggested.

"No!" Karina said quickly, "and do not dare come near me or I will scream and bring your servants to my rescue!"

"I regret to inform you that they will not hear Your Ladyship's distress," Lord Wyman said in a mocking manner that was somehow infinitely menacing. "This room, built by my grandfather because he could not abide music, is soundproof. My grandmother could play a violin here without distressing him.

Therefore, fascinating little Lady Droxford, scream —no one will hear you! But I assure you that I shall find your resistance delightfully exciting!"

For a moment Karina could think of nothing to say.

"You were telling me that your husband would consider himself insulted," Lord Wyman continued. "I think that is unlikely; for whatever happens here to-night. and I assure you I shall find it most enjoyable, His Lordship will not know of it!"

"You must be crazed if you think that I would not inform His Lordship of your despicable behaviour!" Karina retorted.

Lord Wyman gave a little chuckle.

"I think not, my dear! Husbands have a deep disgust for their wives when they have been unfaithful with or without their connivance. Besides, duelling, as you know, is frowned upon in Court circles. If the Earl were to call me out it would damage his prestige and would prove that he was defending the honour of his wife—too late!"

"I do not credit anything you are telling me," Karina said steadily, "And now, Lord Wyman. enough of this farce! If you have brought me here to make love to me, let me inform you that I loathe and detest you!"

She almost spat the words at him and continued:

"I would rather be touched by a snake than by you! If you have any pride you will unlock that door and let me return to Droxford House!"

"Bravely spoken!" Lord Wyman exclaimed. "Unfortunately whether you like or dislike me, whatever your feelings may be, I still desire you and before the night is past I intend you shall be mine!"

His eyes rested on the tumultuous rise and fall of her small breasts.

"There is something different about you from any other woman I have seen for a long time," he went on. "Perhaps it is that air of purity and innocence! Surely Droxford cannot have been so insane as to have married you and left you untouched?"

Lord Wyman's words, spoken in a quiet, silky voice, brought the blood flooding into Karina's cheeks. Just for a moment her eyes fell before his and she heard him give an exclamation of triumph.

"Then I am right! I thought I must be! How adorable, how fascinating you are! How much I shall enjoy holding you in my arms, knowing I am the first man to have received your favours!"

"I would rather die than let you touch me!" Karina cried hotly.

"Few women die under such circumstances," Lord Wyman said dryly. "Mostly they live to enjoy them!"

He moved round the table as he spoke and Karina edged away to the other side.

"Keep away from me," she said, "or I will . . ."

She paused, realising how helpless she was, feeling he was stalking her like an animal. She had little chance of escape.

"What will you do," Lord Wyman asked, "except scream and struggle a little? You are small and weak, and I assure you that I am extremely strong!"

With an effort Karina fought against the panic which was beginning to overpower her.

"I a . appeal to Your L. Lordship," she stammered. "You cannot really intend . . . to . . . k . keep me here in your h . house, to . . ."

Word failed her.

". . . to ravish you?" Lord Wyman asked, finishing the sentence. "But that is exactly what I do intend!"

"Have you no decency, no honour?" Karina flashed at him.

"None where you are concerned," he answered. "You are too beautiful, too alluring. You tempt men and I, like most of my sex, have no intention of resisting such a temptation!"

"Let me go . . . please let me go?" Karina begged.

"No!" he answered. "And I think, Your Ladyship, we have talked long enough. Come, let me teach you the delights of love; for I assure you that I am very experienced."

"What you are offering me is not love," Karina cried. "but a degradation so disgusting that even to be near you makes me feel as if I am touching filth!"

"Did anyone ever tell you that your eyes sparkle when you are enraged?" Lord Wyman asked. "It is very alluring, my dear in fact, it is something which I for one find irresistible!"

He advanced towards her and again Karina retreated moving round the small table finding that with the brilliant light of the chandeliers in her eyes it was hard to keep looking at him while wondering where he would move next or whether he would make a sudden pounce at her.

She knew even as she moved away that the mere fact that he had to pursue her was exciting him. She knew it by the expression on his face. by the smouldering fire in his eyes by the dryness of his lips, which he kept wetting with the tip of his tongue.

She felt herself tremble. wondering how long she could go on dodging away from him. circling the table, preventing him from gathering her once again into his arms.

He moved suddenly and her heart leapt with fear. As she in turn moved quickly to evade him, the reticule which swung from her wrist by its green ribbons knocked against one of the chairs. She heard the sound and for the first time she remembered what she carried with her.

With an effort she made herself speak quite steadily.

"This is ridiculous, My Lord! Could we not sit down and discuss the matter more sensibly? And I would—if it were possible—like a drink!"

She knew by the sudden smile on Lord Wyman's lips that he thought he had gained an advantage over her.

"But of course," he said. "It is hot in this room, and fear, my pretty Lady, always makes its victim thirsty!"

He glanced towards the sideboard.

"May I offer you a glass of champagne, little Temptress?"

"I would like one very much," Karina said, "And if I sit on the sofa will Your Lordship promise that until I have had a drink and discussed matters, you will not attempt to touch me?"

"You have my word on it," Lord Wyman replied. "But I can promise you only a temporary respite!"

"I do . . . indeed feel a little . . . faint," Karina said weakly.

"Then I must certainly revive you with a glass of wine," Lord Wyman told her, "for I do not wish you to become insensible. It is when you flutter and defy me that I find you so entrancing!"

He walked towards the sideboard and Karina sat down on the sofa. Her fingers were trembling so much that for a moment it was almost impossible for her to open the reticule.

Lord Wyman took a bottle of champagne from the crested silver ice-cooler. Wrapped in a napkin he began pouring the golden liquid into a glass.

At last Karina managed to undo the reticule and slip her hand inside. Her fingers found the small, amethyst-decorated pistol. The stones felt cold beneath her touch and she drew it slowly from the satin bag.

Lord Wyman was intent on pouring out a second glass of wine for himself.

"I have only one bullet," Karina thought frantically. "If I miss him there will be no hope for me!"

She realised that her hand was shaking and strove with all her might to think calmly—to remember she must bring the weapon down onto the target!

Robert Wade had told her that the Earl had found the pistol dead accurate. She would aim, she decided, for Lord Wyman's heart. She would kill him because he deserved to die!

"One bullet . . . just one bullet!" she thought, as he turned, a glass in either hand.

"And now my pretty one," he said, "We will drink to the happiness we shall find . . ."

His eyes widened suddenly as Karina rose and he saw what she held in her hand. Then—before he could move or speak the last word that trembled on his lips—she shot him!

She heard the explosion reverberate round the room and for one frantic moment she thought that she had missed him.

Lord Wyman still stood looking at her, a glass in either hand, until slowly—so slowly that Karina could hardly believe it was happening—he collapsed onto the ground.

He fell backwards, the champagne spilling from the glasses and then the crystal goblets themselves smashing into small pieces as they hit the floor!

She gazed at him wide-eyed, the pistol still pointed in her outstretched hand. Then as he lay there, his eyes staring, a crimson stain appeared, spreading over the whiteness of his shirt.

"He is dead! He is dead!" Karina thought triumphantly.

Slowly and deliberately, without hurry, she put the

pistol back into her reticule and walked round the table to pick up her cloak from where Lord Wyman had laid it.

Only as she slipped it round her shoulders did she remember the locked door. She first thought that the noise of the pistol-shot might have brought the servants from the Hall.

Then she remembered that the room was soundproof and that she had walked down a long passage to reach it.

Yet to escape, she had to pass the attendant flunkeys and before that, take the key from Lord Wyman's pocket. In a sudden panic she knew that she could not touch him!

The red stain was increasing. Now it was soaking into his waistcoat. There was something horrible about the way in which he lay slightly crooked, his knees a little bent, his arms outstretched, his fingers still holding the stems of the two shattered wine-glasses.

"I cannot touch him! I cannot!" Karina found herself whispering and knew that her teeth were chattering.

Then she remembered the window! She ran to it, pulling back the heavy damask curtain. There was a casement, quite easy to open, and outside there was a small, walled garden running the whole length of the house.

Karina clambered out. The window was only a few feet from the ground and within a few seconds she found herself in the garden.

At the far end there was a narrow opening and Karina guessed that it led to the stables. Nearly all the London houses, she had found, had passage-ways which led from the houses themselves to the stables and mews behind them.

It was very dark in the passage, which was narrow, with blank walls rising high on each side of it. Moving

214

swiftly—not running because she was afraid of stumbling—Karina hurried away from the garden.

Suddenly she heard, just as she had expected, the whinny of horses and the sound of a groom whistling through his teeth as he brushed an animal down.

She could hear several men laughing and joking together. Karina slowed her pace and crept on tiptoe to the end of the passage where she could see a faint light.

She peeped round the wall and realised that the grooms were in the stalls attending to the horses and the stable was lit only by a lantern!

Moving silently in her satin slippers, Karina slipped across the sanded floor towards the open door which led to the Mews. She reached it unnoticed and started to run up the rough, cobbled way towards Green Street.

She reached the main road and now, running as quickly as she could, with her cloak floating out behind her like green sail, she sped towards Park Lane.

It was only when she reached the sweep outside Droxford House that she paused for a moment to get her breath, to tidy herself before she entered the house.

"No one will ever know!" she told herself. "It is over, it is finished! They will find him—but why should they suppose that it was I who killed him? And if they guess it was his guest—the servants do not know my name!"

She could feel her agitation subsiding, her breath coming more evenly. Her hair was dishevelled and she pulled up the hood of her cloak so that, edged with ermine, it shadowed her pale face and hid her golden hair.

"No one will know if I behave sensibly and calmly!" she told herself.

She pulled her cloak more firmly round her shoulders and smoothed beneath it the green gauze which edged the neck of her dress.

Suddenly she was still! Frantically her hand searched the front of her gown! it could not have gone! It was impossible! But she knew despairingly that the emerald brooch belonging to the Droxford collection —so easily identifiable—lay on the floor in Lord Wyman's Music Room!

Just for one second she contemplated going back. But it was unthinkable! Her whole body screamed out at the very idea of it! Instead, she went up the steps and raised her hand to the silver knocker.

The footman on duty swung open the big polished door. When he saw who had knocked his expression was one of surprise.

"Your Ladyship!" he exclaimed and looked incredulously to see that there was no carriage behind her.

"Where is Newman?" Karina asked in a voice which did not sound like her own.

Even as she spoke, Newman appeared from the servants' quarters.

"I beg your pardon, M'Lady," he said, "but we did not hear the carriage. Otherwise I'd have been here to greet Your Ladyship."

Karina walked across the Hall towards the Library.

"I wish to speak to you, Newman."

He followed her. Coming into the room, he shut the door behind him. By the light of the candles he could see her face.

"Your Ladyship is unwell!" he exclaimed.

"Fetch His Lordship," Karina cried. "You know where he is dining. Fetch him immediately! It is of the utmost urgency! Do not argue, but fetch him here with all possible speed!"

"But Your Ladyship . . ." the Butler began hesitantly.

"I have to see His Lordship. Do not waste time— take a carriage, and beg him to return with you!"

"You Ladyship is ill," Newman said. "Let me bring you a glass of wine?"

"No! No! I want nothing!" Karina declared. "Just do as I have bade you. Fetch His Lordship at once! Do you hear me? At once!"

Newman bowed, but his expression was perturbed as he went from the room.

When she was alone Karina took off her cloak and with trembling hands started to tidy her hair. As she did so she looked down at the torn gauze of her dress where the emerald brooch had been pinned.

She felt a sob rise in her throat and yet she did not weep. She only wondered in the darkness of her despair what the Earl would say to her . . .

Travelling down Park Lane in his closed Brougham the Earl thought of the wistfulness in Karina's face as she had asked him if he could not change his plans for the evening. He would have done so, he thought, had he not felt that it was obligatory for him to dispense once and for all with Mrs. Felicité Corwin.

It had not occurred to him that Mrs. Corwin, like Lady Sibley, ascribed to his wife the lack of attention she had received from him since his marriage.

Neither of them could for a moment credit that it was the Reform Bill which was engaging His Lordship and that almost from dawn to dusk he was in the company of his fellow peers.

Lady Sibley had trusted the Earl when he had told her his marriage would make no difference to their association, and she had believed her own theory that it would actually make it easier for them to meet. Now she was consumed with a jealousy she had never before experienced in the whole of her life.

The Earl was not at all a conceited man. He was well aware of his consequence; he knew from experience that if he looked with favour on a woman it was unlikely she would repulse him.

But he had no conception that he had aroused such a frenzy of infatuation in Lady Sibley's breast, and he

217

would have been genuinely astonished to learn that almost the same emotions were felt by Mrs. Corwin.

He had found Felicité Corwin amusing to be with and pleasurably attractive. He was far too controlled to have any deep feelings where a Cyprian or a Fashionable Impure was concerned.

It was the vogue for all Gentlemen in his position to sport a mistress. Since he had left Oxford there had been a number of frippery bits o' muslin who had thought themselves fortunate to come under his protection. Sometimes they engaged his interest for several months; occasionally the attachments lasted longer.

Mrs. Corwin had in fact held her position for over a year. She was shrewd enough to know that when a Gentleman sought her company he wanted not only to be amused, but also to be comfortable.

She therefore persuaded the Earl to dispose of the rather sordid villa in St. John's Wood where he had housed his previous mistress and move to the more respectable neighbourhood of Eaton Square.

She did not, of course, aspire to the Square itself—which was strictly for the Quality—but the Earl's agent found a pleasant little house in Eaton Terrace where, having engaged a cook who was proficient in the Earl's favourite dishes, and a maid who could open the door in style, she had made the Earl's periodical visits extremely pleasant.

She knew that she could not expect to hold the key to his affections, and she regarded his infatuation for Lady Sibley with tolerance. But she had in fact been extremely startled when he had arrived unexpectedly one morning to inform her that he had been married the day before.

When the Earl had explained the circumstances to Mrs. Corwin she had managed quite convincingly to shed a few sentimental tears and she had believed

218

him when he told her that nothing in their relationship would be changed.

He had then with consummate tact carried her off to Bond Street to assuage her wounded feelings with an expensive gift in diamonds.

Even diamonds were cold comfort when the Earl no longer visited her. Mrs. Corwin had her own method of learning what was happening in the *Beau Ton*. Karina's expenditure on her gowns lost nothing in the telling.

She was also aware of Karina's win at Ascot and it was the report that the Earl was spending immense sums in providing his wife with her own stable which had made her, even without Lord Wyman's insistence, write him a frantic letter insisting that she must see him.

Had she given herself more time to think, she would have remembered that the Earl disliked receiving letters of any sort, and most of all those which reproached him or demanded any action that had not first been suggested by his own wishes.

For the first time in their acquaintance the Earl, reading Mrs. Corwin's badly phrased note, decided that she bored him. The time had come, he told himself, when she no longer held any particular attraction for him.

He thought as he considered the matter that her charms had been waning slightly for several months. Such women had few brains and their conversation was limited.

Once one knew them well and the novelty had worn off, there was little to recommend them save the inevitable love-making which, in this instance, the Earl decided, had lost its savour.

A man of less integrity would doubtless have dismissed his mistress by letter or by sending a secretary or steward to enact the unpleasant task. But the Earl never discussed his affairs with his secretary, nor had he any intention of embroiling any servant in his employment in any matter so intimate.

He had, therefore, decided when he received Mrs. Corwin's letter that he would dine at her home in Eaton Terrace and break it to her gently that this was the last time he intended to visit her.

He would be extremely open-handed, as he always had been, so that she would certainly not want for the immediate future. And he had no doubt that she would quickly find herself another Protector.

She had several times during their association attempted to make him jealous—something she had found to her chagrin was an impossibility!

As his carriage passed through Belgrave Square, Chesham Place, and into Eaton Terrace, the Earl thought irritably that he was not looking forward to the evening ahead. Mrs. Corwin's letter to him had not been couched in the terms in which he expected to be addressed by someone who had no hold on him and who had received a more than generous recompense for any favours he had enjoyed.

When he thought of the carriage and horses with which he had provided his mistress, the jewels which had cost him many thousands of pounds, and dressmaker's bills—which appeared to increase month after month—he told himself that Felicité Corwin could have no possible cause for complaint!

And yet he felt uncomfortably that there was a distinct similarity between Mrs. Corwin's reproaches on paper and those spoken by Lady Sibley which she used to berate him every time they met.

"Damn all women!" the Earl said to himself.

He then found himself thinking of the wistfulness in Karina's green eyes and the manner in which she had seemed distinctly disappointed when he had told her he was not dining at home.

"We will be together tomorrow night," he told himself, and was surprised to find how much he was looking forward to discussing with her the speech he had made in the House of Lords and the new horses she intended to put in training with Nat Tyler.

Mrs. Corwin's maidservant opened the door to the Earl. She was as astonished as His Lordship's footman was when she heard him say:

"Be back here at half after eleven o'clock."

"Half after eleven, My Lord?" the footman questioned.

"That is what I said," the Earl snapped as he walked into the house.

The footman, abashed at having dared to query his master's command, looked up at the Coachman with a lift of his eyebrows.

They were both thinking the same thing. Having been in the Earl's service for a long time, they were aware that occupants of the "houses of joy" to which they conveyed him in a closed carriage without a crest on the panel had seldom lasted as long as this one.

The Earl seemed almost to dwarf the small Hall. He followed the maidservant in her rather theatrical uniform upstairs to the Drawing Room. The room was well-furnished with the Earl's money and lit discreetly by shaded candles.

Felicité Corwin, who had been posed elegantly on the sofa, rose with a little cry as the door opened, and glided towards him, her hands outstretched, an almost exaggerated smile of welcome on her lips.

She was an extremely attractive woman, as quite a number of men had declared during the years she had been "on the town." But it was the first time that the Earl, as he took her hands in his, had thought she looked slightly vulgar and somewhat coarse.

Perhaps it was in contrast with the delicate fragility of Karina; perhaps it was because she no longer had any particular allure for him.

"My Lord, it is far, far too long! How could you

221

have been so cruel, so unkind?" Mrs. Corwin said in what she hoped was a seductive voice.

"I have been very busy, Felicité," the Earl replied, seating himself not on the sofa as she indicated so that she could have sat beside him, but in an armchair on the other side of the hearth.

"You have indeed!" Mrs. Corwin retorted. "I hear so much about your new wife that I fear that you no longer have time for your old loves!"

There was no mistaking the venom in the silken tones.

"Actually, it is the Reform Bill that has kept me fully occupied," the Earl said and knew as he spoke that Mrs. Corwin did not believe him.

"But at last—at last you have come to me," she said. "Oh, Alton, I cannot tell you how much I have been looking forward to this evening!"

She moved to stand close to his chair as she spoke and the Earl knew it was his cue to rise to his feet and clasp her in his arms.

He did not move and it was with a sense of relief that he heard the maid announce that dinner was served.

The menu included all his favourite dishes, but he wondered as he ate them whether the cook had less culinary skill than he had believed, or whether his tastes had changed.

The wine was brought to the table at the correct temperature and as he had bought it himself he was unable to find fault with the flavour.

At the same time he found it did not alleviate a feeling of depression which was almost like a headache.

In the mistaken belief that wine would revive his spirits, he allowed his glass to be filled time after time, noticing with something like concern that Mrs. Corwin was keeping him company.

He looked at her sharply, having a violent dislike of

women who over-indulged, knowing that all too often it resulted in their becoming hysterical.

However, Mrs. Corwin had never shown any signs of addiction to the grape like many of her profession, and he decided that his suspicions were without foundation. She was actually doing her best to amuse him.

She chattered and she laughed, she used every flirtatious trick with which he was only too familiar: fluttering her eyelashes, gesticulating with her long fingers, pouting enticingly with her red lips and flattering him with a blatantness which to the Earl was too obvious to be credible.

He was honest enough with himself to realise that it was not Felicité Corwin who had changed, but he.

He suddenly took a dislike to the small Dining Room, the manner in which the maidservant placed the dishes on the table, the heavy perfume of gardenias which he recognised as coming from a certain shop in Jermyn Street; and most of all the manner in which Mrs. Corwin was trying to engage his attention.

Dinner, which seemed far too elaborate and lengthy, eventually terminated when the port which had come from the Earl's own cellars, was set on the table beside him.

He poured himself a glass and wondered if this was the moment to break the news to Felicité that this was the last time he would dine with her.

Then he thought that perhaps the maid, with her stringed apron and frilled cap, was listening, and decided he would wait until they went upstairs to the Drawing Room.

Mrs. Corwin was still talking. She told the Earl several warm stories he had already heard at his Club, and he was aware that she was putting on a quite professional act to make him laugh and to keep him amused.

In a way he was sorry for her. At the same time there was nothing he could do about it except be even more generous than he had intended in writing out a farewell cheque.

It was nearly a quarter to eleven o'clock before finally they went upstairs to the Drawing Room. The maid served coffee and offered the Earl brandy, which he refused.

The door closed behind her and Felicité Corwin with a throb in her voice, said:

"At last, dearest Alton, we are alone together!"

"There is something I wish to say to you—" the Earl began, only to be interrupted.

"And there is something I wish to say to you," Mrs. Corwin said, her voice breaking with emotion. "When you came here after your wedding Your Lordship told me that your marriage would make no difference to our relationship. But have you any idea what a difference it has made to me?"

She paused for effect, before she continued:

"I was well aware that you have had other interests from time to time. There has been Lady St. Helier, the Countess of Melchester, and then last April you became enamoured with Lady Sibley!"

The Earl started to protest but she put up her hand to stop him.

"No, no! Do not interrupt, for what I have to say to you must be said!"

Mrs. Corwin had bottled up her feelings for so long that now her sense of grievance together with the wine she had drunk had made her lose all sense of prudence and of restraint.

She was well aware that it was incorrect for a woman in her position to mention the names of Ladies of Quality with whom her Protector might be interested. But carried along on the floodtide of her feelings she broke all the rules with impunity.

"And then you married!" she said dramatically. "Without telling me, without my having the least suspicion that such a thing might occur! Oh! I grant that you behaved decently in telling me about it before the announcement appeared in the newspapers. but can you imagine what I felt! The shock! The misery!"

"Now listen Felicité . . ." the Earl began, only to be interrupted once again.

"And since your marriage you have never been near me! I have waited for you day after day, night after night. but you never came! You never even sent a message' You just forgot about me!"

"I have told you." the Earl protested. "I was busy!"

"Busy doing what?" Mrs. Corwin enquired. "Busy with that child who has become your wife; that green-eyed creature from nowhere who in some peculiar manner has become a social success overnight. But . . ."

She paused for a moment and there was no doubt that carried away by her emotions she intended to be shocking.

" . . . but does Your Lordship not realise what is happening behind your back? Do you not know that she is making a fool of you? That you are being cuckolded by the woman who bears your name?"

"Be silent!"

The Earl rose from the sofa.

"How dare you!" he said, and his voice was icy. "How dare you speak to me of my wife or refer to me in such a manner? I came here tonight, Felicité, to thank you for the happiness you have given me and to inform you that our relationship could no longer continue."

"You intend to brush me off?" Mrs. Corwin cried. "Oh. no. Alton! It cannot be true! You cannot mean to be rid of me!"

Her words ended on a shriek.

"Now, listen, Felicité. there is no need for such dramatics," the Earl said. "You know as well as I do that such arrangements as ours inevitably come to an end sooner or later."

"But I love you! I cannot let you go!" Mrs. Corwin cried. "You were fond of me. I know you were fond of me! We were happy together and you know how often you have said that you like coming here, that I attracted you more than any other woman had attracted you before. You cannot change so quickly! You cannot leave me, I will not let you!"

There was something so theatrical in the way that Felicité Corwin was throwing herself about that the Earl could not help feeling that it was more of an act than any expression of a deeply wounded heart.

At the same time, like all men, he detested a scene and was determined to put an end to it as quickly as possible.

He glanced at the clock and saw to his consternation that it was only eleven o'clock. He had unfortunately not ordered his carriage until half past, having a dislike of keeping his horses waiting.

He was wondering whether it would be possible for him to obtain a hackney carriage when, weeping hysterically, Felicité Corwin flung herself against him.

At that moment there was a loud imperious rat-tat on the front door.

"You cannot leave! You cannot leave me!" Mrs. Corwin cried, "not tonight, especially not tonight!"

Her arms went round the Earl's neck to drag his face down to hers. Her eyes were half closed, her lips were raised to his invitingly—a gesture which in the past had never failed to arouse his desire.

Now he unclasped her hands from around his neck and said in a matter-of-fact voice:

"There is someone at the door!"

"A tradesman! What does it matter? Listen to me, Alton," she cried.

Then there was the sound of voices, the door of the Drawing Room opened, and the maid said:

"I beg your pardon, Ma'am, I knows you've told I not to interrupt, but there's a man 'ere who says he be

His Lordship's Butler and insists on speaking with him."

"Newman!" the Earl ejaculated. "I will come downstairs."

"No, no, Alton! It cannot be anything of import," Mrs. Corwin cried.

But the Earl had already passed through the door and was descending the narrow staircase.

Newman was standing in the Hallway, a worried expression on his elderly face.

"What is it, Newman?" the Earl asked.

He realised the maid was listening, and opening the door of the Dining Room, beckoned him into it. The candles were still alight on the table and he knew by his Butler's expression that while he could easily find out from the Coachman where his Master was dining, he would never have presumed to intrude unless it was something of considerable gravity.

"'Tis Her Ladyship, M'Lord. She has returned in a terrible way!"

"Returned?" the Earl asked sharply. "Her Ladyship dined at home!"

"No, M'Lord. A Lady Mayhew called for her and took her out to dinner at Hampstead. But Her Ladyship's returned on foot and has asked that you'll come to her immediate, that it is of the utmost urgency!"

"What has happened, Newman?" His Lordship asked, knowing there was little that went on in his household of which Newman was not aware.

"I've no idea, M'Lord, and that's the truth. But I thinks Your Lordship should come home."

"I will do that!" the Earl said.

Good manners drove him upstairs to the Drawing Room. As he entered the room Mrs. Corwin ran towards him.

"Something has happened at Droxford House, the Earl explained. "I am sorry, Felicité, but I have to leave."

227

"But you cannot go, that is impossible!" Mrs. Corwin said. "It is only just eleven o'clock. You must stay here, you must!"

"I regret . . ." the Earl began.

"But I insist!" Mrs. Corwin interrupted, clinging to his arm in a manner he most disliked. "There are reasons why I cannot let you depart!"

"Control yourself, Felicité," the Earl said in his most crushing voice. "My presence is required at home. There is no more to be said!"

"But there is—there is! You cannot go," Mrs. Corwin cried frantically.

The Earl disengaged her hands from his arm and walked from the room. He heard her give a despairing cry as he ran down the stairs. The door was open and he stepped into his carriage which was standing outside.

Newman had already climbed onto the box beside the Coachman and the carriage set off at a sharp pace.

He could not help feeling thankful that he had escaped from what had promised to be a grand drama, after which doubtless he would have been expected to apologise and give solace to Felicité's injured feelings in the usual manner.

Why should she behave in such a reprehensible manner? he wondered. She was well-versed in the game and should have been far too experienced to let herself overstep the bounds of propriety. She had given him such a disgust for her that he had no wish ever to see her again!

He would be kind, he would be generous as far as money was concerned. She could stay on in the house until she found someone to provide her with another one. But never, he told himself, never would he allow himself to endure another scene such as he had just experienced.

At the same time he had been wondering what had happened to Karina. Why had she gone out? And who the devil was Lady Mayhew? He had never heard of the woman. Gambling, racing. what could Karina have got up to now? At this time of night?

The Earl was still puzzling over the problem when the carriage drew up at Droxford House. The red carpet was rolled down. He walked into the Hall.

"Her Ladyship is in the Library," Newman told him.

The Earl moved quickly towards the great mahogany doors which were opened by a footman. He passed through them and heard them close behind him.

Karina was standing in the middle of the room and one look at her white. frightened face told the Earl that Newman had been right to fetch him.

"What has happened?" he asked.

He saw that she was finding it impossible to answer him. Her lips moved but no sound came from them. Her eyes were dark with fear and he saw a terror in them that he had never thought to see in any woman's.

"What is it, Karina?" he asked. "What has upset you?"

"I have caused a . . . terrible scandal for you!" Karina answered. "I . . . did not mean to. In fact . . . I cannot even credit now . . . how it happened! I have been . . . thinking while I . . . have been waiting for you . . . that I should not have . . . shot him as I did. I should have aimed at his . . . legs! Of course I should have done that . . . but I have killed him . . . I have . . . killed him, My Lord . . . and everyone will know I did it . . . because I have left my brooch behind! The . . . emerald brooch with the engraving on it. It must have fallen off when he tried to . . . kiss me."

Karina's voice came in broken gasps, so low that it was difficult for the Earl to hear her. Then with her eyes on his she whispered:

"I am sorry . . . so terribly . . . desperately sorry!"

Her hands fluttered despairingly and the Earl caught them in his and drew her across the room to the sofa.

"Sit down," he said quietly, "and tell me all about it, Karina. I may be somewhat slow but I do not understand who you have shot and why."

"It was . . . Lord Wyman," she answered. "I was taken to his house by a trick, and then he said he intended to . . . ravish me and that he knew I would not tell you because . . . if you fought a duel with him it would do you harm at Court . . . and besmirch me as well!"

"Is this true?" the Earl asked and there was a note of incredulity in his voice.

"It is true," Karina said with a sob. "So . . . I shot him! I meant to kill him! I aimed for his . . . heart and he is . . . dead! And now I have realised how . . . foolish it was of me. Will they . . . will they . . . hang me?"

The Earl tightened his hold on her hands.

"No one shall hang you," he said reassuringly. "But I must hear the whole story from the beginning. Did anyone see you leave Lord Wyman's house? Why did you go there and who knows you were there?"

"Only Lady Mayhew," Karina replied. "Only she was not a Lady but an actress . . . who Lord Wyman paid to take me . . . to him!"

"Start from the moment I left you, the Earl insisted.

Slowly, growing a little more coherent as she talked, Karina told the Earl how a strange woman had arrived unexpectedly; how she had taken her to dine in Hampstead; and because of the danger of footpads she had slipped the pistol into her reticule; how she had been tricked into entering Lord Wyman's house to meet an old lady who was suffering from arthritis.

She related Lord Wyman's assertion that Mrs. Corwin would keep him with her until dawn; she described how despite all her pleadings Lord Wyman was determined to ravish her; and how he had stalked her round the table until frantic with terror she had shot at him, meaning to kill, and had succeeded.

She related how she had escaped into the mews and how she had supposed no one would know what had happened until she found the emerald brooch was missing.

"I knew then that . . . everyone would . . . know," she said miserably. "Oh, I am so . . . sorry, desperately sorry to have caused such a . . . scandal . . . I know you will never . . . forgive me!"

The Earl rose to his feet.

"There will be no scandal if I can help it!" he said. "Tell me again, Karina, on which side of the mews is the passageway?"

"What are you going to . . . do?" she asked wide-eyed.

"I am going to collect your brooch," he answered with a faint smile.

He raised one of her hands to his lips and before she could say another word he had gone from the room.

"Have you kept the carriage, Newman?" he asked.

"Yes, M'Lord. I thought Your Lordship might wish to send for a Physician.

"There is no need to do that, but take Her Ladyship a glass of wine and insist that she drinks it. Light the fire and ask no questions!"

"Very good, M'Lord."

Newman had resumed the unperturbable expression of the perfect servant.

The Earl stepped into his carriage and drove to Park Street where he told the Coachman to wait for him on the corner. Then he slipped down the mews at the back and found, as Karina had described to him, the small alleyway leading to the back of the house.

The window was open as she had left it and the

Earl, stepping over the sill, saw Lord Wyman, apparently dead, on the floor.

The Earl glanced towards him, then moved to the other side of the room where Karina suspected her brooch had fallen. She had been right! The brooch was lying just inside the door. The Earl picked it up and put it in his pocket.

He then knelt down beside the shot man and felt for his pulse. Lord Wyman was not dead! The pulse was very weak but there was no doubt that there was still life in the body.

The Earl drew from his pocket a pistol such as was always kept handy in the carriages he used at night.

Crossing to the sofa he fired it into a cushion—he remembered that Karina had said the room was soundproof but he was taking no chances.

Then the Earl removed the stem of a champagne glass from the fingers of Lord Wyman's right hand, threw it behind the unlit coals in the fireplace, and replaced it by the pistol.

He felt in the injured man's pocket and drew from it the door-key. The Earl unlocked the door, then crossing the room he climbed through the window to return the way he had come to his waiting landau.

It was only a short distance to Lord Wyman's front door. There the carriage was directed to stop and the Earl descended.

A footman opened the door and the Butler came forward to say quickly:

"His Lordship is not at home!"

"Lord Wyman is expecting me," the Earl replied firmly. "We are supping together."

"I regret that His Lordship is not at home," the Butler repeated.

"I am the Earl of Droxford. You will kindly announce my arrival to His Lordship."

The Butler hesitated. For a moment he was undecided what he should do. Then as the Earl started to move towards the end of the Hall which Karina had described to him as leading to the long passageway, he capitulated.

"His Lordship did not inform me that he was expecting a guest."

"Very remiss of him!" the Earl exclaimed. "But I assure you His Lordship will not be surprised to see me."

When they reached the door into the Music Room the Butler knocked.

The Earl watched him with a grim expression on his face. He knew that Lord Wyman's orders not to be disturbed must have been received by his staff on many previous occasions.

There was no answer and the Butler knocked again.

"Perhaps His Lordship has fallen asleep," the Earl suggested.

Tentatively the Butler opened the door. Then he gave an exclamation and ran across the room to his fallen master.

"Good God!" the Earl ejaculated in apparent surprise. "There must have been an accident!"

The Butler stood staring down at the pistol in Lord Wyman's hand and his blood-stained shirt, before he faltered:

"His Lordship is injured. What shall I do?"

"You will send one of your footmen immediately for a Surgeon," the Earl replied. "Do not move his Lordship—cover him with a blanket—and prop a pillow carefully under his head."

"His Lordship is not—dead?" the Butler asked.

"No indeed," the Earl replied. "I can feel his pulse. It is faint but he is alive!"

He bent forward to examine Lord Wyman's chest.

"In my opinion the bullet has not punctured the heart," he said. "It is lodged somewhere above it. It was obviously an accident."

He paused and repeated.

"An accident! Do you understand?"

"Yes, M'Lord. I'm sure you're right, M'Lord," the Butler agreed in an agitated manner.

"Then hurry, man, and do as I have told you," the Earl commanded.

"Of course, M'Lord. At once, M'Lord!"

The Butler hurried from the room to order a footman to fetch the Surgeon.

The Earl glanced round to make quite certain that Karina had left nothing else behind, then strolling slowly towards his carriage he left the house.

At Droxford House he strode across the Hall in such a hurry that he opened the door himself into the Library.

Karina was sitting staring into the fire. She had not expected him back so soon. As he approached her she raised her head lethargically. When she saw the Earl she started nervously to her feet.

He smiled at her and taking her hand put the emerald brooch into the palm of it.

"My brooch!" Karina said in a voice hardly above a whisper. "You have . . . it . . . back! How . . . clever of you!"

"Yes, I discovered it exactly where you said it would be," the Earl said, "and Lord Wyman is not dead!"

"Not . . . dead!" she ejaculated.

"You were somewhat rough with him," the Earl said, still with a smile on his lips. "But he is alive!"

She stared at him with an almost uncomprehending expression in her eyes and then folded up like a flower . . .

He caught her just before she reached the ground, and lifting her in his arms, he carried her from the room and across the Hall towards her bedroom.

Karina came back to consciousness half-way up the stairs. She was aware who carried her and she knew that never before had she felt so secure, so safe! With a little murmur she turned her face to the Earl's shoulder, like a child who seeks comfort after it has been frightened.

Newman, who had ran up the stairs beside them, opened the door of Karina's bedroom and the Earl carried her inside.

"Fetch Her Ladyship's maid," he said over his shoulder.

He set Karina down very gently on the bed. She gave an inarticulate murmur as he lowered her onto the pillows, then she looked up at him, her eyes wide in the pallor of her face and he thought he saw a question in them.

"It is true!" he told her. "You have not killed anyone! If you had—he deserved it! Do not worry, Karina, everything will be all right!"

He looked at her for a long moment, his eyes searching her face before bending down he kissed her very gently on the lips.

Then even as she moved her hands towards him, he went from the room.

10

Good night, M'Lady. May you sleep deep and dreamless!" Martha said.

She had undressed Karina and given her a drink of warm milk laced with honey. Now she blew out the candles and went from the bedroom, closing the door.

Karina lay still in the darkness and knew that something breathtaking had happened! She was not recalling the perfidy of Lord Wyman or the horrors through which she had passed that evening.

She was thinking of the feeling of security and happiness she had felt as the Earl had carried her upstairs and the touch of his lips on hers! They had swept away the last vestige of pretence and evasion. She faced the truth—she loved him!

She knew now she had loved him from the very first moment she had seen him. She had loved him when she had clambered down the tree to ask him to marry her; she had loved him when he had come to the house and carried her away from her father's brutality and the anxiety she had felt for her future!

She had loved him when she had married him, and the reason that she had sent him from her bedroom that first night was because she had been afraid not of him but herself!

She had known then, she now admitted, that had the Earl touched her or kissed her she would have flung herself into his arms and been only too ready to surrender her body, like her love, which had already passed into his keeping.

Karina put her hand to her lips. When the Earl had kissed her a flame had leapt ecstatically within her and she had known that this was what kissing should be like! Not the rough passion of Sir Guy or the bestial lust of Lord Wyman, but some strange magnetic force which ran thrillingly like quicksilver through her body.

And she knew she would yearn achingly and endlessly to feel such ecstasy again.

"I love him! I love him!" she murmured into her pillow.

But her elation was short-lived and she became miserably aware that she could never tell him so. The Earl had no feeling for her save that of a kindliness such as he might give to a frightened child.

She knew how easily she irritated him. She could

hear again the anger in his voice after she had raced against the Marchioness of Downshire.

She could recall vividly the icy coolness with which he had threatened her when, returning from Windsor Castle, she had tried to justify her friendship with Sir Guy.

And tonight, she remembered, he had had no wish to dine with her but instead had gone to his mistress, finding her embraces infinitely preferable to being alone with his wife!

There was no chance, Karina told herself of ever winning her husband's love. There were already two other polished and experienced women in his life. A tiresome green girl falling into scrape after scrape was hardly likely to appeal to a man who had a partiality for sophisticated females and who only required a wife who would grace his table and behave circumspectly.

"Complacent and conformable!"—the words seemed to echo and re-echo in her ears, taunting and jeering at her until at last she knew despairingly there was only one thing she could do—she must go away!

She could not stay and feel her love consuming her day after day, or run the risk of revealing her feelings and seeing the disgust in the Earl's eyes.

She could visualise all too clearly the manner in which he would turn away from her because she had broken every promise she had given him when they had made their bargain together.

"I must go away! I must go away!" Karina repeated the words aloud in the darkness, and felt the tears trickling down her face.

Then as dawn broke over the trees in Hyde Park she drew back the curtains and finding there was enough light in the room to see, she went to the secretaire which stood near one of the windows.

She made half a dozen attempts at writing a letter to the Earl, and when finally she finished one to her satisfaction she crept back to bed to wait, wide-eyed, unti she dared ring her bell for Martha.

It was eight o'clock when Martha answered the summons, exclaiming:

"Your Ladyship's early! You're not indisposed, M'Lady?"

"No, indeed," Karina answered. "There is nothing wrong with my health, Martha, but I want you to do something for me. Something secret which no one else must be told."

"There s nothing I wouldn't do for you, M'Lady," Martha replied.

"I was sure I could rely on you," Karina said. "I want you, to go to the Posting Inn in Piccadilly. I think it is called the White Bear, and ask them to have a chaise with two horses here at a quarter after eleven."

"A post-chaise, M'Lady? But why not use your own carriage?"

"I have to leave London," Karina replied. "And I desire that no one shall be aware of my destination. Can I be sure you will do this for me and not speak of it to the other servants?"

"I swear you can trust me, M'Lady!"

"Then go at once, Martha. Order the post-chaise and then come back to pack a few garments for me, not many, and all my most simple gowns. I shall not need anything elaborate."

"Very good, M'Lady. You're sure you're well able to travel?"

"I am well enough!" Karina answered.

"Then I'll tell the Housemaid to bring in Your Ladyship s breakfast-tray and I'll make all haste to reach the White Bear and be back before Your Ladyship rises."

"Thank you, Martha."

Karina lay back against her pillows thinking sombrely of what lay ahead.

The Housemaid brought her breakfast and with it *The Times* newspaper. Karina opened it to look for the description of the race she had won on Tuesday, which Robert had assured her would be included in this morning's paper.

Then turning the pages she gave an exclamation as she read—

"FATAL ACCIDENT TO LORD SIBLEY"

Under the headline was a description of how Lord Sibley, driving a light curricle, had collided with a coach of the Royal Mail. His curricle had been overturned down a steep bank. The vehicle had fallen on top of him and he had died of his injuries before a Physician could reach him.

Karina put down the paper. This meant that Lady Sibley was free! Free to marry the man she loved and who loved her; free to become the Countess of Droxford had not His Lordship already taken a wife!

Feeling as if the whole world was dark and without hope, Karina rose from her bed and went again to her secretaire.

She opened the letter she had written to the Earl and hurriedly and without thought she added a postscript. She sealed the letter again and stood looking at it for a moment before she raised it to her lips!

"Oh, my darling . . . my darling," she whispered. "Good-bye."

She crossed the room to the bell. The Housemaid, an elderly woman who had been at Droxford House for over twenty-five years, came hurrying to her call.

"Mr. Wade should be in his office by now," Karina said. "Will you ask him to be so obliging as to let me have notes for the sum of a hundred pounds. I have some bills to pay this morning."

"Very good, M'Lady."

Karina thought that this would be enough money

for her immediate needs. The Earl would have placed her winnings at Ascot into the account he had opened for her at Coutts Bank, and as soon as she reached her secret destination she would write and ask them to send her notes of hand for whatever sums she required.

When the money was brought to her, Karina placed it carefully in her reticule and sat waiting for Martha's return. No one seeing her in her lace-trimmed wrapper with her gold hair falling over her shoulder would have believed anyone so young or so lovely could be in the depths of utter despair.

"If I were only dead' Karina was thinking. "How can I bear this pain for the rest of my life?"

The Earl, tooling his High Perch Phaeton towards Ascot, was conscious of something nagging at the back of his mind which for the moment he could not put into words.

Something was worrying him and yet he was not certain what it was. It was a strange feeling and an irritating one, and deliberately he thought instead of all he had done before he had left Droxford House at eleven o'clock.

He had not slept well, finding himself remembering not only Karina's frightened face but the manner in which she had turned her head confidingly against his shoulder.

Then unforgettable and disturbing was the memory of her lips. He had not known any woman's lips could be so soft, so sweet, so defenceless. He had kissed her on an impulse as he might have kissed a child who was distressed and whom he wished to comfort. But he had known as his mouth touched hers that it was not a child who awakened a response within him.

He shied away from recalling how he had wanted to put his arms round Karina, to hold her close! He would not think of her, he told himself! Instead his thoughts went to Mrs. Corwin and immediately there was a frown between his eyes.

Karina's revelation that Lord Wyman and Mrs. Corwin had contrived the events of last evening between them had so incensed the Earl that his first impulse was to dismiss his former mistress with no pay-off. The insulting things she had said about Karina were due, he knew, in part to the amount of wine she had drunk at dinner.

Women without breeding were, under the influence of alcohol, invariably uncontrollable, and there might be some excuse if she had been speaking the truth when she claimed she had an affection for him.

But what he would never forget was that she had intrigued with a man of Lord Wyman's disreputable character to trick Karina into a position from which only by the grace of God had she managed to extricate herself.

After breakfast the Earl had sat down at his desk and written a cheque for a sum which was exactly a quarter of what he had intended to give Mrs. Corwin.

He had left it for Robert Wade to post with his other letters and beside it he had set a note ordering his secretary to put the house in Eaton Terrace up for sale.

Having ruthlessly dispensed with his mistress, the Earl had opened a newspaper and read the same information about Lord Sibley's accident that Karina had seen, but with different feelings.

His first reaction was one of relief. If Lady Sibley was in mourning for the next year at least she could not pursue him from Ball to Ball, Assembly to Assembly, to moan of his inattention. He was heartily bored with being reproached for not continuing an affair for which he had no longer any enthusiasm.

He had known at the Richmond Ball when they had argued and quarrelled in the Ante Room downstairs, that Lady Sibley's attraction for him had vanished, and he must somehow withdraw from the position of her lover without unduly lacerating her feelings.

It was a manoeuvre such as on other occasions he had been able to carry out with considerable adroitness. There were few Ladies of Quality who were prepared to parade to the world a broken heart even if they suffered from one.

It was easier to pretend an attitude of good friendship, and in many cases they did in fact become friends with the man who had once aroused so many conflicting emotions in their hearts.

But Lady Sibley was made of more enduring stuff than her contemporaries. For the first time, in a long sequence of clandestine love affairs, she had found a man who had aroused her deepest emotions and she was determined to hold him even if he wished to escape.

But the Earl had proved elusive, and now he thought optimistically that by the time Lady Sibley could return to the social scene she would have forgotten him.

He had the sudden sensation of being free—free of the scent of tuberoses, of the cloying perfume of gardenia, free of clandestine meetings, whispered asides, secret messages.

He was free from deception and conspiracy, from creeping along dark bedroom passages; free from leaving a warm bed in the middle of the night and dressing again to face the chill outside.

Free! And his thoughts were once again of Karina. He had thought as he had carried her upstairs, that she smelt of honeysuckle. Whatever the scent she used, it was very faint and very fresh and had made him think of the gardens at Droxford in the spring.

Her hair had the same golden glory as the daffodils blowing in the wind around the lake!

It was then that he remembered with an exclamation what had been teasing him at the back of his mind!

He had gone upstairs to Karina's bedroom before leaving for Ascot and had knocked. Martha had opened the door, slipping through the narrowest possible aperture and closing it behind her.

"Her Ladyship is asleep, M'Lord. She's been restless during the night and I wouldn't wish to disturb her."

"No, of course, not!" the Earl answered. "When Her Ladyship awakes give her my respects and say that I am hoping she will be well enough to dine with me this evening."

"I'll convey your message, M'Lord," Martha promised, curtseying respectfully.

The Earl turned away. As he did so he had noticed two footmen walking along the passage. He had thought, although he was not certain, that they came from the Wardrobe Room adjacent to Karina's bedroom.

He had not thought about it at the time but hurried downstairs so as not to keep his horses waiting. But now he remembered that the footmen carried between them a round-topped trunk!

Why should they be conveying a trunk from Karina's room towards the back stairs? What could such a trunk contain? And why, when there had been no suggestion of Karina going on a visit, should a trunk have been brought down from the attics?

He remembered something else. When Martha had come from Karina's room the opening of the door had revealed that there was light and sunshine inside. If Karina had been asleep surely the curtains would have been drawn?

"There is something wrong!" the Earl decided.

Something so wrong that it gave him a premonition of danger.

He reined in his horses.

"What is it, M'Lord?" his groom asked anxiously, looking to see if there was any fault with the harness.

"I am returning," the Earl replied. "There is something I have forgotten!"

He turned the High Perch Phaeton round and started back towards London. He had not been driving for more than twenty-five minutes so he calculated he would arrive back at Droxford House before noon.

He decided he would make some plausible excuse for his return, but he would insist on seeing Karina before he left again.

He might miss the first race, but that was not of import; he only knew that he could not go on to Ascot feeling apprehensive—though why he should feel that way he did not know!

By pushing his horses the Earl reached Park Lane at exactly ten minutes to twelve o'clock. The sound of his carriage-wheels brought the footmen on duty to the door and by the time the Earl had given the reins to the groom, stepped down from the Phaeton and entered the Hall, Newman was in attendance.

"I would wish to speak with Her Ladyship," the Earl said casually. "She should be awake by now."

There was an expression of consternation on Newman's face.

"Her Ladyship has left, M'Lord! I thought you were aware of Her Ladyship's plans."

"What plans?" the Earl asked harshly. "And where has Her Ladyship gone?"

"I do not know, M'Lord," Newman replied. "Her Ladyship had ordered a post-chaise which called here shortly after Your Lordship's departure for the races."

"A post-chaise!" the Earl ejaculated.

"There is a note for Your Lordship," Newman said in a low voice. "I have placed it on Your Lordship's desk."

Realising the footmen were listening the Earl walked into the Library followed by Newman.

As the Butler shut the door behind him, the Earl asked angrily:

"Why the devil did you let Her Ladyship travel in a post-chaise? The stable is well-stocked with my horses!"

"I know, M'Lord. T'was a great surprise for me," Newman said, "and I think I should inform Your Lordship that about a quarter of an hour after Her Ladyship had departed, Sir Guy Merrick called!"

"Sir Guy?" the Earl questioned.

"Yes, M'Lord, he asked if I'd any knowledge of where Her Ladyship had gone."

He saw the Earl was listening intently and continued:

"I have my suspicions, M'Lord, that one of the footmen—a man for whom I've never had a liking —has been receiving bribes from Sir Guy to inform him of Her Ladyship's movements. I'm convinced, Your Lordship, that is how Sir Guy was cognisant of Her Ladyship's departure.

"But he did not know her destination!" the Earl said, as if he were talking to himself.

"No, M'Lord, except that he asked me if I'd any idea from where the post-chaise had been hired. And James, without asking my permission, informed Sir Guy that it was from the White Bear. I've reprimanded him sharply, M'Lord, for imparting unnecessary information!"

"The White Bear!" His Lordship repeated, as he opened Karina's letter.

Newman withdrew from the Library and the Earl stared down at the white sheet of parchment as if for a moment he could not comprehend what it said.

The letter was exquisitely written except for the postscript which had obviously been added in a hurry.

My Lord,

After all the Trouble in which I have Involved Your Lordship, I think it Best that I should Go from London and stay quietly in the Country. I shall be quite Safe and I Beg Your Lordship neither to Worry nor to try to Find me. I hope to Return as soon as I feel Rested. I can only Apologise deeply to Your Lordship for the Manner in which I have Behaved and Pray that I may Obtain Your Lordship's Forgiveness.

I remain your Most Apologetic and Humble Wife.
Karina

Postscript: I have just Seen in the Newspaper that Lord Sibley is Dead. I can quite Understand that Your Lordship now Wishes you were Free to Marry the Lady who Holds your Heart. I want your Happiness, My Lord, and it would be Best if I have not Returned in Three Months for You to Announce that I have Died. No One will know this is not True and Your Lordship will Never see Me Again.

The Earl read the letter through, then read it again as if his brain could not take in the information it imparted. Then hastily he walked from the Library into the Hall.

He took his hat and gloves from a footman, and without a word to Newman he hurried from the House and climbed into his Phaeton.

He drove to the White Bear, asked for the Head Ostler and demanded the destination of the Phaeton which had been ordered by the Countess of Droxford and which had picked Her Ladyship up at Droxford House about three-quarters of an hour earlier.

"That be strange!" the Head Ostler exclaimed. "You be the second Gentleman who's asked me that! Severn be the name of the village, Sir, to which the Lady wished to be conveyed."

Throwing the man half a guinea, the Earl drove his horses from the yard, tooling them down Piccadilly at a speed which made his groom look at him in surprise; for he was well aware of the Earl's frequently expressed conviction that horses should not be driven fast in heavy traffic.

Once outside London the Earl gave his horses their heads. He guessed that Guy Merrick would be driving his bays, and the only hope of catching up was that he was more familiar with the road to Severn, which was a village not far from Droxford Park.

The Earl drove superbly; but there was a scowl on his face and it was obvious he was deeply preoccupied with his thoughts. He was in fact seeing a little but white frightened face and two green eyes dark with terror.

The speed the Earl obtained from his chestnuts—although the edge had been slightly taken off them by having already been driven for three-quarters of an hour earlier in the morning—made his groom grit his teeth and wonder on several occasions whether his last hour had come.

However, in under two hours they reached the outskirts of the village without mishap, but without a sight or sign of Sir Guy's Phaeton. It was then, as they reached the first cottages, that the Earl saw coming towards them a post-chaise.

He set his horses across the road the post-chaise slowed up to come to a stop about ten yards from them.

"Wot the devil be ye adoing?" the Coachman asked aggressively.

The Earl drew his Phaeton alongside the vehicle.

"I wish to know where you have taken your passenger," he enquired. "I can find out without troubling you, but it will save me time if you tell me what I wish to know."

247

He drew a sovereign from his waistcoat-pocket as he spoke and the Coachman looking at it with greedy eyes replied:

"Lavender Cottage, Sir. 'Tis at th'far end of th'village—right 'and side—standing at th'edge of a fir wood."

The sovereign changed hands and the Earl drove on.

Sir Guy must have got there before him, but the Earl guessed that Karina would not have arrived more than half an hour ahead of them both.

He had noticed the post-chaise was drawn by good horses, but they could not be compared with the prime stock such as was tooled by himself and Merrick.

Lavender Cottage was easy to find and as he drove towards it he perceived Sir Guy's Phaeton was pulled up outside. His famous bays were steaming, and it was obvious that they had only arrived a few moments ahead of the chestnuts. But only the groom was in the Phaeton—there was no sign of Sir Guy!

The Earl threw the reins to his groom and, alighting, strode through a white-painted gate and up a path edged with forget-me-nots to the door of the small black and white thatched cottage.

He knocked, and after a minute or two the door was opened by an elderly woman. Her grey hair was drawn back into a bun at the nape of her neck and in her neat grey gown covered by a white apron the Earl recognised the traditional figure of a child's Nurse.

"I wish to speak with Her Ladyship," he said quietly.

"Miss Karina—I means Her Ladyship—has gone into the wood," the old woman answered. "There's already been a Gentleman asking for her."

Her wrinkled old face looked worried and the Earl said:

"I am the Earl of Droxford. If Her Ladyship is in the wood I will find her."

248

"Follow the path at the end of the garden, My Lord," Karina's Nurse told him.

Then as the Earl turned to go she said tentatively:

"You'll not be harsh with her, M'Lord? I knew the moment my baby arrived that she were unhappy. She has not confided in me but I'm sore afraid for I knows without words there is something sadly wrong!"

"I promise you that I shall try to right the wrong," the Earl replied.

Then as the anxious old eyes lightened he walked swiftly away towards the pine trees.

His Lordship's feet, moving swiftly along a sandy tract made little sound. As he looked from right to left searching for some sign of Karina, the path, twisting through the trees, led him further and further into the wood until finally he heard voices.

He slowed his pace until in front of him he saw the brightness of the sky and realised that he had come through the wood to the other side of it. It was then, in a clearing almost directly in front of him that he saw Karina. And beside her was Sir Guy!

Karina in a white muslin gown was sitting on the fallen trunk of a tree and behind her was a vista of the countryside stretching away towards the horizon. Sir Guy had his back to the Earl, who stopped behind the trunk of a great fir tree.

He could hear quite clearly what Karina and Sir Guy were saying and he thought that his wife's golden hair silhouetted against the blue of the sunlit sky was incredibly lovely.

"How can you go away alone?" Sir Guy was asking and his voice was sharp.

"I shall not be alone," Karina replied. "I shall take my old Nurse with me."

"How do you know that your relatives in Ireland, whom you have never seen, will accept you?"

"If they will not then I shall buy a small cottage

somewhere in an isolated part of the country. Nana and I can live very cheaply and no one will find us."

"And you really expect me to allow you to do that?" **Sir Guy** enquired. "Karina, do not be so non-sensical! If you wish to hide yourself away—then I will hide with you. Come with me, we can go anywhere in the world that it pleases you!"

"You have suggested that to me before," Karina said.

"And you refused me! I let you go then, Karina, because I believed that your happiness lay with Alton. But now that you have run away from him you have removed the last obstacle—the last fetter of restraint that you imposed on me when you told me you did not love me and offered me only your affection!"

"My feelings have not changed," Karina answered. "I have, as I told you, Guy, a deep affection for you. I always shall have. But I do not love you and I will not live with you."

"And you expect me to allow you to journey alone to Ireland accompanied only by an aged Nurse? My dearest, be practical! Can you imagine for one moment you would not be pursued by men, and continually forced into a position of embarrassment, even of danger? You are far too beautiful, too vulnerable, to be alone and unprotected."

"Nevertheless that is what I intend to do," Karina said firmly.

"And that is what I will not let you do," Sir Guy retorted. "You will come with me now and at once, Karina. You can come willingly or I will take you, bound, drugged or senseless, whatever way is easiest, to my yacht which lies in Dover Harbour.

"It will carry us across the Channel, and once we are on the Continent we can make plans for our furture—yours and mine, Karina. I love you, I have, as you well know, long since laid my heart at your feet and I swear that in time I will teach you to love me!"

"No, Guy, I am sorry . . . desperately sorry that I must make you unhappy. But I cannot . . . come with you."

"Then I will take you without your permission," Sir Guy said roughly, putting out his hand and drawing Karina to her feet. He would have taken her in his arms and she gave a little cry of protest.

The Earl stepped forward into the clearing.

"I think before you go any further, Guy, you should remember that I have a say in this matter."

"Alton!" Sir Guy ejaculated.

Karina gave a little gasp and put both her hands to her breast as if she would quell the tumult in her heart.

The Earl faced Sir Guy and for a moment the two men stood looking at each other. They were about the same height and there was in a way a strange resemblance between them.

It was as if their breeding, their education, their upbringing and their expertise in the same sports, had set a stamp on them.

They might in fact have been brothers—brothers facing each other with a hatred on their faces that was unmistakeable.

"I have stood enough from you, Guy," the Earl said menacingly. "I intend now to fight you. I shall teach you a lesson that has been overdue for a long time."

"And are you suggesting that whoever is the victor of this Herculean contest should take Karina as the prize?" Sir Guy asked mockingly.

"I am suggesting nothing of the sort," the Earl replied. "Karina is mine—she is my wife!"

"A wife of whom you are mighty careless!" Sir Guy jeered. "A wife who finds you so attractive that she is running away to hide herself in the depths of Ireland where she imagines you will never find her!"

"I will not bandy words with you," the Earl re-

251

torted. "Karina, go back to the cottage and wait for me!"

He put down his hat and gloves on the fallen tree and started to take off his coat.

The spell which had seemed to hold Karina speechless broke and she moved forward to put her hand on his arm.

"Please . . . please do not . . . fight . . . him."

"You heard what I told you, Karina," the Earl replied not looking at her. "Go to the cottage."

Karina's fingers tightened and her eyes were dark and worried.

"I would not wish him to . . . hurt you," she said in a whisper.

He looked down into her face and for a moment was very still.

"He will not hurt me! Go, Karina!"

She knew there was nothing more she could say and with a sense of despair turned away. She did not look at Sir Guy, she was only conscious of the Earl throwing his coat down on the tree and standing tall and muscular in his white shirt as he started to unwind the stiff folds of his cravat.

She walked slowly for a few yards and then she started to run. She ran because she could not bear to hear the sounds of their clenched fists battering each against the flesh of the other.

She was afraid she might hear a cry of pain! She was still more afraid she might hear a body fall to the ground!

She reached the cottage and opening the door, flung her arms round her nurse.

"Oh, Nana, Nana," she sobbed. "They are fighting . . . what am I to do?"

"Now do not be fretting yourself, my dearie," her old Nurse replied. "Come and sit down. I'll bring you some milk to drink."

Karina went into the tiny parlour and sitting down on the hard, horse-hair sofa, covered her face with her hands.

"Pray, child, that the best man may win!" the old woman said as she went away to the kitchen.

"The best man!" Karina whispered the words to herself.

She loved the Earl, she thought helplessly, and all that was happening was her fault!

11

"Please God let him win! Do not let Guy hurt him! I love him . . . I love him so . . . much!"

Karina tried to pray but her brain was in such a whirl that she could not formulate a proper prayer. She only knew that her whole being—body, heart and soul—yearned with an intensity that was almost unbearable for the Earl.

When she had seen him walk from the fir trees into the clearing she had known that the only thing she wished to do was to throw herself into his arms. Somehow she had kept her self-control but she wondered now how she could ever face him again!

It had seemed imperative to run away, and yet now he had found her she knew that agony as it had been to leave him, the agony of being in his company again on the same terms as before would be infinitely worse!

How long she sat in the parlour trying to pray, fighting a sense of helplessness which made her want to scream, she had no idea! She could not touch the milk her Nurse brought her—she could only suffer as she had never thought it possible to suffer.

Then she heard a step on the flagged floor. She started to her feet, her face drained of all colour, finding it impossible to breathe as she waited to see who came through the door!

Would it be the Earl or Sir Guy who had won the fight? Then as she felt she must faint with the intensity of such suspense, she saw her husband come into the room!

She looked at him apprehensively, expecting to see him bruised and battered, his knuckles bleeding. But he appeared very much as usual save that his cravat was not tied quite so immaculately as it had been on his arrival.

He stared at her in what she felt was a cold, disinterested manner.

"Come, Karina," he said, and it seemed to her there was no warmth in his voice, and his expression was stern.

She thought for a moment she must refuse to go with him. Then as he turned away and she heard him giving orders for her trunk to be set upon the Phaeton, she walked to the door.

Without realising what she was doing she put on the gay bonnet her Nurse handed her and inserted her arms in the green silk pelise in which she had driven down from London.

"His Lordship's a fine Gentleman!" Nana said as Karina kissed her. "Do what he wishes, dearie, it'll be best for you!"

But Karina could only feel like a schoolgirl who has played truant and was being taken back to school!

She climbed into the Phaeton and they drove away, leaving Sir Guy Merrick's bays standing—it seemed to her—forlornly outside the cottage.

Because the groom behind them was within hearing

Karina knew she could not ask what had happened, and in fact she would have been unable to frame any coherrent question with her lips.

The Earl's horses were sweating and she knew he must have travelled from London at a great speed. She wondered why he had turned back from Ascot to discover she had left the house.

But these were things she could not ask until they were alone, and the mere thought of being alone with him made her long to run away and hide.

They drove along an unfamiliar road until she realised that they were not returning to London but moving in the direction of Droxford Park.

The great house lay only two miles from Severn Village and as they drove through the wrought-iron gates into the Park she could see the ethereal beauty of it glowing like a jewel among the dark trees which sheltered it.

The black swans were reflected in the silver lake; the windows were glinting iridescently; the romantic sweep of the turrets, statues and gabled rooftop was silhouetted against the blue of the sky.

The Earl drove up to the front door and flunkeys came hurrying down the long flight of stone steps to assist Karina to alight.

"You are doubtless fatigued, My Lady," the Earl said as they walked into the Greet Hall. "I suggest you retire to your bedroom and rest. We will talk later in the day. In fact, we will meet an hour before dinner, I wish Your Ladyship a quiet repose."

His tone was formal, as was the bow he made her.

Feeling small and insignificant Karina followed the Butler up the stairs to where the Housekeeper in rustling black silk, her chatelaine clanking at her side, was waiting at the top of the landing.

"Good day, M'Lady! This is an honour, M'Lady! We have long been awaiting the pleasure of welcoming Your Ladyship!"

"Thank you," Karina replied shyly.

The bedroom into which she was taken was magnificent. But she was too perturbed and overwrought to have eyes for the gilt mirrors decorated with cupids, the colourful carpet with its pattern of roses and lovers' knots, the painted ceiling depicting Venus; or for the huge bed with its carved canopy and white satin hangings embroidered with hearts and doves.

At any other time Karina would have asked questions about the room, but now, vaguely realising that she was being treated as a bride and had been taken to the Bridal Chamber, she could only think of herself as a fraud, and having undressed she crawled miserably beneath the lace-edged sheets.

The Housekeeper tried to entice her to eat a light meal but, although to save argument she sipped a little soup and ate a few mouthfuls of spring chicken, she was too tired and too unhappy to want anything but to be alone.

Finally the curtains were pulled, the door closed and she knew she need no longer keep up any pretence. She had thought then that she must either burst into tears or else lie awake distressed and distraught over what had occurred.

But after a night of sleeplessness she was more tired than she knew. Before she realised what was happening the curtains were being drawn back and she was astounded to find she had been asleep for nearly four hours.

A bath was prepared for her, in front of the fire, and the Housekeeper explained:

"It may be the summer, M'Lady, but unless these large rooms are constantly in use they feel chill even on the warmest day!"

The water was scented, the towels smelt of lavender, and by the time Karina was dressed she felt that some of her agitation and fear had left her.

Martha, on her instructions, had packed only her

plainest gowns and in the grandeur of Droxford Park Karina regretted that she had nothing smarter to wear than a white English organdie trimmed round the hem and *décolletage* with white lace and bows of satin ribbon.

It revealed her tiny waist but it was very simple compared with the elaborate and expensive dresses Yvette had especially designed for her.

She was met when she reached the Hall by the Butler who preceded her across the marble floor and along several corridors to throw open a door which led into an extremely beautiful room which looked onto the garden.

The sunlight was coming through its long windows to reveal the treasures with which the room was furnished and to be reflected in the huge carved Chippendale mirrors which decorated the walls.

Karina stood just inside the door. She appeared, in her white gown, with her wide troubled eyes and golden hair, very young and defenceless.

Then her heart leapt in her breast as the Earl rose from the desk in the centre of the room at which he had been writing.

He was extremely elegant in his close-fitting long-tailed velvet evening coat and embroidered waistcoat. His frilled shirt and high cravat were ornamented only with a large black pearl encircled with diamonds.

"Come here, Karina," he said.

She moved towards him and then in dismay she saw that lying open on the desk was the letter she had left for him in London.

"There is something I wish you to explain to me. In the postscript of your note, you wrote: *"I want your happiness, My Lord."* Why did you want that, Karina?"

Karina looked down at the letter, seeing it swim before her eyes. She felt that her mouth was dry, that her voice was somehow constricted in her throat. She was quivering because the Earl was so near to her and also because there was a gentleness in his voice which she had not expected.

"Well?" he asked as she did not answer him. "Can you not explain it? Then perhaps you will tell me why you ran away?"

Again Karina could find no words and after a moment he continued, his tone now more insistent:

"I desire to know the answer, Karina."

"I thought . . . it . . . best," she murmured, her voice very low.

"Best for whom? For you or for me?" the Earl enquired. "And in what way?"

There was silence. Karina's head was bent so that he could not see her face. After a moment he said:

"I want the truth. You promised me once that we should always be frank with each other, that there should be no pretence between us. That was part of our bargain, was it not? Now I am asking you a simple question: why did you run away?"

Karina, feeling her fingers were trembling, clasped her hands together, looking down at them sightlessly.

"Look at me, Karina!" the Earl commanded. "And give me an answer!"

She could not move, could not raise her eyes.

"Obey me!" he insisted.

As if he finally broke down her resistance, Karina felt the words rush to her lips—words over which she had no control.

"Your Lordship wants the truth, then I will tell it to you! When you married me . . . we made a bargain between us . . . I promised I would be a complacent and conformable wife! As Your Lordship knows . . . I have not been . . . conformable! I have been in scrapes! I have given rise to gossip! I never meant to do so . . . but that is what I have done! Now I have . . . broken the second part of my promise . . . I am no longer . . . complacent . . . either."

There was a pregnant silence, and then as if the last vestige of self-control left her, Karina cried:

"You asked for the truth! Now I have to . . . go . . . can you not . . . understand?"

She would have turned and run from the room, but the Earl put out his hand and caught her wrist so that she was arrested almost in full-flight.

"Why are you no longer complacent?"

She heard the question almost in surprise. Then she looked up at him, her eyes full of tears, her lips trembling.

"Do you really want me to tell you the answer to that?" she asked, her voice breaking, but with a note of anger because she felt he was deliberately torturing her. "It is because . . . I love . . . you . . . because I cannot help . . . loving you . . . let me . . . go!"

She would have pulled herself free, but the Earl released her wrist only to put his arms round her and sweep her against him, holding her so closely that she felt as if she could hardly breathe.

"You love me!" he cried in a voice she could hardly recognise. "Oh my darling, why did you not tell me so?"

His lips found hers and Karina felt as if the room whirled around her and she knew a sudden ecstasy such as she had never known before in her whole life.

She felt as though she was carried upwards into the sun. The birds were singing around her and she felt thrill after thrill sweep through her body, lighting a flame deep within her.

"You love me!" she heard the Earl say and there was a note of triumph in his voice that was unmistakeable. "You love me, my absurd, incorrigible, unconformable wife!"

He was kissing her again! Kissing her with those

slow, possessive, demanding kisses for which she had longed. Kisses which seemed to draw her very soul from between her lips and make it his for all time.

Then as she felt the happiness which had encompassed her was almost too great to be borne, the Earl raised his head and looked down at her flushed cheeks, at her parted lips and the radiance in her green eyes.

"You are lovely!" he said. "So incredibly, unbelievably lovely! How can you imagine for a moment that I would let you go?"

"I thought you . loved . ." Karina stammered.

"I love you! No one but you!" he interrupted. "There is no other woman in my life. Can you not understand, Karina, that I have loved you since the moment I married you? Since the night I came to your room, believing—fool that I was—that I was insisting on my rights as your husband! But it was really because I wanted you, because I loved you, even though I would not acknowledge it to myself."

His voice deepened.

"When you sent me away I thought you had a distaste for me and I knew I had been crazed to marry you as I did and had not tried first to gain your heart."

"Are you . . . really saying . . . this to . . . me?" Karina whispered. "Is it . . . true?"

"It is true, my own darling, and if you only knew what it has meant to keep away from you these weeks! I wanted you and yet my pride held me back because I thought you preferred Merrick!"

His arms tightened.

"I hated him and I was so crazily, wildly jealous that I would not compete! I would not try to win you from him!"

He drew a deep breath before he continued:

"It was only today, when I had your letter, that I knew that if you had left me my life would be empty

260

and pointless without you. I love you, Karina, more than I have ever loved any woman!"

"Do you . . . mean that?" Karina whispered. "I have . . . dreamt that you might say such . . . things to me but I never . . . thought they would come . . . true."

"You are not dreaming, my sweetheart."

The Earl kissed her again—a long time later he said softly:

"Can we not forget the unhappiness and all the foolish things that have happened since we have been married? Let us go back to our wedding day, my lovely one, and start from there!"

He was pleading with her as he asked:

"Could we pretend that the ceremony has just happened and now we are on our honeymoon—you and I together, getting to know each other, discovering the depths of our love and realising how much it means?"

"C   could we do . . . that?"

Karina looked up at him and her face was transfigured with happiness. He thought that never in his life had he imagined a woman could look so warm, glowing and beautiful.

Taking his arms from her he raised both her hands to his lips.

"I salute my bride!" he said with the smile she found irresistible. "Welcome to your new home, My Lady, and I hope Droxford Park will meet with your approval!"

"I thank Your Lordship . . . Oh, but I wish . . . I were wearing one of my best gowns!"

He laughed at her tenderly.

"There speaks the eternal female. What is amiss with your gown? You look adorable in it!"

"It is so plain," Karina complained with a shy smile. "As your bride I want you to think I look . . . beautiful."

261

"And could I think anything else?" he asked.

Once again his lips sought hers and she felt herself thrill and quiver beneath his kiss!

"I have a present for you, my darling," he said after some minutes, "which will perhaps mitigate your disappointment over your attire!"

"A present?" Karina enquired.

The Earl went to his desk, and from the drawer he brought out several velvet boxes and he opened them. There was a tiara fashioned of turquoises and diamonds, a wide necklace, bracelets, a ring and ear-rings.

"They are magnificent!" Karina exclaimed.

"They belonged to my mother," the Earl told her. "When she died she left them to me and told me I was to give them to my wife on the happiest day of my life. Heart of my heart, this is I believe that day! Will you wear them?"

"You know I will!"

He set the tiara on Karina's golden head, clasped the necklace round her neck, the bracelets on her small wrists and the ear-rings in her ears.

She looked at herself in a mirror and gave an exclamation of joy.

"Now I look beautiful for you . . . all for you!"

He drew her once again into his arms, but even as he did so the door opened and the Butler announced:

"Dinner, My Lady, is served."

The Earl offered Karina his arm. Conscious of her glittering jewellery and her happiness, which seemed to make the whole world so glorious as to dazzle her eyes, she let him lead her towards the Hall.

To her surprise they turned not towards the great Banqueting Room with its murals, its marble-topped tables and its magnificent painted ceiling, but proceeded up the stairs.

On the landing the Butler held open the door adjacent, Karina realised, to her bedchamber. Then, as she entered, she gave an exclamation. The room, small and oval-shaped, was decorated from floor to ceiling with white flowers.

There were garlands hanging from the cornice; there were banks of lilies, carnations, white lilac, and roses, all of which scented the room with an almost overwhelming fragrance and made it a bower of incredible beauty.

Karina looked at the Earl.

"You have done this for me?"

"For my bride!" he replied.

The dining-table was lit by candles set in gold candelabra and encircled with white orchids. The Earl sat on a high-backed velvet chair, Karina was beside him.

He raised his glass.

"To us both," he said softly so that the servants could not hear, "And to our love—my beloved one!"

It was difficult to know what they ate. Karina felt that the food tasted like ambrosia and the wine like nectar.

It was indeed impossible to think of anything but the man beside her; his eyes were continually seeking hers so that she was conscious of the waves of magnetism passing between them until she quivered and found it hard to speak.

"In a few days I shall take you to Paris," the Earl said. "There is so much I want to show you!"

"That would be wonderful!" Karina exclaimed.

"And we shall be alone together," he said quietly and the look in his eyes made her blush.

At last dinner was finished and the servants withdrew. The Earl turned his chair away from the table and holding a glass of brandy in his hand sat back at his ease crossing his legs.

Karina thought that no man could look more elegant and yet so disturbingly masculine.

As the Butler closed the door of the sitting-room

the draught had blown open the door into the Bridal Chamber. It was in a corner of the flower-filled room but Karina was suddenly conscious of it and that she was alone with her husband.

"Are you happy, my lovely one?" he Earl asked gently.

"You know I am," Karina replied. "But please, there is one thing I must . . . know."

"About Guy?"

"What . . . happened?"

"I know that Guy has told you his version of what occurred all those years ago," the Earl said. "I want you to hear mine. I loved Guy, Karina, I would never have betrayed him!"

"You did not?"

He shook his head.

"Guy had been my friend, my confidant, my brother, ever since I could remember. We thought alike, laughed at the same things, and delighted in each other's company."

The Earl stopped speaking and seemed to be looking back into the past before he continued:

"When Guy told me he intended to run away with my cousin, I was worried not because of Cleone, but because of Guy! I knew, you see, what Cleone was like. She was temperamental, unbalanced, almost to the point of abnormality—and bad!"

"What do you mean?" Karina asked.

"Guy was not the first man she had seduced by her wiles," the Earl replied. "There had been a scandal with her brother's tutor when she was only fifteen. There was even greater scandal the following year when she behaved abominably with Lord Ward's agent—a married man with three children!"

The Earl paused before he continued:

"Of course it was always said to be the man's fault, but I was not deceived by Cleone's innocent face! I

264

was extremely disturbed when I realised she was ensnaring Guy!"

The Earl sighed.

"She was attractive—very attractive—and there was no chance of his keeping his head under such circumstances. But when he told me he was running away with her I felt I must prevent it if possible.

"I knew it was useless for me to argue with him, so I told my father, a most fair-minded man, hoping that he would make Guy see sense."

"Then it was your father who told Lord Ward?"

Again the Earl shook his head.

"No, it was while my father and I were discussing what we could do, that we discovered to our consternation that Guy and Cleone had already left the house.

"It was at that moment, by the most unlikely coincidence, that Lord Ward arrived to take Cleone home with him. The Duke had decided the marriage should take place earlier than had been intended."

"So you were forced to tell him Cleone had already left?" Karina asked.

"That was exactly what happened," the Earl replied. "We could not lie, it was impossible! Then Lord Ward, infuriated to the point of madness, behaved in the outrageous manner of which Guy will have told you. He caught up with the runaways at Baldock. He thrashed Guy insensible and informed Cleone she would marry the Duke."

"But surely she was distraught at the idea?" Karina asked.

She was thinking of how she would have felt had she been told she was to marry someone like Lord Wyman.

"Cleone, although poor Guy did not realise it, forgot about him almost as soon as she reached home," the Earl answered. "She suddenly discovered that it might be rather fun to be a Duchess! Perhaps the only man who could have dealt with her turbulence was indeed the dissolute, but extremely sophisticated Duke!"

"But she committed . . . suicide!" Karina murmured.

"She did nothing of the sort," the Earl replied. "That was the lying story that was circulated by the gossips after Cleone, as usual wilful and disobedient, had broken her neck because she insisted on riding a stallion that was not fit to be mounted by a man, let alone a woman."

"Guy said she was having . . . his baby."

"It might have been Guy's, it might easily have been someone else's," the Earl replied. "Cleone was bad through and through, and because of her I lost the best friend I ever had."

"Why did you not help him after they were separated?"

"I tried to," the Earl answered, "but Guy would not meet me! He was convinced I had played traitor, and because I was so deeply hurt by the assumption, I soon stopped trying to get in touch with him."

The Earl gave an exasperated sigh.

"How stupid and headstrong the young are! A few words could have bridged the gulf between us. Instead we decried each other to outsiders, who repeated and re-repeated what we had said! The condemnation lost nothing in the telling!"

"So you built up a wall of hatred!" Karina said.

"A wall that I thought was indestructible until today," the Earl told her.

"What happened?"

There was just a little pause before the Earl replied:

"When you had left Guy said to me: 'Do you love Karina? I know full well she has no love for me. If you care for her as she deserves, then I will go away.'"

"And what did . . . you reply?"

"I told Guy the truth—that I loved you," the Earl

266

answered, "and I knew as I said it that I could not fight him even had he wished it. We had meant too much to each other in the past."

"But what will . . . he do?"

"Guy is travelling immediately to Jamaica. He has vast Estates there left him by his Uncle. He says that when he returns he will be Godfather to our— children!"

The Earl put down his glass of brandy as he spoke and rising from the table drew Karina to her feet.

"Was Guy right, my darling?" he asked, holding her close. "Do you love me?"

"You know . . . I do!"

"Then our children will be beautiful and clever. Is that not what you told me they would be—were they born of love?"

"Yes . . ." she whispered so shyly he could hardly hear her reply.

He drew her to the big cushion-covered sofa beside the hearth. He pulled her down beside him and taking her in his arms kissed her very gently. He felt her lips respond to his and knew that she trembled in his arms with a sudden ecstasy. Then his kisses grew more possessive and more demanding.

After a little while he reached out and took the tiara from her head, setting it carelessly on a side-table before he drew the pins from her hair, letting the golden wonder of it fall down over her shoulders.

He raised a handful of it to his lips and kissed it! Gently he turned Karina's face up to his and pulled her hair like a veil over the shyness of her eyes to kiss her through the golden screen.

Then sweeping her hair aside, the Earl took off the turquoise necklace to kiss the whiteness of her throat and the little pulse that was beating excitedly because he moved her so tremendously.

"This is how I have longed to see you, my darling,"

he said, his voice deep. "When I came to your bedroom the night we were married I knew I had never
set eyes on anyone so beautiful, so alluring, as you
with your wonderful hair streaming over the pillows
and over . . ."

The Earl stooped. His arms tightened around her.

"There is something I have wanted to ask you, my
precious, something I have ached to know—do you
always sleep naked?"

Karina felt the blood rising in her cheeks and her
eyes fell before his.

"No . . . no . . ." she whispered "It was because
. . . my nightgown was so old and shabby . . and
I did not expect . . . you!"

"I know you did not!" the Earl answered. "But I
must confess, my sweetheart, that ever since I saw
that fleeting glimpse of your lovely body its beauty has
haunted me! I have longed with a longing I cannot
even describe to see you like that again."

With an inarticulate murmur Karina hid her face
against his shoulder.

"I love you!" he murmured. "God, how I love you!"

"Are you . . . sure?" Karina asked

"More sure than I have ever been of anything in my
whole life! Tell me again that you love me! I am so
afraid of losing you!"

"I love . . . you," she whispered, and now her
voice, like his, was deep with the passion he had
aroused in her—a passion she did not fully
understand—she only knew that she thrilled with an
almost unbelievable excitement at the demand of his
lips and the touch of his hands.

"I want you!"

Rising to his feet the Earl drew Karina from the
sofa into his arms.

"You are mine!" he cried possessively "Mine, now
and for all time. You will never escape me again, my
darling! I will never let you go!"

His lips were on hers, holding her captive

Then as her arms went round his neck, drawing him close and still closer . . . he lifted her high against his heart and carried her through the open door into the shadows of the great white bridal bed!

Romantic Tours
inspired by
Barbara Cartland

With the same research and care that goes into writing her novels,
BARBARA CARTLAND has designed a series of tours to the
romantic and exciting places you have read about in her novels.

- You will meet the author herself in her
  home at CAMFIELD PLACE.

- You will lunch with the EARL AND
  COUNTESS SPENCER (Barbara Cart-
  land's daughter) at their home
  ALTHROP PARK

- You will spend one unforgettable week
  touring ENGLAND with special events
  arranged for you wherever you go.

All this is offered to you plus second optional weeks to such other
historical and exciting destinations AS: SCOTLAND AND
WALES, FRANCE, AUSTRIA AND GERMANY, TURKEY,
EGYPT AND INDIA.

PRESENTED IN COOPERATION WITH
THE WORLD OF OZ AND BRITISH AIRWAYS

Send for your Romantic Tours folder now! Do not miss the
opportunity of sharing this unique travel experience with other
admirers and fans of Barbara Cartland.

SEND TO: DEPT. J

WORLD OF OZ, LTD.
A Cortell Group Affiliate
3 East 54th Street
New York, N.Y. 10022
Tel: 212-751-3250   800-223-1306

NAME_____

STREET _____

CITY _____

STATE _____ ZIP_____